CAROLINA KISS

Jaqueline Kiss

A Jaqueline Kiss Book

Published by JamesCafe.com

ISBN: 978-0-9899211-1-4
Print Edition

Cover Design by www.CoverToCoverDesigns.com

ACKNOWLEDGEMENTS

Some people are born into your life and some people come into your life as you walk the path you have chosen. Many thanks to my sister Cindy for her support, positive thoughts, and editing talents. You have always been there for me and I will always be here for you. Many thanks also to Alicia, the sister I chose for myself. She is my best friend, my first editor, and my confidant on so many things in life. None of this would be possible without Jamie, my biggest fan and the reason I write romance novels. You are an amazing person!

Many thanks also to the wonderful people who work so hard behind the scenes. Kari, at Cover to Cover Designs, puts so much heart into her work and the results are brilliant. Paul at BB eBooks does an outstanding job with print and e-book formatting. Check him out at http://bbebooksthailand.com.

"The sweet kiss of emotion rocks the soul."

—*James Johnson*

CHAPTER 1

The elevator dinged and the doors opened to the beautiful reception area at Stanley, Wilson, and Krenshaw, Certified Public Accountants. A pretty, young woman sat behind the black granite reception counter, her bright smile fading when she saw who had emerged from the elevator. She could tell by the grim face that Jillian Stanley was not having a good morning. When Jillian had a bad morning, everyone at SW&K had a bad morning too. Drawing in a steadying breath, Allison, the receptionist, plastered her smile back on as a tornado of red hair on top of a shapely body flew into the room.

"Good morning, Ms. Stanley," Allison said, bracing herself for a verbal tirade.

"For you maybe," Jillian snorted. "I'll be in my office. Make sure no one disturbs me. And I mean NO ONE. Reschedule my ten o'clock appointment for next week. I'm not in the mood today to hear old Mr. Henry whine about how much we charge him. And call some moving companies for me. I need appointments for tomorrow or Saturday for estimates to move things to my new condo. They need to meet me at my house in Falls River. You know the address."

"Um, OK," Allison stammered. "It's not my business, but I thought you were going out of town tomorrow morning."

"You're right, it's not your business," Jillian barked.

With that, Jillian stomped down the hall into her office and slammed the door. Allison let out a sigh as she looked up Mr. Henry's phone number on her computer. She missed the Jillian Stanley who used to reside in that office. Just two short years ago, Jillian had been sweet, caring, and fun loving. Everyone at the office had adored her. Now Jillian was a miserable, cranky, short-tempered shrew most of the time. To be fair, so many things had happened in the last two years to poor Jillian that Allison couldn't really blame her.

Down the hall, Jillian tossed her briefcase and purse onto the large teakwood desk and then threw herself into the chair behind it. Her office reflected her personality with sea-foam green carpet, eggshell walls, and comfortable teakwood furniture placed around the room. The walls were alive with photographs Jillian had taken of the places she loved in the Carolinas. The beach, the mountains, and all the beauty in between had been captured in her photographs. Today, however, the warmth she normally felt here was missing.

She turned to look out the window toward the landscape of downtown Raleigh, N.C. She hated that she had been so short with Allison, but when the black moods took over, she couldn't seem to help herself. Her life was in complete disarray and she just couldn't deal with it sometimes. It seemed the only time she felt any happiness at all was when she was with Victor.

Victor….he was a big part of the problem today. The early morning phone call from him certainly hadn't helped her mood. Once again, he had cancelled their weekend plans with the excuse that he had to do something with his wife. That was the fifth time in as many months. She had thought that she could handle an affair with a married man….one who claimed he was in a loveless marriage. But it was becoming very clear that his commitment to his marriage would always take precedence over his relationship with her. She was truly wondering if the incredible sex they had when they were together was worth all of the evenings and weekends alone.

Tears glistened in Jillian's eyes as she gazed out the window, but she wasn't seeing the stunningly blue sky or the gorgeous late-summer day. She was thinking about what had happened to her life. Between the loss of her father, her mother's move to Asheboro, and her divorce, nothing was as it used to be. Jillian had felt adrift until Victor came into her life. But the affair with him hadn't become what she expected either. Why was she, a smart, successful businesswoman, willing to be a hidden mistress? How had her life gotten so lonely and out of control at the age of thirty-two?

Thinking that maybe it was time to make some changes, Jillian continued to stare out at the downtown landscape. A knock on her office door brought her back to reality. Hadn't she told Allison she didn't want to be bothered? Did the girl never listen?

"What?" Jillian bellowed.

The door opened and Victor stepped in, closing it behind him. Jillian was so startled she was speechless. He had never been to her office and only a few people at SW&K knew that he was her real estate agent. No one knew at the office he was her lover…at least she hoped no one knew. He always called her on her cell phone or at home so she could take the calls when she was alone. The only person who knew anything about him was her best friend Kellie. And Kellie was not very happy about the affair.

"Hey babe, why the angry voice?" Victor asked. "Are you still mad at me?"

Victor's dark eyes sparked with passion and hunger. Jillian once again was breathless with desire for this man who exuded sex. She wanted to be angry, but with him standing there looking at her that way, she just couldn't maintain her anger. His piercing stare seemed to drill straight into her and she felt heat engulf her entire body. His athletic body, jet-black hair, and custom-made suit made her ache with desire.

"I'm upset that our weekend is cancelled….again. I'm beginning to think we'll never have a weekend together," Jillian snapped, trying to keep her voice from cracking with tears. "And how did you get in here anyway? I told Allison I was not to be disturbed."

"I told the girl out front that I'm your real estate agent and I needed to speak with you about a very urgent matter," Victor responded. "She tried to stop me, but I was determined to see you. Please babe, don't be upset with her. I wanted to be sure you're not angry with me. You hung up on me this morning before I could really explain."

Stepping away from the door, Victor crossed the office in three strides. He took off his suit coat and threw it on one of the teak chairs placed in front of Jillian's desk. Then he came around the desk and perched on the corner. He pulled Jillian up out of her chair and between his legs. He put his arms around her and nuzzled her neck. She breathed in his unique scent and was filled with a deep longing to feel him inside her. He always had this affect on her and he knew it. When he touched her, her entire brain seemed to shut down except for the part that controlled sexual response.

"I'm so sorry, babe," Victor whispered as his tongue darted out to lick her ear. "I wish I could change things but I can't."

Jillian turned her head to look at him and her black mood disappeared completely. She felt alive, desired, and as close to happy as she could be these days. She leaned forward and when his lips touched hers, she moaned softly and felt a heaviness bloom in her lower abdomen. They kissed deeply, tongues playing a sensuous dance as Victor's hands slid over her butt. When she felt the zipper on her skirt slide down, Jillian tried to step out of Victor's embrace, but he held her tightly and pushed her skirt to the floor.

"Victor, no," Jillian gasped as wetness started to form between her legs. "Someone might walk in."

"Don't worry," he whispered as his hands continued their caress of her butt. "I locked the door behind me when I came in. I need you babe. Please, I need you."

When his hands slid beneath the elastic on her silk bikini panty and began to push it down, Jillian surrendered to the sensations consuming her. She wanted him, wanted to feel alive. As her panties fell to her ankles, Victor's hands caressed her naked butt and Jillian moaned out loud.

"Ssshhhhh," Victor grinned and licked her lips. "No need to advertise to the whole office how much you want me."

They kissed again, tongues sliding in and out of the other's mouths. Victor's hands moved up and found what they were looking for under Jillian's shirt. He squeezed her breasts until her nipples were standing at attention. He broke the kiss and leaned down to take one hard nipple in his mouth and then his hand slid down her belly to the V between her legs.

"Oh yes," Jillian breathed as she instinctively spread her legs.

Victor slid his insistent fingers over her clit and plunged them into her heat. Jillian swallowed another moan as he slid his fingers in and out of her. She gripped his shoulders to stay upright and quickly exploded with a huge orgasm. He continued to stroke her with his fingers, bringing her to a second orgasm and than a third one. Her legs weak, Jillian was panting from the heat that suffused her body. Victor removed his fingers and put them in his mouth.

"Ah babe, you taste sweeter than heaven," Victor whispered. "Let me have a real taste of you."

He slipped off the desk and pushed her briefcase and purse to the other side. He turned to Jillian and kissed her deeply, letting her taste her own juices on his tongue. Then he grabbed her hand and ran it over the bulge in his pants.

"See what you do to me?" he asked as she unzipped his zipper and freed his hard penis. "Lean over the desk and let me see that perfect butt."

Jillian stepped out of her panties, turned, and leaned over the desk, her naked butt twitching in anticipation. Victor dropped his pants, covered his penis with a condom, and moved to her. He ran the head of his penis down her butt crack and over her now wet pussy lips. Jillian moaned again, wanting him inside her, wanting to cum again. Victor kneeled and licked her from behind. She grabbed the edge of the desk and pushed back against his tongue. In seconds she had another orgasm as his tongue flicked over her clit again and again.

Victor rose and quickly pushed his throbbing penis into her. He began to stroke her in a slow, sensuous rhythm until she was again at the edge. When he sensed she was close to orgasm, he increased his pace, thrusting harder and harder. He grabbed her hips and pushed deeper and deeper into her heat and wetness. Over and over his hard penis stroked her inside until she gasped and came with a muffled moan. Victor groaned then, cumming too as he felt her muscles tighten around him.

They stayed bent over Jillian's desk for several seconds, as both fought to regain their breath. Finally, Victor stepped back, pulled the condom off, dropped it into the wastebasket, and pulled his pants up. Jillian stood up and turned toward him. He picked up her skirt and panties and kissed her as he handed them over. As she got dressed, Victor moved to the other side of her desk and sat down.

"Wow, babe, you are incredible," Victor remarked as he watched Jillian zip her skirt. "I always heard redheads were wild in bed. You're my first redhead and have definitely proved it to be true again and again."

"I wouldn't exactly call this desk a bed, but thank you for the compliment," Jillian answered as she walked around the desk. "I wish it was a bed so we could snuggle for a few minutes."

Victor rose from the chair and put his arms around her. He held her close for a long minute and then kissed her softly. Jillian sighed at the sweet kiss.

"Listen babe, I really have to get to work but I need to tell you something first," he said as he stepped back from the embrace. "I know I've disappointed you about a weekend away several times. I hate that hurt look in your eyes."

"It's OK," Jillian said quickly. "I know your marriage has to take priority. I knew that early in our relationship. But it's so hard when you promise we will go away and then cancel at the last minute."

"That's what I want to talk about," Victor added. "You see…..well…..I know I've promised you several times that we would go away, but the reality is that I don't think that will ever happen. I can't think of a reason to be gone for a weekend that won't make Mary suspicious."

"Why would you even make a promise like that to me if you know you can't keep it?" Jillian asked.

"Mary and I have been married for almost fifteen years. It's not the best marriage and I'm not in love with her anymore," Victor explained. "But she's my best friend and I can't imagine life without her.

"To be totally honest, I'll never divorce her. I'm sorry babe. It doesn't change how I feel about you. You're hot and sexy and I want to be with you. We can still have lots of fun together."

Jillian stepped away from him, trying to understand his convoluted logic. All she could think about was that he had intentionally lied to her about the weekend trips. She should have known. Now it was out in the open and it felt like a slap in the face. She was suddenly so angry and disgusted that she didn't want to be anywhere near him.

"Get out!" she shouted. "Just get out of my office!"

"Hey, quiet babe," Victor said, stepping towards her. "We don't need the whole office listening to us fight."

"You have ten seconds to get out that door," Jillian responded, her back rigid with the fury she was feeling. "If you're not out of my sight in ten seconds, I'll call security. I should have known I couldn't trust you. It should have been obvious since you're willing to cheat on your wife. This relationship is over, Victor. Get out!"

Victor looked at her, grabbed his jacket and strode to the door. He turned, looked at her, and smirked at her anger. Then he fled out the door. To Jillian, he looked like a rat scurrying under a rock. She slowly walked back around her desk and turned towards the window once again. Her shoulders heaved as she sobbed. Her life was such a mess and she didn't know how to make it right again.

CHAPTER 2

Friday morning dawned with the promise of another sun-filled summer day. Jillian was up early, anxious to begin packing while she waited for the moving company representatives coming to do estimates. She had appointments today and tomorrow to begin the process of moving from the home she had shared with Gary Lindstrom, her now ex-husband. Almost everything she was keeping would have to go to a storage facility as the condo she was renting temporarily was furnished. As a Certified Public Accountant, Jillian knew she should purchase a new home for the tax benefits. However her life was too unsettled and she just couldn't get excited about it right now. She had opted for a short-term rental instead, while she decided where in Raleigh she wanted to live.

Jillian had taken all of the pictures off the built-in mahogany bookshelves in her home office and stacked them on her desk beside the bubble wrap and moving box. Now she was sorting through them to decide which ones to take to her new place. When she came across a picture of her parents, Gary, and her at her college graduation, she almost burst into tears. The picture had been taken ten years ago and the dreams she had then had mostly been shattered.

When she joined Stanley, Wilson, & Krenshaw upon graduating from college, she was on top of the world. She was so excited to be working with her father, Jesse Stanley, a senior partner at SW&K. Her entire life, her father had told her his dream was to have his very own daughter become a partner in his firm. She and Gary had dated through college and were married shortly before she began working at SW&K. They had soon purchased a brand new home in Falls River, Raleigh's most sought after neighborhood, thanks to help from Gary's wealthy parents. Life was so good then.

However, it had all started to go downhill two short years ago. Her father had a massive heart attack on the tenth hole of Wildwood Green Golf Club and passed away before the ambulance reached Duke Raleigh Hospital. Her mother, Barbara, grieved deeply and Jillian didn't know if Barbara would ever recover from the loss. Less than a year after her husband's death, Barbara decided to move back to her hometown of Asheboro, NC. Although it was only seventy miles away, it seemed like a thousand miles to Jillian. She felt a huge void in her heart and her life without her parents close by.

A few months after her father's death, Jillian was hit with another loss. After many late-night discussions, she and Gary decided to divorce. They had tried for five years to have a baby. After the first couple of years with no luck, the doctors performed all the necessary medical tests to see why Jillian hadn't become pregnant. It was found that Gary had a very low sperm count and Jillian had an anomaly in her uterus. With both issues against them, the doctors advised it was not likely that they would ever conceive.

They had talked about adopting, but Gary was dead set against it. She didn't understand his statements that he couldn't love and raise someone else's child. She would have been ecstatic to have a baby to love and care for, no matter how that baby came into their lives. Gary, however, didn't feel the same way and it had become a major issue for them.

As time progressed, they had begun to grow apart. When her father died, Jillian had hoped they would grow closer, but they had actually grown even farther apart. The tension of the continuing adoption discussions finally caused a permanent rift in their marriage. They agreed to an amicable divorce and Gary graciously moved out of the house when it was listed for sale.

With the downturn in the real estate market, the sale had taken much longer than either of them anticipated. Jillian had rambled around the big four-bedroom house feeling lonely and distracted most of the time. It was such a beautiful home, but much too big for a single person. Then one day, Victor arrived to show the house to a couple new to Raleigh. After the couple left, he stayed to talk about decreasing the price of the house so it would sell faster.

Up to that point, Gary had been Victor's primary point of contact and Jillian had never met him. She made it a point to be gone when the house was shown. It was too painful to think about leaving her beautiful home, the home she had hoped to fill with children and laughter. As fate would have it, she was running late that particular day. Victor was attractive and attentive and exuded a sexuality that took Jillian's breath away.

When Victor suggested they have dinner the next night, Jillian was thrilled. She dressed carefully for their date and was a bundle of nerves when his silver Mercedes pulled into the driveway. Victor was a gentleman, holding her coat while she slipped her arms into the sleeves, opening the car door, and lightly touching her back as he guided her into the restaurant.

The restaurant was small, out of the way, and very romantic with candles and flowers on each table.

After dinner, Jillian had invited Victor in for a nightcap. Before she realized it, she and Victor were kissing and she wanted him in a way she had never felt with Gary. She had taken him into her bed and made passionate love with him. Shortly after, he got up to go home and Jillian was devastated. She tried to understand when he said he had an early morning appointment with his real estate team, but his leaving still hurt. Two days later, they had another date, but never even got out of her house. The heat and sexual attraction between them exploded when Victor kissed her in the foyer and they ended up in bed within minutes of his arrival.

Jillian grunted at the thought of what came next. After the best sex of her life, Victor told her he was married, but the marriage was without love. He was up front that he would never get divorced and he would never be able to stay the night with her. They never went out except to out-of-the-way places. He had asked Jillian to keep their relationship a secret from her family and friends. But then he had promised they would have weekends together occasionally. Thinking that would be enough for her, Jillian had decided to continue the affair.

Shaking her head, Jillian carefully wrapped the picture in bubble wrap and finally admitted that maybe she wasn't cut out to be the "other woman." It wasn't bringing her the peace and contentment she so desperately wanted. To be totally honest, very little in her life was bringing her peace and contentment these days. Maybe it was time for a complete life change….definitely something to think about.

The doorbell blaring from the front hall brought Jillian back to the present. She headed down the hall to let the moving company representative in and start the process of closing the door on her past. By four o'clock that afternoon, she had four moving estimates and had called the first company back to set up a move for two weeks later. She wanted to get moved and settled in her new condo by Labor Day weekend.

With most of the knickknacks from her home office and the family room packed, Jillian was ready to call it a day. She heard her cell phone ringing and ran to the kitchen to grab it off the counter. Kellie was on the line, asking what she wanted for their take-out dinner. They were going to continue packing this evening after dinner. They decided on Chinese, since that was on Kellie's way.

While waiting for Kellie to arrive, Jillian decided to call her mother. She hadn't talked to her in a few days and wanted to check in. She constantly worried that her mom was hiding from the world instead of trying to move on from her loss. Jillian was at a loss as to how to get her mother to rejoin the living.

"Hi Mom," Jillian said when her mother answered. "How's my favorite person in Asheboro?"

"Oh hi, sweetie," Barbara responded. "I'm good, just cooking some dinner. How are you?"

"Doing OK, I guess," Jillian replied. "I'm packing for my move. The house sale closes in two weeks and I have to be out the day before. Did I tell you I have a condo lined up temporarily until I decide what to do?"

"You said that's what you were going to do. I'm glad you found something. You sound kind of down, Jillian," her mother noted. "I have some news that might cheer you up. Want to hear it?"

"I could use some good news Mom," Jillian answered. "What's up?"

"Remember when I went to dinner at my old friend Linda's house a couple of weeks ago?" Barbara asked.

"Sure I remember," Jillian laughed. "I had to call you every day for a week to convince you to go and have fun with your old school friends."

"Well," Barbara divulged in a near whisper. "There was a man there that I had a crush on in high school. His name is Thomas Anderson."

"And????" Jillian giggled at the change in her mother's voice.

"And he's a widower now. He asked me out that night," Barbara confided breathlessly. "We went to the North Carolina Zoo last Saturday afternoon. I had such a good time! He makes me laugh and is such a charming gentleman. He asked me out again and we went to lunch on Tuesday."

"Mom, that's great!" Jillian shouted into the phone. "I'm so glad you're getting out! I hate to think that you spend your days sitting at home."

"Jillie, you kept telling me that your dad wouldn't want me to be alone. I finally decided you're right," Barbara explained. "I'm having so much fun with Thomas! I still feel a little guilty sometimes, but I also feel like I finally have something to look forward to again."

Jillian could almost see the smile on her mother's face. She could definitely hear it in her voice. She smiled too at the knowledge that maybe her mother was finally moving forward.

"Mom, I'm so happy for you," Jillian asserted. "I know Dad would be too. You're only fifty-five, way too young to be alone for the rest of your life. I can't wait to meet your new beau and see if he passes inspection!"

"If he's still around next time you're here, you will definitely meet him," Barbara insisted. "Actually, I'm expecting him for dinner in about an hour. I'm cooking my world famous fried chicken with mashed potatoes."

"If he has any brains at all, that will seal the deal, Mom," Jillian said with giggle. "No man in his right mind would ever walk away from someone who cooks as good as you do!"

"Thank you, sweetie! Now, I hate to be short with you, but I need to get back to my chicken," Barbara said. "I'll call you tomorrow so we can properly catch up. I want to know all about what's going on with you and when I can expect to see you. I sure do miss my beautiful, smart daughter."

"Don't burn the chicken, Mom," Jillian laughed. "Kellie will be here with dinner shortly, so I need to go anyway. She's going to help me pack some more tonight."

"Tell Kellie hello," Barbara replied. "I love you sweetie!"

"I love you too, Mom. Have fun tonight and I'll talk to you tomorrow."

Jillian was still smiling when she hung up. Finally some progress with her mother! At last she was moving forward. Maybe this was a good sign that the Stanley ladies were on their way back up. Maybe it was time for a new beginning for both the Stanley women.

By the time Kellie arrived with their Chinese food, Jillian's good mood was waning. She had spent the last hour thinking about how she was packing her life away in boxes and she only had a temporary home. Once again, she was starting to feel alone and unsettled with her life. As they ate in the kitchen, Kellie studied her friend closely. Jillian looked so sad that Kellie was worried.

"Hey Jillie, talk to me," Kellie said. "What's going on in that head of yours?"

"I don't know Kell," Jillian replied in a shaky voice. "I feel uprooted, like my whole life is being packed up and put in storage. Dad's gone, Mom is in Asheboro, and my marriage is truly over now that the house is sold. The relationship with Victor is going nowhere and never will. I'm over the whole thing with him, if you want the truth. What do I do now? I'm feeling kind of lost."

"I'm so sorry about your parents and Gary," Kellie spoke softly. "I can't imagine how it feels to have your life torn apart like that. However, all I can say about Victor is good riddance. If I ever meet him, he's gonna be walking funny for a long time from a kick in the balls. I can't stand how he lies to you and hurts you! And he's a cheat, too."

"I know, Kellie," Jillian answered, tears rolling down her cheeks. "I can't believe I was stupid enough to fall for his lies. But honestly, I knew up front that the affair wasn't going to go anywhere. He was a diversion from everything else going on. I've decided I'm done with men in general and Victor in particular.

"I have to move on and get my life back on track. The problem is that I don't know what to move on to. I feel so confused. I have no interest in my work anymore, I'm bitchy with the office staff, and my life just seems to be at a standstill. The only thing I really know is that I need a change."

"Hey girlfriend, give yourself some time," Kellie advised as she rose from the chair and put her arms around Jillian. "You don't have to decide right now what you want to do with the rest of your life. Get moved and settled in the new apartment. Then we'll do a girls' weekend at the beach and talk all night, every night we're there. I'm sure we can figure it all out with some sun, sand, conversation, and good wine!"

Jillian smiled at the thought of a road trip with her best friend. They had taken their first trip together to the beach the summer before they graduated from high school. There were several trips during college that were always fun. After she and

Kellie had married, the road trips were very infrequent and there had been none since her father's death. Maybe that was exactly what she needed.

"OK, let's do it!" she cried, feeling a surge of happiness at the thought of a long weekend at the beach with her best friend. "How about a trip to Ocean Isle Beach for Labor Day weekend? I'll be moved into the condo and ready for a break."

"Great idea!" Kellie agreed. "Hey, let's take a look online and see if we can find a place to stay."

Jillian rose from her chair then sat back down. Kellie looked at her, a question in her eyes.

"What?" she asked.

"What about Stephen?" Jillian inquired. "He's not going to like you going off without him for a long weekend."

"No issue there," Kellie replied. "He has a Labor Day weekend fishing trip planned with his dad. He won't even miss me."

The two friends cleaned up the remains of their dinner and took their wine glasses to Jillian's office. An hour later they had reservations for a two-bedroom condo beginning Friday night of Labor Day weekend. Jillian seemed to be in much better spirits. They spent the next few hours packing the hundreds of books that were still waiting on the office shelves.

Around eleven o'clock, Kellie left and Jillian drug herself upstairs to bed. She put on her favorite pajamas and settled in to read a bit while she finished her glass of wine. When she lifted the book from her bedside table, a piece of paper floated out. Jillian picked it up and read it for probably the tenth time. It was a hand written note Victor had left under the pillow several weeks earlier. It described how hot and sexy he thought she was. How he liked her fiery red hair, especially when she was leaning over him, sucking on his penis. How he thought about her all the time, wanted her with an intensity he had never known before. Jillian tore the note into little pieces and threw it off the bed. She burst into tears and buried her face in the pillow, crying herself to sleep.

Jillian awoke to a darkened bedroom, certain she had heard a noise. The bedroom door opened and the night light from the hallway showed the silhouette of a man with broad shoulders and long legs. He looked familiar so she wasn't afraid, but she couldn't bring his name to mind. He crossed the room, pulled the covers back, and stood looking down at her. Even in the darkness, Jillian could feel his eyes taking in every inch of her body. She was sure she had pajamas on when she went to bed, but now she was naked under his gaze. His eyes were raking the length of her body, setting her on fire inside.

In one swift move, the man removed his shirt and pushed his pants to the floor. Jillian could see his penis spring free, hard and pulsing. She sucked in a breath, thinking about how it would feel inside her now wet pussy. Reluctantly she moved her eyes up and caught sight of a tightly muscled chest, followed by the darkest, most intense eyes she had ever seen. Jillian's breathing became ragged as the mystery man's eyes bore into her. Her nipples hardened and her stomach muscles clenched in an agonizing need to have this man, have him now.

"Jillian," the man whispered, so softly she wasn't sure he had actually spoken.

"Take me," she whispered in return.

In the next instant, Jillian felt him kneel on the bed be-tween her wide spread legs. She had no memory of opening herself to him, only an acute desire to fill her heated core with his throbbing penis. He leaned forward and slowly ran the head of his penis over her dripping wet pussy lips and across her clit. Jillian moaned as electric jolts shot through her entire body. He did it again and again until she was writhing on the bed, begging for release.

It seemed he had teased her for an eternity when he finally lowered his body on top of hers. His scent, the feel of his skin against hers, and the depth of his eyes overwhelmed her already quivering body with another rush of erotic sensations. In all of her thirty-two years, she had never felt such desire for a man. It was the only thought in her mind right now. Her world was reduced to the incredibly sensual feelings rushing through her body and the need to take him inside her.

"Please," she whimpered. "Oh god, please."

Without a single word, he put his lips to hers and slid his tongue into her mouth. Her pelvis arched up, desperate for him. He obliged by once again sliding his length across her pussy lips and clit. Jillian screamed as a powerful orgasm took over her body. She pushed up against him and his hard penis slid inside her, setting off another extraordinary orgasm. She felt him begin to thrust in and out of her, his breathing now becoming as labored as hers. He stroked her faster and faster, pushing her higher and higher with each thrust.

"Jillian!" he growled as he began to explode inside her.

Jillian screamed again as her body pulled him deeper inside and she orgasmed with an unbelievable ferocity. The man lay on top of her, both of them struggling for breath. Jillian closed her eyes, unable to think, unable to speak.

When she opened her eyes again, Jillian was alone in her bed. She looked around as the morning sun streamed in the bedroom window. She was disoriented for a minute, wondering where her late night lover had gone. When she saw she was wearing pajamas, she almost cried as she realized it had only been a dream. Letting out a huge sigh, Jillian got out of bed and headed for the shower. She had a lot of work to do to finish packing away her life.

CHAPTER 3

Jillian spent Saturday morning packing pictures and knickknacks in the living room and dining room. When she took a break for lunch, she noticed she had a text message on her iPhone. It was from a number she didn't recognize. She opened the message and realized it wasn't meant for her as soon as she began to read it.

Hi Angel, this is Will. Sure enjoyed dancing with u at the tiki bar last night. Hope to see u again before the weekend is over.

She ignored the message, deciding that Will, whoever he was, would figure out on his own that he had been given a wrong number. As she fixed a tuna sandwich, her phone buzzed again. She picked it up and saw a new text message.

It's Will again. Can we meet for drinks tonight?

Jillian immediately replied, wanting to shut this down right away. After all, she was done with men until she figured out what her future was going to be.

You have the wrong number. I'm not Angel.

In just a few minutes, her phone buzzed again as a new text came in. She read it and shook her head.

Come on beautiful, u gave me this number. After that incredibly sexy slow dance last night, don't get shy on me today!

This was immediately followed by another text.

Let's meet for a drink tonight at the tiki bar. U said ur staying close by. Drinks at 8?

Trying to decide how to convince this guy that he had a wrong number, Jillian took time to eat her lunch while she was thinking. As she cleared her plate and glass from the table, her phone rang. She looked at the screen and saw it was Kellie.

"Hey Kellie," she answered. "What's up?"

"Just wanted to check up on my best friend today," Kellie replied. "How are you?"

"OK, I guess," Jillian responded. "I'm making progress in the living and dining rooms. Gary is coming by tomorrow to get his furniture and the rest of the things that he stored in the spare bedroom. I'll wait to pack the kitchen until the last day. I might actually be ready when the movers get here."

As she was talking, her phone beeped again. Another text message had come in.

"Hang on a second, Kellie," she said. "I have a text message I need to read. Be right back."

I'm persistent with beautiful women that dance as good as u do. Come on sexy Angel, how about that drink?

"Well, he just doesn't give up!" Jillian exclaimed as she went back to her phone call.

"Who?" Kellie asked. "Please tell me it's not Victor!"

"Nope, not Victor," Jillian replied. "I'm getting text messages from some guy named Will. He says I gave him my number at a tiki bar last night and he wants to get together for drinks. I told him he has a wrong number, but he thinks I'm being shy with him."

"Oh wow! Almost like a secret admirer!!" Kellie squealed. "You should reply. Maybe the Masters of the Universe are trying to bring a new man into your life."

"Yeah right, Kellie," Jillian giggled. "I'm sure the universe uses text messages to hook up random people. Besides, I'm done with men, remember?"

"So? Play along, Jillian. What have you got to lose?" Kellie said. "It's a text message, not a marriage proposal!"

"I don't know, Kellie," Jillian responded. "It seems kind of mean to lead him on. He thinks I'm someone named Angel."

"Come on, Miss Stick in the Mud," Kellie teased. "Have some fun with it. If it gets too far along, you can always stop replying to him. It's not like he can find you. He doesn't know where you live or work. Heck, he doesn't even know your real name!"

"I'll think about it," Jillian said and then changed the subject. "What are you and Stephen doing this weekend?"

"His grandparents are visiting so we have to go to his parent's house for dinner tonight," Kellie answered. "Tomorrow we're tied up with them all day at an outing at Falls River State Park. Want to come along tonight and tomorrow? I could use the moral support. You know how ugly his mom gets with me."

"Let's see, a quiet evening at home tonight or dinner with the wicked witch of the east?" Jillian laughed. "My friend, as much as I love you and Stephen, I'm not up to dinner with the wicked witch. Sorry, but you're on your own!"

"I totally understand," Kellie sighed. "If I could get out of it, I certainly would. How about tomorrow? I would love having someone to hang with. I know Stephen, his dad, and his grandfather will be fishing all day. I'm going to be stuck with the wicked witch and her mother!"

"I really can't," Jillian replied. "I want to be here when Gary comes and I hope to get more of the packing finished. I have less than two weeks until the movers get here."

"Wow, it's coming up fast, isn't it?" Kellie noted. "So, are you going to return the text from your new admirer? Don't think I'm going to forget about that!"

"I don't know Kellie," Jillian answered. "It seems kind of dishonest but I'll think about it."

"Well, I still think you should," Kellie responded. "Like I said before, have some fun with it. What do you have to lose? Anyway, I better get going. I have a bunch of things to do before we go to the witch's castle."

As the two friends hung up, Jillian pulled up her text messages. Maybe a different tactic would get him to go away.

Hi Will. You are definitely persistent! Can't do drinks tonight. Had to leave unexpectedly this morning.

Now maybe this annoying man would leave her alone. Jillian headed back to the dining room, phone in hand. As soon as she laid it on the table, it buzzed with a new text.

Too bad u had to miss the last day of ur vacation. Beautiful day here. Hope everything is OK in Raleigh!

Jillian hesitated before replying again. Maybe if she left it alone, he would move on and stop texting her. She was debating what to do when her phone buzzed again.

Did I tell you that I'm originally from Raleigh? Maybe we can get together next time I come to see my dad. Let's stay in touch.

Yikes! Jillian drew in a sharp breath wondering if this was someone she knew. Maybe someone she went to school with? In the next breath, she decided that was silly. Raleigh was a good-sized town and she certainly didn't know everyone. She decided one last text and she would be finished with this guy.

Sure, let me know if you ever get this way. We can go dancing again.

Jillian looked at the message as it went into cyber space. What in the world prompted her to offer to go dancing with him? Oh well, she thought, I'll never hear from him so it doesn't really matter. She picked up the roll of bubble wrap and a box and opened the glass doors of the china cupboard to begin packing her wedding china. As she set a stack of plates on the table, her phone buzzed one more time. She began to read the text from Will and sighed.

Sounds good! Until then, let's chat and get to know each other. All I really know is that ur a beautiful woman from Raleigh and a great dancer. When's a good time to call u?

Reading the message, Jillian thought oh no, this is definitely not what I wanted. Now what am I going to do? But deep inside, she realized she was getting a little thrill out of pretending to be someone else. What would be the harm in texting or chatting with him? Men twisted the truth to their liking all the time, so why shouldn't she? Like Kellie said, it was a text message, not a marriage proposal! She decided to put him off for a day or so while she thought about it.

Busy today but maybe we can chat tomorrow. I'll text you.

Seconds later, a new text from Will buzzed in.

OK. Don't want to intrude on whatever took u back to Raleigh. Looking forward to hearing from u beautiful Angel!

Jillian refocused on her packing but her thoughts were swirling with the deception she had just started. Part of her felt guilty at leading this guy on, but another part was excited at the thought of talking to someone who knew nothing about her. She could be anyone she wanted to be, invent the life she wanted to live. And right now, a different life looked so much better than the one she was living.

Sunday morning was hot and sunny with endless blue skies. Jillian woke early, determined to do as much packing as possible. Maybe after Gary came by to get his boxes and furniture, she would go for a late afternoon swim at the community pool.

She had finished packing the living and dining rooms the evening before and was now attacking the family room. Since Gary had already taken his things from this room, it wouldn't take as long as the other rooms had. She was almost done when the doorbell rang around noon.

Jillian hurried down the hall and opened the door for Gary. He had a big truck parked in the driveway and a couple of friends ready to help load it. As they piled into the foyer, Jillian was aghast at what she saw on the street. Victor had pulled up in front of the house and was getting out of his car!

What in the world was he doing here? Seeing her expression of surprise, Gary turned to look out the door.

"Oh good, there's Victor," he said. "Hope you don't mind that I asked him to stop by."

"Uh, well, no," Jillian stammered. "But why is he here?"

"He has some papers for us to sign before the closing can go forward," Gary replied. "I thought it was easier if he just came here since we would both be here. Are you OK? You look upset."

"No, I'm fine," Jillian lied as she struggled to keep her composure.

Victor arrived at the door and Gary greeted him like a long lost brother.

"Victor, have you ever met my ex-wife Jillian?" Gary asked. "I remember that when we signed the sales agreement, she had to stop in at your office without me. I don't know if you met her then."

"We met here at the house once," Jillian rushed to speak first, not trusting Victor to keep his mouth shut. "He was showing the house and I was late getting out that day. That's the only time we ever met."

"Nice to see you again, Jillian," Victor said with a knowing smirk on his face. "Gary, I tell you, if I wasn't married, I would have to ask this gorgeous woman out. The fiery red hair and deep green eyes, now that's an alluring combination."

"She's beautiful, smart, and still one of my best friends," Gary responded. "And she makes all of those horrible ex-wife stories sound like total lies."

"Hey guys, I'm standing right here," Jillian sighed. "How about letting me get back to my packing and then you guys can talk about me all you want."

"I only have a few minutes anyway," Victor responded. "On my way to do an open house here in Falls River. It's at the Waverly's over on Riverton Drive."

With Jillian leading the way, they trooped into the kitchen and Victor produced the papers he needed them to sign. With that done, he formally shook Jillian's hand and Gary walked him out. Jillian was sitting at the kitchen table, her heart racing, when Gary returned.

"You OK, Jillian?" he inquired upon seeing the flush on her face. "You look flushed."

"Yeah, sure," she replied, her brain scrambling for an excuse. "I guess signing those papers makes it real, doesn't it?"

Gary sat down and took Jillian's hand. Even though they had agreed a divorce was best for both of them, he felt bad for her and sincerely hoped she would move on soon. The last couple of years had been one nightmare after another for her.

"Yes, I guess it's really going to happen," he began, looking into her eyes. "I know you've had a very difficult time the last few years. I'm so sorry that the divorce had to happen, but remember, we agreed it's best for both of us. One thing you need to know is that I will always be here for you if you need anything. The divorce has nothing to do with our friendship."

Jillian looked down at their hands intertwined and then back into Gary's eyes. He had no idea her flushed face had to do with the piercing looks Victor had given her while Gary signed the papers, looks that sent heat straight to her lower abdomen. And he had no idea that shaking hands with Victor had set the rest of her body on fire. She was upset that her body still responded to the slightest touch from that man. She stood and went to the refrigerator for a bottle of water.

"I know, Gary," Jillian replied walking back to the table. She smiled at him. "I appreciate your friendship more than you can imagine. I'll be fine once I get moved into the condo. Did I tell you that Kellie and I are going to Ocean Isle Beach for Labor Day weekend? A girls' road trip is exactly what I need. I can clear my head and be ready to take on whatever comes my way next."

"Now that's my best friend talking!" Gary said, smiling back at her. "I better get out there and get the guys started before they decide to go home. Promise me you'll call me if you need to talk, OK?"

"Of course," Jillian responded, trying to sound upbeat while her mind screamed no way, no way, no way can I talk to him about Victor. "Now go put those guys to work and make them earn that six pack of beer."

By four o'clock, the house was once again quiet. Gary and his friends had finished moving his furniture and boxes. Jillian wandered through the rooms that were now only partially furnished. The house looked so lonely. She found herself back in the kitchen, wondering what to do next. Pack some more? Go for a swim? Neither sounded good to her right now. Instead she pulled out a wine glass and filled it with what was left in the bottle she and Kellie had shared Friday evening.

Jillian sat out on the back patio in one of the remaining lounge chairs sipping her wine. She thought about her life and where she wanted it to go next. The wine was making her warm and a little fuzzy headed. She had finished the glass of wine and was deep in thought when a familiar voice startled her.

"Hey babe, mind if I join you?" Victor asked, looking down at her.

"Victor, I thought I was clear that I didn't want to see you again," Jillian spoke quietly without looking up at him. She didn't trust herself to look at him, knowing one look could easily undo her resolve to end things. "Why are you here?"

"I knocked on the front door, but you didn't answer. It was unlocked so I let myself in," he answered in a pleading voice. "I miss you, Jillian. I couldn't stop thinking about you while I was at the open house. I need to see you, be with you again. Please talk to me."

"Victor, we are over, done, finished," Jillian stated forcefully, trying to convince both Victor and herself. "You need to leave now."

Victor stepped closer and Jillian could feel the sexuality radiating from his body, smell his unique scent. With the wine in her blood and the sun beating down, she felt a rush of heat overtake her body. She was instantly filled with desire for him, her body aching to be held and loved. Then she made the mistake of looking up at him. Her eyes met his and her brain shut down.

"I miss you babe," Victor whispered. "I need to be with you, Jillian."

Jillian reached up and took his hand in hers. She pulled him down on top of her, wanting him urgently. Their lips met and Jillian sighed as he settled his weight on top of her. How could this feel so good when she knew he was the wrong man for her? Not wanting to think about that, she slid her tongue into his mouth and their kiss deepened.

Victor groaned and rubbed his crotch against her. Her body responded with an intense need to feel his skin against hers. Jillian broke the kiss for a few seconds while she pulled her shirt over her head and then unbuttoned his shirt. Her hungry mouth found his again while his hands began to caress her bare skin. Victor unhooked the front clasp of her bra, moved it out of the way, and covered one naked breast with his hand. He squeezed her breast as he sucked her tongue deeper into his mouth. Jillian moaned against his lips at the feel of his rough hand touching the delicate skin of her breast.

When he pinched her nipple, she broke the kiss to gasp in pleasure.

Victor rolled to one side and pulled Jillian's shorts and panties down over her hips. She kicked them off and instinctively opened her legs for him. He brushed his lips over her hard nipples, biting each one gently to make her moan again. His hand traveled over her belly and down to her pubic hair while his mouth continued to assault her nipples.

Jillian was crazed with need. She arched up against his hand, her body begging to be touched more intimately. Victor complied with her unspoken request and slid his fingers towards her white-hot center. He stroked her hard little clit with his thumb, sending shock waves through Jillian's entire body. A few more seconds and she went rigid with an intense orgasm. He continued to touch her clit as his fingers stroked her wet pussy lips. She screamed as a second orgasm followed quickly on the heels of the first.

"Ssshhhh, babe," Victor murmured. "Maybe we should go inside. We don't need the neighbors watching."

"Neighbors can't see back here. Trees and fence block view…." Jillian gasped, as she tried to calm her breathing.

Victor lifted his head and looked around. Satisfied that no one could see them, he stood and removed his shirt and pants. He rolled a condom over his fully erect penis and lay back down on the lounge chair, this time between Jillian's legs. He leaned over and sucked on her nipples once again. Jillian's breath caught in her throat as Victor slid his fully erect penis into her dripping wet pussy. He began to thrust into her, slowly at first. His lips locked onto her breast again, sucking hard on her nipple as his penis moved faster and faster inside her.

"Oh god, baby," Victor moaned. "You feel so good. So hot, so wet, so damn good."

He pushed deeper into her wetness as she instinctively spread her legs wider. Jillian could feel another orgasm building and pulled him closer to her, rubbing herself against him with each thrust. Victor suddenly growled and pulled his penis out of her. He pulled the condom off, then grabbed his erection with his right hand and began jerking himself off. In a few seconds, his cum gushed all over her belly and breasts. When he was done, Victor laid down beside Jillian. He seemed to be taking great care not to touch her cum-covered breasts or belly.

"Oh my God, babe," he groaned. "That was awesome! You really know how to make a man feel good. That was so hot, cumming on you like that."

Feeling unsatisfied from Victor's abrupt move, Jillian lay quietly. She wanted to ask him to touch her and make her cum again. She wanted him on top of her instead of beside her. She wanted him to make her feel cared for instead of used. Without warning, Victor jumped up and grabbed his clothes.

"Babe, can I take a quick shower before I go?" he asked, grinning at her like the cat that caught the canary. "Don't want to go home smelling like sex!"

Jillian looked up at him and instead of the desire she had felt before, she felt total disgust. Disgust at him for treating her so poorly, but more than that, disgust with herself for allowing him to use her once again. She sat up and slipped into her clothes, the thin fabric of her summer top clinging to her sticky belly. All she could think was that she needed a scalding, hot shower to rid her body of him.

"Get out, Victor." Jillian spoke in a low, firm voice. "Get out of my house and out of my life. We are finished. You disgust me and make me disgusted with myself."

"Oh, come on babe, you know that's not true," Victor scoffed and grabbed his crotch. "You know you can't live without this."

"GET OUT!" Jillian shouted this time. "You will never see me again. You will never have another opportunity to use me."

"Oh, but I will see you," Victor gloated. "At the closing next week. We can't close the sale of this fine house without your signature. And then we can celebrate afterwards, babe. Just you and me and my big cock."

Victor grabbed his crotch again and then turned and went through the kitchen door. Jillian followed him through the house. When he went out the front door without another word, she slammed it behind him. Then she carefully locked the deadbolt and clicked the chain into place. She wanted to be sure he couldn't get back inside her house and her head.

Jillian ran up the stairs and into her bathroom. She turned on the water as hot as she could stand it and stepped into the shower. As the water cascaded over her body, she began to cry. She felt used and violated even though she had invited Victor to make love to her. Jillian cried even harder when she finally admitted to herself that they hadn't made love. She had allowed Victor to use her for sex, something she vowed she would never again permit.

Stepping from the shower, Jillian looked at her reflection in the mirror. She wanted someone to talk to, someone who would understand how hurt she felt. Kellie was the only one who knew about Victor and she was tied up with Stephen's family today. Oh God, she needed someone to talk to, someone to help bolster her resolve to put Victor out of her life for good.

As she walked into the bedroom and rummaged her dresser for clean clothes, Jillian's mind was racing, trying to think of someone she could call. Just as she was about to give up, she thought of Will. Will wanted to talk to her, get to know her better. He didn't know she wasn't Angel from the bar. He said he didn't know anything about her except her name and that she was a beautiful lady from Raleigh. She didn't know anything about him either so it would almost be like talking to a therapist.

Jillian picked up her phone and went to her text messages. Then she put it back down, arguing with herself that this wasn't fair to Will. Almost immediately she picked it up again and began typing a text message to him. What was that old saying? All's fair in love and war. Well, this was war....war against men who used women.

Hi there, it's Angel. Still interested in chatting?

In less than a minute, her phone buzzed with a new text message.

Hey beautiful Angel. Glad to hear from you. Call me, would love to chat.

Taking a deep breath, Jillian dialed Will's number. She wasn't sure what she was doing but she decided she would plunge ahead anyway. All her life she had played by the rules and what did she have to show for it? Her life was in shambles and she was alone. So now she would play by her own rules, consequences be damned.

CHAPTER 4

As she climbed in bed later, Jillian thought about the conversation she and Will had just concluded. It started out a bit awkward, but in fifteen minutes, she had felt comfortable with this stranger. He was a good listener and had quickly put her at ease. She admitted to feeling a little weird talking to someone she barely knew. He laughed and told her it was OK.

"Just pretend this is a first date," Will said. "We didn't really talk much the other night so we still need to get to know each other. I'll tell you a little about me and then you can tell me about yourself."

Will told her he owned a small business that catered to large companies. He traveled all over the world, wherever his current client needed him. He had a house at the beach where he lived when he wasn't traveling. Last week was a rare week that he didn't have a project, so he had come home for a few days. He was heading out of town again the next day for an assignment. He thought he would be gone for a few weeks but didn't know exactly how long.

Before she could ask Will what kind of business he was in, he began asking her questions about herself. Being careful not to relate too many identifying details, Jillian told him that she was in a transition phase of her life. She said she had just gotten out of a bad relationship and decided it was time to examine her life and where she wanted it to go.

"Wow," Will exclaimed. "That guy must have done a real number on you if you're examining your entire life."

"It's more than just my failed relationship. I lost a close family member just before my relationship went south," Jillian replied, deciding not to give the detail that it was her father she lost. "I really looked up to that person and my career choice was tied to my respect for him. Now that he's gone, I'm realizing that I might be in the wrong job."

"Oh, Angel," Will murmured in a sympathetic voice. "I'm so sorry you had to go through a death and a bad relationship back to back. No one deserves that. It's completely understandable that you're taking a step back to look at your life. However, let me caution you not to make any rash decisions based emotions. Take time to think it through."

"You sound just like my best friend," Jillian responded. "She was telling me the same thing the other day. I have to take time to think about my options because I honestly don't know what I want to do."

"Well, anytime you want to talk, just give me a call," Will sympathized. "I'm an excellent listener. Maybe I can be your second best friend."

"You can be my best phone friend since you travel all the time," Jillian chuckled.

"It's a deal!" Will shouted. "I like that. I'll be the best phone friend of beautiful Angel. Maybe when you feel more settled, we could be more than phone friends. I would love to take you out dancing again."

"Will, I truly appreciate the offer," Jillian began. "But for now, I need to keep this as phone friends. I'm so confused about so many things. I feel really vulnerable right now.

Honestly, I don't trust my own judgment when it comes to the people I let into my life."

"Of course, Angel," he replied. "I don't mean to rush you at all. I had a great time the other night and find you interesting and beautiful. However, the little bit I now know has made me realize two things. First, I definitely want to get to know you better. You sound like an amazing person. Second, I have to give you as much space as you need so I'll have the opportunity to get to know you better. You'll discover that not only am I a good listener, but I'm good at reading people. I can see that you're skittish about this whole thing and I understand why. I won't push you or ask for something I don't think you can comfortably give."

"Thanks, Will. I want to get to know you too, but I have to take this slow," Jillian responded. She quickly changed to subject to get the focus off of her. "Tell me about your work. Where have you traveled? What have you seen of the world? I've haven't traveled out of the country much."

Will entertained Jillian with tales of things he had seen and done all over the world. He told her about his first trip to China and how surprised he was to find the food wasn't anything like any Chinese restaurant he had ever frequented in the United States. He gave her a graphic description of the strange fish, live eels, and unusual vegetables he found in Chinese outdoor markets. Jillian laughed as he talked about trying to figure out what to buy for dinner when faced with long beans, pei tsai, komatsuna, and bitter melons.

He talked about seeing live sea bass and Chinese carp swimming in tanks and watching the Chinese fishmonger grab one out with his bare hand. Jillian giggled when he admitted that he had no idea what to do when the fishmonger tried to hand the live fish to him. She went into fits of uncontrollable laughter when he described using his own version of sign language to let the Chinaman know he wanted his fish dead and filleted.

Other tales were told of trips to Amsterdam, Rome, and Egypt. Will was a good storyteller and made Jillian laugh again and again. It was so much fun listening to him talk about getting in trouble with the guards at the Vatican in Rome, riding and falling off of a camel in Egypt, and how the beer in Amsterdam was so good he had tried to go to every pub in the city. Jillian was shocked when she looked at the clock and saw it was almost ten o'clock. They had been talking for over three hours! When Will took a break from his monologue, Jillian told him she needed to hang up.

"I'll let you hang up on one condition," he told her. "You have to promise we will talk again soon. I still don't know much about you. I'm curious by nature so the mystery of Angel has really peaked my interest."

"I'd love to talk again," Jillian answered. "I had such a good time listening to your stories. Call me when you get back from your trip and we can continue this."

"Maybe I'll call while I'm gone, if I get a break. Just have to remember the time difference," Will noted. "I get really wrapped up in my work and tend to forget the time when I'm in the middle of a project. I sure don't want to call you in the middle of the night and scare the crap out of you."

"I appreciate that," Jillian laughed. "I need my beauty sleep!"

"You're already beautiful, Angel," Will said solemnly. "I think you've had plenty of beauty sleep. Now what you need is some fun, like dancing until the wee hours of the morning or playing in the surf at the beach. But I'd like to ask you to save the dancing until we can get together again. That last slow dance was so hot.....I want to be the one pressed up against your sexy body."

Jillian was momentarily speechless. She had been having so much fun that she forgot Will thought she was someone else. She forgot that he obviously had enjoyed dancing with this woman named Angel. Oh, what had she started by calling him?

"Sure," Jillian stuttered. "No dancing until we meet again."

"I'm sorry. I certainly didn't mean to make you uncomfortable," Will spoke quietly, thinking he had made her nervous with his statement about her sexy body. "I'll try to behave until we know each other better."

"Thank you. Well, I really need to go Will," Jillian said in a rush.

"Me too, Angel," Will responded, hoping he hadn't blown it with her. "I'll text you while I'm gone and, if we can find a moment, maybe we can talk."

"That works for me," Jillian replied. "Goodnight Will. Sleep well."

"Goodnight to you too, beautiful Angel."

As she sat in bed, Jillian went over the personal part of the conversation again. She still wasn't sure exactly what Will did for a living, but she did know he enjoyed life to the fullest. She also knew that whenever she was ready to open up, he would listen to her. For some reason, that made her feel better than she had in a long time. Since it wasn't too late, she decided to check on her mother before going to sleep.

"Hi, Mom," Jillian said when her mother answered. "How was your date on Friday?"

"Hi, sweetie," Barbara responded. "I'm so glad you called. Thomas and I had a lovely dinner. He's such a gentleman! And he loved my fried chicken, mashed potatoes, and gravy."

"Mom, no one can resist your fried chicken!" Jillian exclaimed. "I'm glad you had a good time and that he's a gentleman. You deserve nothing less."

"That goes for you too," Barbara replied. "How are you doing?"

"Actually, I'm doing really well," Jillian announced. "I'm almost finished packing and the movers will be here next week on Thursday. Then Kellie and I are going to Ocean Isle on Friday. I think I'm finally ready to move forward. Now if I could just figure out what to do when I move forward, life would be perfect."

"Oh Jillian, I'm so happy you're ready to move on," her mother said. "We both have to do that. You know your father wouldn't want either of us to be sad forever. Life is too short to be in a situation that makes us unhappy."

"Mom, I need to tell you something." Jillian hesitated. "I know it was Dad's dream for me to follow in his footsteps and work with him. I loved being at the firm when Dad was there. But part of what I'm struggling with right now is whether accounting is the right career for me. I don't want to hurt you but…"

"Jillian," Barbara cried, interrupting her daughter. "You've far exceeded your father's wildest dreams. He loved having you at SW&K. Your dad is gone now and you have to follow the path that is best for you. He would never want you to stay there if you really want to do something else. Follow your own dreams, sweetie. Do what makes you happy."

"Mom, you're the best!" Jillian responded, happiness welling up inside her. "I don't know yet what I want to do, but I'll figure it out. I love writing and you know I'm good at it. If I could find a way to make a living at that, it would be awesome."

"Sweetheart, take your time and think this through," her mother said. "Don't make an emotional decision. Make the decision that is right for you. Now when are you coming to see me? I can't wait to introduce you to Thomas."

"Soon, Mom," Jillian answered. "I need to get moved and settled and then take my trip with Kellie. I have a big project at work once I get back from Ocean Isle, so it may be mid to late October before I can squeeze a trip to Asheboro in."

"I'm going to hold you to that," Barbara threatened with a smile in her voice. "I know you're all grown up but you're still my little girl. I miss you and worry about you, you know."

"I miss you too, Mom. I'll call you again in a few days. And don't worry about me. I'm doing OK."

Jillian and her mother said their goodbyes and hung up. Jillian lay back in her bed with a smile on her face. She was so happy her mother was finally coming out of her self-imposed exile and enjoying life again. Now if she could only do the same. Her phone buzzed, signaling a text message. When she read it she smiled an even bigger smile.

I really enjoyed talking to u this evening beautiful Angel. Will do it again very soon. Take care of yourself while I'm gone my best phone friend!

Phone friend! At least for the time being, Will seemed OK that they were only going to be phone friends. Jillian was glad she had opened up to him somewhat. And she couldn't wait to talk to him again. Picking up her phone, she typed a reply.

I enjoyed talking to you too! Be safe on your travels and we'll talk again when you get back.

CHAPTER 5

The next ten days flew by. Jillian and Gary closed on the sale of the house. Victor tried to make eye contact with her during the closing but she ignored him. Afterwards, when Gary went to the restroom, he tried to talk to her but she walked away without responding. She knew the affair was truly done and all she felt for Victor was loathing.

Other than a few text messages, Jillian had not heard from Will and she found she missed him. Early on the Thursday morning before Labor Day weekend, she directed the movers as they emptied her beautiful house of all signs that she had ever lived there. It was sad to say a final goodbye to her old life, but she also found she was looking forward to beginning a new life.

The furniture was delivered to storage and Jillian's personal items were then delivered to her furnished condo. She spent the rest of the day organizing her new home and thinking about her trip with Kellie. They were leaving at noon Friday and had a girls' weekend planned. She was happy and excited to have time with her best friend at her favorite beach. They had three days for sun, sand, seafood, wine, and as much talking as possible.

As she finished putting her clothes away, Jillian heard her phone buzz with a text message. She smiled when she saw whom it was from.

Hi beautiful Angel! How's it going?

Jillian quickly typed a reply.

Hi Will! Good. How are you?

While she waited for a reply, Jillian began organizing her linen closet and bathroom. In a few short minutes, her phone buzzed again. She was hoping Will was back and wanted to talk again.

Looking forward to getting back home. Be back in NC Saturday afternoon. Any weekend plans for u?

When she read the message, Jillian was surprised at how disappointed she felt. She would have loved to talk to Will this evening. She knew she couldn't talk to him over the weekend with Kellie around. Especially since she hadn't told Kellie that she had actually spoken to him. Kellie thought they were still just exchanging text messages.

Going away for the weekend with my best friend. Leaving tomorrow. Back home Monday. How about you?

With the towels, sheets, and other items neatly stowed in the linen closet, Jillian began filling the under-sink storage area with items for the bathroom. She had finished and was on her way to the kitchen when her phone buzzed again.

*No plans except to relax and rest. Glad ur going to enjoy
some time with your best friend. Where r u going? Was
hoping I might see you at the Tiki bar.*

Realizing that she didn't know which North Carolina beach Will lived at or where he met Angel, Jillian was suddenly hesitant to tell him where she would be. Maybe he lived at Ocean Isle, where she was going. That was a long shot, since there were dozens of beaches within four hours of Raleigh. However, she didn't want to take any chances so she decided not to tell him the truth.

*Going to the mountains. Family cabin at the lake. Probably
the last time until spring that I can go. Snows early up there.*

As she fixed a cup of tea, Jillian wished she could tell Will the truth. He sounded like a really good guy and all she had done was lie to him. It was too late now, she decided. At some point she would either have to break it off or come clean with him. Both results were something she didn't want to think about. Her phone buzzed again and she put her cup down to read the text.

*Love the NC mountains! Have a great weekend beautiful
Angel. Can I call u while ur there?*

Oh wow, now what should she say? Jillian hated this lying thing more and more. She thought quickly and responded.

*No cell reception at cabin. R u leaving again soon? Maybe
talk next week?*

In seconds her phone buzzed again.

Not sure how long I'll be around. Talk next week for sure.
Let me know when u get back. I missed talking to you while
I was gone.

Jillian breathed a sigh of relief. While it was true the Stanley's mountain cabin had no cell reception, deceiving Will was not feeling very good to her. She responded with another text.

Absolutely! Lets talk next week sometime. Looking forward
to it!!

At least that text was completely true. Now she had the weekend to think about how she might tell him the truth. Maybe she would confide in Kellie and see what she thought about it. The phone buzzed once again.

Me too! Late here, need to go to bed. Have a GREAT
weekend!

Finished with her tea, Jillian headed to the bedroom to organize her closet and pack for the weekend. She was excited that she and Kellie would have some time away from Stephen. She loved Kellie's husband like a brother, but a long weekend where they could talk uninterrupted was exactly what she needed right now. She had to figure out what she wanted to do with the rest of her life and what to do about Will. Her best friend always had good, solid advice and Jillian wasn't comfortable lying to Will anymore. She sighed as she put her bright blue bikini into her suitcase. What to do?

At noon the next day, Jillian pulled up in front of Kellie and Stephen's house. She honked the horn and Kellie came flying out the door with a backpack hanging over one shoulder, pulling a suitcase behind her. Jillian popped open the back hatch and waited for her friend to stow her luggage.

The hatch slammed closed and Kellie jumped into the passenger side of the Jeep.

"Let's go!" Kellie shouted. "I am sooooooo ready for this trip. I wanted to put a muzzle on Stephen when he was getting ready for work this morning. All that whining about how he has to be alone for tonight and tomorrow until he and his dad leave. You would think I was going to be gone for three months!"

"Let's do it then!" Jillian bellowed as she pulled away from the curb. "Ocean Isle here we come!! They won't know what hit them when the Dynamic Duo of Jillie and Kellie get to town."

Both women burst into a fit of giggles as they headed toward the interstate. In less than three hours they would stop in Shallotte, a small town on the mainland, to pick up some groceries and wine for the weekend. Then a short hop over the Intracoastal Waterway and they would be in Ocean Isle Beach, ready for a fish dinner and a glass or two of wine.

Holiday weekend traffic was heavy leaving Shallotte and bumper-to-bumper over the causeway onto the island. After checking in with the rental agency, the women finally arrived at their rental condo on West First Street shortly after five o'clock. They unpacked the car, put on their bikinis, and uncorked the wine.

As they walked down the elevated wooden walkway that took them over the dunes, Jillian sighed with relief. Here on this beautiful strip of beach, she felt her worries begin to dissolve. She had always loved the ocean. Being here brought back bittersweet memories of trips with her parents when she was a child. It also brought back memories of fun trips with Kellie during their college breaks.

After setting up her beach chair and placing her glass of wine in the cup holder, Jillian sat down and looked at the waves gently lapping at the sand. She didn't know how or why, but looking out over the ocean was always a calming experience for her. She was so happy to be here with Kellie for the long weekend.

"Oh wow, I forgot how much I enjoy this," Kellie exclaimed. "Especially this time of day when all the kids are either napping or playing mini-golf! It's almost like having the beach to ourselves."

"I know what you mean," Jillian replied. "For a holiday weekend, the beach is really quiet right now. This is exactly what I need."

"I know, Jillie," Kellie answered. "We've both been going non-stop for weeks now. I'm so glad we decided to do this. We really need some time to unwind."

"And I need your thoughts on what to do with my life," Jillian said. "I think I told you that my mom is OK with me leaving the firm. That's good, of course, but now I have figure out where to go and what to do."

"I'm happy to share my thoughts tomorrow," Kellie responded. "Tonight is for relaxing, drinking wine, and laughter. No heavy duty discussions for the Dynamic Duo!"

"Absolutely!" Jillian laughed as she raised her glass to Kellie's. "Here's to the Dynamic Duo! We haven't had a real Double D weekend since we graduated from college. It was always so much fun when we used to take off and go at a moment's notice. Batman and Robin have nothing on this Dynamic Duo."

Both women chuckled as they remembered how they used to wander up and down the North and South Carolina coast, calling themselves the Dynamic Duo or the Double D's for short. It was on trips just like this that their already strong friendship had forged an unbreakable bond. They had been there for each other in fun times as well as crisis times. Jillian knew she could count on Kellie no matter what, and Kellie knew the same about Jillian.

As the sun began to sink low over the horizon, Jillian and Kellie decided to go back to the condo. They showered, dressed, and ordered a pizza for dinner after deciding to stay in for the evening. As they sat on their balcony overlooking the ocean, they had wine and pizza and made plans for the next day.

"I'm thinking we catch some sun early, before the beach gets crowded," Kellie said. "Then we can read, nap, or whatever we want in the afternoon. You know how the afternoon heat and humidity bothers my asthma a little. What do you think?"

"I like it," Jillian responded. "I can't remember the last time I actually took a nap in the afternoon. Sounds very decadent! I think I could get used to this lazy lifestyle."

"How about a short walk on the beach before we hit the sack?" Kellie asked. "The moon is big and beautiful tonight, so we should be able to see pretty good."

"Sounds perfect, Kell," Jillian replied.

As they walked along the shoreline, Jillian felt the rest of her tension drain away. She knew she would figure out what to do with her life. She still didn't know what to do about Will and decided to bring the subject up to Kellie.

"Kell, I need to tell you something," Jillian began in a somber tone.

"Wow, sounds serious my friend," Kellie replied.

"Remember Will, the guy who texted me thinking I was someone named Angel?" Jillian asked.

"Sure, I know you two have been texting back and forth. Are you still feeling bad about that?" Kellie answered.

"Well, I have a confession to make," Jillian noted, hoping the darkness wouldn't reveal the embarrassment on her face. "We progressed beyond texting."

"What? When? Tell me girl!" Kellie exclaimed.

"About two weeks ago we talked on the phone," Jillian disclosed. "He wanted to talk and get to know me and I was feeling down. It was the day Gary moved his things out of the house and Victor came by. Remember me telling you about that?"

"Sure I remember," Kellie declared. "I remember how depressed you seemed that day. And I remember that was the day you broke it off for good with Victor. You haven't seen him since then, have you?"

"No, I haven't seen or spoken to Victor," Jillian said. "He called several times but I didn't answer or call back. And I think part of the reason is that Will cheered me up and made me feel good about myself. We spoke for the first time that night. He was so sweet and funny. He told me stories of his travels around the world for hours. I felt so positive about life after I talked to him."

"How much did you tell him about yourself? Oh, did you tell him you aren't Angel?" Kellie asked.

"He still thinks I'm Angel, but the details I gave him were of my own life," Jillian answered. "I talked to him about going through a bad break up and how I was questioning my entire life. He's a really good listener, but I was careful about how much I revealed. He travels a lot with his job and the next day he left for Europe. We've texted a couple of times since then, but we haven't talked again."

"Be careful, Jillian," Kellie warned. "You don't really know this guy. He may not be telling you the truth."

"I know what you're saying Kell, but the reality is, I feel bad lying to him," Jillian said. "I think he was being honest with me and here I am, dishonest from the start. He told me when we talked that he wanted to see me again and get to know me.

"I stalled, telling him I was feeling vulnerable from the break up. He said he understood and wouldn't push me to do anything I didn't want to do. We agreed to be phone friends. He seemed okay that I wasn't shutting him down completely."

"Well maybe you won't hear from him again," Kellie remarked. "If he travels for his job, he probably has women all over the world."

"But I did hear from him," Jillian announced. "He texted me yesterday. He's coming home tomorrow and wanted to talk to me this weekend."

"Uh oh," Kellie interjected.

"Uh oh is right," Jillian stated. "I told him I was going away for the weekend with my best friend. He asked where I was going. I know he lives at a beach, but I have no idea which beach. I didn't want to tell him we were coming here in case he lives here. So I told him we were going to the mountains, to my family's cabin. I said there was no cell service there."

"Chances are he lives at some other beach, but that was a smart answer. What did he say then?" Kellie questioned.

"He said he missed talking to me and we agreed to talk next week," Jillian responded. "Now I don't know what to do. I hate lying and I'm not good at it. But I really enjoy talking to him. I'm so confused! I need some good advice here, Kell."

"First of all, don't stress over it," Kellie advised. "We're on a Double D trip and no stressing out is allowed. Second, you have no commitment to this guy. Just do what feels right to you. If you want to talk to him, then talk to him.

"But be careful how much you tell him. When you do feel it's time to tell him the truth, you don't know how he might react. You certainly don't want him to know where you live or work in case he doesn't react well."

"I think I need to tell him the truth when we talk next week," Jillian replied. "I just can't continue to lie. He probably won't want to have anything more to do with me, but I have to chance it."

"See, you didn't really need my advice," Kellie smiled in the darkness. "You just needed to talk about it out loud. You'll figure it out Jillian and everything will be all right. If he stops talking to you, then all he was interested in was getting into your pants. If he's really interested in you as a person, he'll get over the rest."

"I hope you're right," Jillian said. "He seemed so nice and so interesting. I think I'd like to get to know him for real. I just hope he understands why I lied to him."

"By the way, do you know how old he is?" Kellie asked. "Maybe he's in his twenties. That's probably a little young for someone our age."

"Damn, I have no idea!" Jillian cried. "I guess I better find out next time we talk. Based on his travel experience, he sounds like he's close to our age. And people our age get to have fun too you know. Thirty-two isn't exactly old enough for the senior discount at the Golden Corral."

"OK, OK," Kellie laughed. "I didn't mean to imply that you're old. But if he's twenty-two, he's not going to be interested in a thirty-two year old. And if he's fifty, he's too old for you."

"I know what you mean and I'll certainly find out," Jillian giggled, then continued on in a more serious tone. "Once he finds out I've been lying it probably won't matter anyway. But I have to tell him, so I guess that's settled."

"Good! One problem down, one to go," Kellie noted. "Now let's have one more glass of wine and then head to bed. We have lots of sun to soak up tomorrow!"

"Race you back to the condo!" Jillian shouted as she took off at a run. She felt better than she had in months. Yes, this mini-vacation was exactly what she needed.

CHAPTER 6

Early Saturday morning, Jillian and Kellie crossed the dunes once again and found the perfect spot on the beach. The sun was up and brilliant, making the blue water sparkle as they set up their chairs. The waves were huge and the sound of them crashing onto the sand was very soothing. Jillian reached into the small cooler sitting between the chairs and pulled out two bottles of water. Kellie was busy covering herself with sunscreen.

"Here, Kell," Jillian said. "Drink plenty of water today. All that wine last night and the hot sun today will dehydrate you. I want you healthy so we can go out for dinner tonight."

Kellie grabbed the bottle and took a long drink. She grinned at Jillian and took another drink.

"Where do you want to go?" she said as she resumed slathering sunscreen on her legs. "There are a few places here on the island or we can go down to Murrell's Inlet. I love those seafood places down there."

"It really doesn't matter to me," Jillian responded. "I definitely want to go to Murrell's Inlet, but we can do that either night. Let's play it by ear and see how we feel later."

"Sounds like a plan," Kellie answered. "Now be quiet while I work on my tan. This is serious business. Winter will be here before we know it so it's probably my last chance to have the perfect golden bronze glow."

They both broke into giggles and then settled in for some sun bathing. After a bit, Kellie got up and spread out the blanket they had brought with them. She lay face down, trying to get some sun on her back. Jillian was sitting with her eyes closed, thinking about joining Kellie on the blanket when a shadow fell over her. She looked up to see a handsome man standing in front of her. He had a giant camera hanging from a strap around his neck.

"Sorry to bother you," the good-looking stranger began. "Do you mind if I take your picture?"

"What?" Jillian asked in confusion. "No, I don't think so. Thanks anyway."

"I'm sorry, let me start again," the stranger said. "I'm a professional photographer. I take pictures of interesting and beautiful people and places. I think you're beautiful and interesting and would like to photograph you."

"If that's a pick up line, it's pretty good," Jillian replied. "But I'm not interested in a pick up. I'm here with my friend and we're having a girls' weekend. Sorry, but I'm really not interested."

"No, really, I'm a professional photographer," the man exclaimed as he pulled a business card from his pocket and handed it to Jillian. "I'm R. J. Williams, owner of R.J Williams Photography, and I have a photography studio in New York. I was just at that little inlet about five hundred yards down the beach taking pictures of a starfish that must have come in with the tide.

"I'm collecting interesting photographs of different beaches. I photograph people, sand dunes, wild life, fish, and anything else that catches my eye. You caught my eye and I'd love to take a few photos of you. I'm hoping to eventually put it all together in a book about the beauty found at the beaches of the world."

Jillian took the card and read it. Sure enough it said *R. J. Williams Photography* with a New York address and phone number. She looked back up at the stranger and something about him seemed familiar. She couldn't quite place it, but she felt like she knew him.

"What are you doing in North Carolina, Mr. Williams?" she inquired, looking over at Kellie. Kellie was sitting on the blanket now, wide-eyed and listening intently.

"Hanging out, relaxing, and taking some photos until I leave for my next assignment," he replied. "Until then, I'm enjoying the sun and surf and this beautiful beach."

"Thank you for the offer, but I think I'll decline," Jillian stated. "I hope you enjoy your weekend."

The man nodded and started to walk away. Kellie was sitting with her mouth open ready to say something, but swallowed her comment when Jillian shook her head no. The stranger turned back toward Jillian and spoke again.

"If you change your mind, feel free to call my studio number. I check my messages every few hours," he said and ambled on down the beach.

"What is wrong with you?" Kellie demanded to know when the man was far enough down the beach that he couldn't hear her. "A handsome man, who just happens to be a professional photographer, wants to take your picture and you tell him no?"

"Nothing's wrong with me. I don't know this guy and I've never heard of him in a professional capacity. How do I know my picture won't end up on some weird internet site?" Jillian responded. "I just don't think it's smart to let a random stranger take pictures of me."

"But you will talk on the phone to a stranger who sent you a random text message?" Kellie asked with a smile.

"OK, you have me there, but at least Will can't put my picture up on some internet porn site," Jillian exclaimed. "Besides, you're the one who told me to respond to that text message!"

"Well, now I'm telling you that you should have let Mr. R.J. Williams take your picture," Kellie said as she looked down the beach in the direction the man had gone. "But it's too late now I guess. I don't even see him anymore. He must be staying somewhere close by."

"Get busy on that tan, Bronze Goddess," Jillian chided. "It won't be long before the beach is swarming with parents, their precious little munchkins, and surly teenagers. Once they arrive in force, I'm out of here."

True to her prediction, an hour later the beach was filled with rambunctious children, worn out parents, and teenagers checking out the opposite sex. Jillian and Kellie gathered their belongings and headed back to the condo. Jillian jumped into the shower while Kellie checked her phone for messages. As she was drying off, she heard voices in the living room. It sounded like Stephen, so she assumed Kellie had him on speakerphone.

Jillian dressed and walked out of the bedroom. She was startled to see Stephen standing on the balcony. Kellie turned and saw Jillian walking through the living room. She rushed back into the condo with a look of irritation on her face.

"What's up with him?" Jillian asked, pointing to Stephen. "Wasn't he supposed to go fishing all weekend?"

"Apparently his dad got sick last night so they cancelled the trip," Kellie replied. "He decided to surprise me. I swear Jillie, I didn't know he was coming until I answered the door. I'm not too happy about it either. I wanted a girls' weekend with you, but he doesn't seem to be able to understand that. We were just arguing about it actually."

"Kellie, don't worry about it," Jillian said. "It's all right. We'll just hang out together and still have a fun trip."

Kellie stepped forward and hugged her best friend. She was so grateful that Jillian wasn't upset at the change in plans.

"Thanks for understanding," she murmured. "I love him, but sometimes he makes me a little crazy. It's like he can't stand to be alone for even twenty-four hours."

"Hey, he's a man. He likes to be near his woman," Jillian laughed and hugged her friend back.

Stephen walked into the living room at that moment and put his arms around both women. He bear-hugged them until they were laughing and wriggling to get free.

"Sorry to break up the girls' party, but I just couldn't stand the thought of being all alone at home," Stephen said. "I hope you're not too mad at me, Jillian. I know my wife isn't too happy right now."

"It's OK, Stephen," Jillian assured him. "I understand. We'll all just hang out together. Now, how about some lunch?"

They fixed sandwiches and iced tea and took their lunch out on the balcony. As they ate, they talked about what they had done since arriving yesterday. When Kellie told Stephen about the photographer, his eyes went wide in shock.

"Let me see that business card," he exclaimed. "I think this guy is legit."

Jillian retrieved the card from the kitchen counter and brought it out to Stephen. He asked Kellie to tell him again what the man had said. When she finished, he jumped up and grabbed Jillian by the shoulders.

"This guy really is a professional photographer!" Stephen shouted. "I can't believe it! I just saw a photo spread he did in one of my fishing magazines. He took some incredible pictures of great fishing lakes in the northwest part of the US. I'm sure it was the same name. Oh, wait a minute, I have that magazine in my car. I think there was a picture of him in it."

With that, Stephen took off at a run through the condo. The women watched as he streaked out the door and then they broke into laughter.

"Well, I guess it's a pretty good photo spread to make him move that fast," Kellie giggled. "There are very few things that get him running. He much prefers to sit and fish or sit and watch sports on television!"

In a few minutes, Stephen was back on the balcony thumbing through a magazine. As he reached the middle, he slapped the magazine down on the table in front of the women. He had a triumphant look on his face.

"Is this the guy?" Stephen asked, pointing to a picture inset at the side of an article about fishing lakes of the northwest.

Jillian and Kellie stared open-mouthed at the picture. It was definitely the man who had stopped on the beach and asked to take Jillian's picture. When she regained her composure, Jillian began looking at the pictures that accompanied the article. They were some of the most beautiful pictures she had ever seen. They weren't just basic shots of a lake. Each one had captured something special about that particular body of water. And each one made her long to see it up close. Without a doubt, this man had some real talent.

"Oh my god, I can't believe you told him no picture!" Stephen blurted. "He's pretty famous for his nature photography. I'm sure he wasn't lying when he told you he was taking pictures for a book."

"She didn't know who he was, honey," Kellie said defensively. "But he told her to call anytime if she changed her mind. You should call him, Jillie!"

"No, I don't think so. I'm not interested in being in his book," Jillian stated vehemently. "Let's just drop this please."

"Come on. What's the harm? At least think about it," Stephen argued. "It would be so awesome to be in a book!"

"If it will shut you up, I'll agree to think about it," Jillian chuckled. "But don't get your hopes up. I can't see me changing my mind about this. Now if you will excuse me, I hear my bed calling. Do you hear it? It's saying that it's time for a nap. I'll see you two in a few hours."

Later that evening, Jillian, Kellie, and Stephen went out for dinner. They had decided on The Isle Restaurant, a local's favorite on the island. The restaurant was known for its fresh local seafood and beautiful view of the intra-coastal waterway. Since it was Saturday, there were still a lot of people arriving for the holiday weekend. They certainly didn't want to get stuck in another long line of traffic crossing the causeway from the mainland. It seemed like the best bet was to walk the six blocks to The Isle.

"I love this place," Stephen exclaimed once they had finished their meal outside at the tiki hut. "It's got everything! Good food, lots of beer choices, and a nice view of the boats. Damn, I wish I had a boat down here!! We could be fishing right now."

"Well, I love the water view, boat or no boat, and I'm not missing fishing at all," Kellie responded with a laugh. "This outdoor tiki hut right on the water is fabulous. I think this is new since the last time we were here."

"I certainly don't remember it, but it's really nice," Jillian commented. "It must have doubled the seating capacity. I'm glad the food is still great. And the tiki hut is set so close to the water that the view is spectacular. I wouldn't be surprised if a fish jumped up and landed right on the table."

They all fell silent as they looked around the tiki hut and out to the water. For some reason, Jillian felt compelled to scan the tiki hut again. She stifled a gasp when her gaze found that R.J. Williams was sitting at the bar staring directly at her. She quickly looked away and caught Kellie's eye.

"Oh no, he's here," Jillian said quietly to Kellie, who was sitting directly across the table from her. "He's at the bar, but don't turn around and look."

"Who's here?" Kellie asked.

"That photographer, R.J. Williams," Jillian whispered. "He's sitting at the bar and when I looked up, he was staring at me. I think he nodded at me, but I looked down so he would think I didn't see him."

"The photographer is here?" Stephen asked a little too loudly.

"Yes, the one from the beach this morning," Jillian answered. "Don't make a scene, Stephen! Keep your voice down so the whole place doesn't know what we're talking about."

"But I want to meet him," Stephen whined. "I've never met a famous photographer before. Shoot, I've never met anyone famous."

"Stephen," Kellie said in a warning tone. "Leave it alone. You're making Jillian uncomfortable. She was nice enough to not be mad at you for showing up unannounced, so don't blow it now."

"How about if I go up and introduce myself? I just want to tell him how great I think his pictures are," Stephen suggested.

"I would prefer you didn't," Jillian stated vehemently.

"Come on, Jillian, don't be such a spoil sport," Stephen whined again. Then his tone changed as he said, "Guess it doesn't matter what you prefer. He's coming this way."

Jillian looked up and saw the photographer heading directly to their table. His eyes locked onto hers and she couldn't look away. It felt like he was staring into her soul. In less than ten seconds, he was standing behind the empty chair next to Jillian.

"Sorry to intrude but I wanted to apologize again for this morning," R.J. said looking down at Jillian. "I realized after I left that I made you very uncomfortable with my request. In today's world, you never know if people are who they say they are. I should remember that, so I'm sorry for trying to push you to let me photograph you.

"It's no problem," Jillian stuttered. She was shocked that something about this man was sending all kinds of strange feelings through her body. He seemed so familiar to her, but she couldn't quite place why.

"I told her you were really a photographer," Stephen chimed in. "I showed her your photo spread in the latest *Fishing Life* magazine. She's knows now that you're legit."

"Thanks, but she has a right to decide if she wants to be photographed," R.J. declared. "I get so passionate about my work that I sometimes forget that."

"I'm Stephen, this is my wife Kellie, and this is our friend Jillian," Stephen said as he jumped up and extended his hand. "Why don't you join us?"

Jillian's mouth dropped and she shot Stephen a look that was like a death ray. He grinned at her as he and R.J. shook hands and sat down at the table. The waitress appeared just then and they ordered wine for the ladies and Lagunitas beers for the men. Stephen was ecstatic to find he and R.J. shared a love of craft beers. When the waitress walked away, Stephen began talking again.

"So Jillian says you're doing a book on beaches," he said to R.J. "How do you know what you want to photograph?"

"Most of the time my clients tell me what kind of pictures they want," R.J. replied. "The *Fishing Life* people told me the kind of article they wanted to write and they gave me a list of lakes they were going to feature. I traveled to the lakes they had chosen and took lots of photos of each one to start out. Once I got back to my studio, I pulled out the ones I thought were best and sent them off to the magazine. I didn't even know what ones they were going to use until the magazine article came out."

"Wow, that is so awesome!" Stephen cried. "I mean how cool is it that someone pays you to take pictures of lakes? Did you do any fishing while you were there?"

"As much as I wanted to, I didn't have time," R.J. answered. "When I'm on an assignment, I have to stay focused on my work or I'll never meet the client's deadline."

Before Stephen could say anything else, R.J. turned his gaze on Jillian.

"Again, I apologize for making you uncomfortable," he said. "I think you're beautiful and you have an interesting face. I don't know if I would use your picture in my book, but I would never use it for any other purpose without your consent."

"Really, it's not a problem," Jillian gasped. Her mouth was dry and her heart was beating so loudly she wondered if he could hear it. "You don't have to apologize anymore. I know you meant no harm."

"At least let me buy the drinks for you and your friends," R.J. remarked. "I would feel better about the whole thing if you did. And who knows, maybe you'll decide I'm an OK guy and agree to a photo or two."

Jillian started to say no but before she could say a word, Kellie interrupted.

"Jillian will accept that drink and stop being so stubborn," Kellie announced. "Won't you, Jillie?"

Unable to protest without feeling like a fool, Jillian nodded yes. She glared at Kellie who just grinned at her in return. The waitress had arrived with the drinks and R.J. told her to put the round on his tab. She smiled at him and said OK, then walked back to the bar. Stephen had been fidgeting since R.J. sat down and now he looked ready to pop. He took advantage of the lull while everyone else sipped their drinks.

"So do you just do outdoor photography? Have you ever taken pictures of any wild animals? Is it hard to get started in that business?" Stephen shot rapid-fire questions at R.J. while he had the chance.

"To pay the bills, I photograph pretty much anything my client wants, pretty much anywhere they want me to go," R.J. told Stephen. "But my real passion is for the outdoors and all the beautiful things you can find to photograph. I spent a lot of time in the mountains of North Carolina when I was growing up. I always took my camera along and spent all of my allowance on film and developing the photos I took."

"How did you end up doing that for a living?" Kellie asked. "I can't imagine you just open up a studio and people flock to you. Especially if you're opening a studio in high-priced New York City."

"When I was about twenty-two, right before I graduated from college, I submitted some of my photos of the North Carolina mountains to a contest," R.J. began. "It was held by the State of North Carolina tourism department. They wanted photographs to put in a tourism magazine that was being distributed all over the US. I guess they figured amateur photography would be a lot cheaper than professional."

"Since I gave up rights to the photos and the winning prize was only $500, I think they were correct," he chuckled as he continued. "Anyway, two of my photos were selected for the magazine and off they went to people all over the country. About a year later, I was working in my dad's business and hating life. I got a call from a guy in Rhode Island who had seen my photos in the magazine. He wanted to know if I would come up there and take photos of a sailing event that they hold each summer. I quit my job, went up there, and it all just fell into place after that."

"It just fell into place?" Stephen questioned. "You go from pictures of a sailboat race to famous photographer just like that?"

"Well there was a little more to it," R.J. agreed laughing. "One of the sailboat owners asked me to do a photo montage of all his boats after he saw the ones I took of the sailing event. This guy had lots of bucks, lots of influential friends, and lots of boats. He liked what I did with his boat collection and before I knew what was happening, his friends were calling me. It kind of mushroomed from there."

"How did you end up in New York if North Carolina is your home?" Kellie wanted to know.

"Once I had a little money coming in from my photos, I moved to New York. Most of my clients then were in the northeast. I worked out of a tiny apartment in New York City. I could get to most anywhere in the northeast corridor by train from New York so it just seemed logical to me. As my name and reputation became better known, my financial status improved. About six years ago, I got rid of the apartment and opened my New York studio."

"That is so cool!" Stephen was in awe. "I mean how lucky can one guy be?"

"It wasn't luck, Stephen," Jillian admonished. "You saw those photographs. He has a real eye for capturing something special in each of his subjects. Those lake pictures took my breath away. I wanted to go to each lake and see it for myself."

"Thank you for the compliment, Jillian," R.J. was beaming. "That's exactly what I want people to feel when they see my photos. I want them to see the beauty in our world and reach out for it. We all spend so much time in the glass and steel jungle we call offices. I want people to see my pictures and remember what it feels like to be one with nature."

"I really want to go fishing in each of those lakes," Stephen cried. "You got to me, that's for sure."

"I don't know whether to thank you or smack you," Kellie giggled. "I should thank you for getting my thick-headed husband to see the beauty in nature. But I want to smack you because I will never hear the end of it until he has gotten his fill of fishing in those lakes."

"Speaking of fishing, we should get going," Stephen said. "It's getting late and I have an early reservation on a fishing charter tomorrow morning."

"Why don't you stay and let me buy you another drink?" R.J. asked Jillian.

His eyes bore into hers and Jillian realized she couldn't say no if she wanted to. She was mesmerized by his dark brown eyes and fascinated by how comfortable she felt with him. Once again he seemed so familiar to her, but she knew she had never met him before.

"Sure, let's have another drink," Jillian stammered as she pulled her gaze away to look at Kellie. "I'll walk back to the condo in a little bit. It's just a few blocks down."

"I know you're a big girl," Kellie began with a smile in her voice. "But be careful, OK? Call me if you decide you need an escort and I'll send Stephen to meet you."

"I'll make sure she gets back," R.J. said to Kellie. "I'll walk her right to the front door and wait until she is safely locked inside."

"Um guys, I'm here, remember? Don't talk about me like I'm a ten year old, please." Jillian laughed and then looked at Kellie. "I'll be fine and I have my cell phone if anything happens."

Kellie grinned at Jillian and then grabbed Stephen by the arm. They weaved through the crowded tiki hut and down the steps. Jillian watched for a few seconds and then turned to find R.J. staring at her again.

CHAPTER 7

"What?" Jillian asked as R.J. continued to stare at her.

"You just seem really familiar to me," he answered. "It's like I know you from somewhere, but if I had ever met you, I would certainly remember. I never forget a face and yours is so beautiful I'll be dreaming about it for a long time. And I would NEVER forget such stunning red hair and brilliant green eyes."

Jillian blushed, her face turning a bright crimson. She looked down in embarrassment. When she looked back up, R.J. was staring at her once again.

"Thank you," she stuttered. "I'm sure we never met, but you seem familiar to me too."

"So tell me about yourself," R. J. said. "Maybe we can figure out if we do know each other. At least we will learn a little about each other."

"I have a better idea," Jillian exclaimed as the band began to play. "Let's dance! Oh, I guess I should ask if you like to dance."

"I love dancing," R.J. replied as he stood and grabbed her hand.

As they moved to the dance floor, Jillian felt a tingle of electricity where his hand held hers. She wondered if maybe dancing was a mistake, but then decided to throw caution out the door. She was on vacation and was going to enjoy herself. Her girls' weekend was blown, so she would have to have fun on her own.

R.J. pulled her close and they began to move to the music. Jillian loved to dance and was quite good at it actually. She soon discovered that R.J. was good at it too. Having his arms around her and swaying to the slow music felt just right. She fit perfectly against his chest and when she laid her head on his shoulder, he smelled so good she almost swooned. Jillian briefly wondered what it would be like to dance like this with Will, but pushed the thought away. She had to accept that Will was a temporary phone friend who would dump her when he realized she had lied to him.

For the next several hours, Jillian and R.J. danced almost every dance. They stopped only when the band took a break. The conversation was kept to how humid it was on the dance floor and how much they were enjoying the music and the dancing. Finally, the band finished for the night and Jillian looked at her watch.

"Oh wow," Jillian cried. "It's after midnight!"

"I haven't had this much fun in a very long time," R.J. declared. "You're a fantastic dancer!"

"So are you!" Jillian agreed. "I can't remember the last time I went dancing. This was a lot of fun, but I better get back to the condo. If Kellie wakes up and I'm not there, she will totally freak out."

"Let me walk you home, young lady," R.J. threw his hand out and bowed deeply. "I promised to see you to the door. I don't really know Kellie, but I have a feeling that she could do me a great deal of harm if I don't keep that promise."

"Kellie and I have been best friends since high school," Jillian chuckled as R.J. stood back up. "Let me tell you from experience that you don't want to get on her bad side! You would be in for a world of hurt. Sometimes I almost feel sorry for Stephen....almost."

The crowd had thinned considerably and they had no problem getting to the parking lot. As they started toward the street, Jillian wondered where R.J. was staying and whether he had his car.

"I walked too, so I'll walk you home first," he said as if he had read her mind. "Are you staying near where I saw you on the beach?"

"Yes, we were almost directly in front of the condo," she replied.

They reached the corner and crossed the street. The line of traffic that had been backed up all day was gone. Now there were only a few cars and a couple of golf carts roaming in the darkness. As they reached the Ocean Isle pier, R.J. grabbed Jillian's hand and pulled her toward the beach.

"Let's walk in the sand," he said. "We can look at the stars and the moon while we talk."

"Sounds good to me," Jillian replied. "I love the beach, the sand between my toes, and how salty the air smells."

They reached the beach and stopped to remove their flip-flops. Flip-flops were considered appropriate dress for every restaurant on the island. As a matter of fact, wearing anything more than flip-flops, shorts, and a tank top was considered over-dressed. That was one of the things Jillian really loved about this place.

"You know you lied to me this morning," R.J. noted with a grin as they walked at the water's edge.

"About what?" Jillian was searching her memory for details of that conversation. Before she had gotten to the end of it, R.J. clued her in.

"You said you were having a girls' weekend when you thought I way trying to pick you up."

"That wasn't a lie!" she cried.

"Uh huh—and Stephen just showed up out of nowhere?" R.J. was teasing her now and she could hear it in his voice.

"Actually he did. He was supposed to go fishing with his dad, but his dad got sick," Jillian said. "When we got back from the beach, there he was. He can't stand to be by himself, so he's here for the rest of the weekend."

"Ah, good story," R.J. laughed. "I guess I'll believe it."

"You guess you'll believe it?" Jillian laughed too. "You'd better believe it. You never would have had so much fun dancing tonight if he hadn't shown up. As much as I love Kellie, sometimes I need a break from Stephen."

"Now you've gone and crushed my fragile male ego, Jillian," R.J. said with a sigh. "All night I thought you stayed because of my amazing dancing ability and my cute butt. And now I find out it was only to get away from Stephen. What a blow!"

"Oh, get over yourself," she giggled. "I get the impression that your male ego is anything but fragile. And I really did enjoy dancing."

"I knew it!" R.J. shouted at the stars. "She thinks I'm hot and sexy and a great dancer!"

"Don't get ahead of yourself, Mr. Professional Photographer," Jillian teased. "I said you were a good dancer."

"Hmmmm, well then I guess I'll just have to show you how hot and sexy I think you are," R.J. responded as he pulled her against him.

Putting his arms around her and pressing a hand against the small of her back, R.J. bent his head slightly and put his lips to Jillian's. She leaned into the kiss as the heat from his lips scorched hers. His chest pressing against her breasts sent shock waves through her and her nipples were immediately hard. As the kiss deepened, Jillian put her arms around his neck and sighed against his lips. When his tongue pushed into her mouth, she welcomed the astonishing heat it sent to every part of her body.

A rogue wave crashing over their legs caused them to finally break the kiss. However, R.J. continued to hold Jillian tight against him. He could feel her heart beating just as fast as his was. She smelled so good, tasted so good, that he didn't want the moment to ever be over. Jillian was feeling the same thing and was content to lean her head on his shoulder while she tried to slow her heart rate. When R.J. finally let go of her, she felt suddenly chilled.

"So?" R.J. asked, holding her hands and looking into her eyes.

"Uhhhh," Jillian stammered as his eyes searched hers in the moonlight. "That was….oh wow….that was…."

"That good, huh?" R.J. grinned at her. "Yeah, 'oh wow' pretty much sums it up."

"I have to admit that was one amazing kiss," she smiled back at him. "And yes, you are hot and sexy too. Is your ego all better now?"

"I'm not thinking too much about my ego right now," he replied. "I'm thinking about kissing you again."

He pulled her to him once again and touched her lips with his. Jillian put her arms around his waist and held on tight as R.J.'s tongue explored her mouth. Her entire body was now on fire, heat racing from her lips to her breasts and streaming down her body. He pulled back slightly and licked her lips with his tongue, then kissed her cheek, her ear, and her forehead. He returned to her lips and kissed her deeply once more. His hands had begun sliding from her shoulders down to her hips and back up again.

With each caress, Jillian's body pressed closer against his. He felt so good to her, unlike anyone she had ever known before. She felt like they fit together in all the right places. As R.J. continued to kiss her and caress her back, a flame grew inside her. She wanted to know every inch of his body, wanted to feel every inch of him inside her. She needed him so intensely it surprised and scared her. She broke the kiss and backed slightly away.

"What's wrong?" he asked, his face showing confusion at her action.

"Nothing, nothing," she said, confusion evident in her own voice. "I think I'd better get back to the condo. It's right down there."

Jillian pointed to a condo building just down the beach. She started walking slowly toward it, aching for another kiss from R.J. However, she was terrified of the feelings she knew it would bring.

R.J. followed Jillian as she started across the wide beach toward the dunes. A cloud skittered across the moon and it was suddenly darker. Only a few condos had lights on and because they were behind the dunes, the light barely reached the beach. As they got close to the walkway over the dunes, Jillian suddenly cried out and fell to the sand. R.J. rushed to her and saw she was trying to look at her foot.

"What happened?" R.J. asked.

"I stepped on something and I think I cut my foot," Jillian responded. "It's too dark to see but it feels like it's bleeding."

"Let's get you inside and see what's going on," R.J. said as he helped her up.

Jillian leaned on R.J.'s arm as she limped up the wooden steps and across the walkway. They took the inside stairs and when they started down the hallway, she looked back and saw a trail of blood on the concrete.

"Oh no," Jillian whispered as she pointed back down the hallway. "I'm bleeding pretty good."

"Don't worry, I've got you," R.J. murmured in her ear.

He held on to her arm until they reached the door to the condo. Jillian pulled the key from her pocket and unlocked the door. She turned to tell R.J. goodbye and accidentally put her foot down on the floor. Pain shot up her leg and she fell against him. As she struggled to right herself, R.J. scooped her up into his arms.

"Which way to your bathroom?" he asked. "We need to get that cut cleaned up right away since you don't know what you stepped on."

Jillian pointed to the door on their immediate right as the outside door closed behind them. R.J. opened the bedroom door and carried her inside. He put her down on the queen size bed and went into the attached bathroom. He flipped on the light and wet a wash cloth. Jillian could hear him looking into the medicine chest and under the sink. In a moment, he stood at the bathroom door.

"Don't you have any bandages or antiseptic around here?" he questioned. "It's all empty in there."

"This is a rental unit. Bring me the bag on the dresser over there," Jillian said pointing across the room. "I have some stuff in there that will work."

R.J. brought the bag and while Jillian dug around in it, he gently cleaned her foot with the wet cloth. When he touched the cut area, she winced but didn't cry out. She didn't want to wake Kellie and have to explain why R.J. was in her bedroom. She pulled out some antibiotic cream and band-aids. R.J. applied the cream and covered it with a good-sized band-aid.

"I think you'll live," he confided in a hushed tone. "But you should watch for infection. Maybe I should take another look at it tomorrow. Maybe over dinner?"

Jillian didn't immediately realize he was asking her a question. While he was talking, his hand was softly caressing her foot and calf. The heat his touch was generating in her had taken over her brain. When he removed his hand, she looked up at him and suddenly understood he had asked a question.

"I'm sorry, what did you ask me?" Jillian inquired, her mind screaming at him to continue the caresses.

"I asked you to dinner tomorrow evening," R.J. answered as his hand began sliding over her calf again. "I want to make sure the cut isn't red and inflamed. I certainly don't want to be responsible for your foot becoming infected and falling off."

Jillian tried to form an answer but her brain was focused on his hand as it glided up her shin and around the back of her calf. She looked up at him and saw her own desire reflected back at her.

"Dinner….tomorrow….yeah, sure," she breathed as his hands massaged her legs. "But can you look at my lips? I think I may have cut them when I fell."

R.J. moved quickly to her side and inspected her face silently. The light from the bathroom had shown brightly on her foot but her face was in shadows. He reached up and ran his hand over her cheek and chin, sending shock waves through her body. As he began to move his hand away, she took it in her hand and kissed each finger.

"Your face is so beautiful," he confided and he reached out to touch her lips. "Your lips seem to be OK."

"Maybe you should kiss me to be sure," Jillian murmured.

He leaned forward and this time touched his lips to hers. Jillian moaned as her insides burst into flames. No man had ever made her feel this kind of heat. She needed him, needed to touch him, taste him, feel him against her and inside her. It was a deep physical need that astonished her.

Hearing her moan set R.J. on fire. This stunning redhead had ignited a flame in him the first time he saw her, and with each word, each touch, the heat had intensified. He knew in just a few moments it would be completely out of control. The ferocity of his need for her startled him. He broke the kiss and looked into her eyes.

"I think I had better go," he said quietly, but his eyes begged her to ask him to stay.

"I think you'd better stay," she said just as quietly, her eyes burning with need.

R.J. kissed Jillian again, a deep kiss filled with a promise of things to come. His hands slid over her bare arms, then down her thighs. He moved his lips away from her mouth and kissed her neck and her shoulders. She felt his hands move back up her thighs and slide her shirt up and over her head, freeing her naked breasts. When his lips locked onto her nipple, she groaned at the pleasure that burst through her. He licked and sucked her breasts, making her nipples hard and her breasts swell and flush.

When she felt she could take no more, Jillian put her hands on the sides of his head and lifted his face to hers. She licked his lips as she pulled his chest against her tingling, swollen breasts. Her hand pulled on his shirt, trying to remove it. He leaned back to pull it over his head and she felt chilled without him against her. When he leaned back against her, his bare skin came in contact with her hard nipples and she almost screamed as electricity shot through her body. Suddenly she needed to be totally naked, to feel his skin against the length of her body.

Once again it was as if R.J. was reading her mind. He sat back and pulled on the waistband of her shorts. She lifted her hips and he slid her shorts and panties off, tossing them to the floor. Then he stood and slipped his pants off. Jillian gasped as his penis sprung free, erect and throbbing. He was the most beautiful man she had ever seen.

"Slide down on your back," he murmured, his eyes never leaving her body. "Oh my god, you're so beautiful, so sexy. More beautiful than I imagined."

He climbed onto the bed and lay on top of her. His body fit perfectly against hers, her skin flushing red with the heat they generated. She could feel his chest pressing against her hard nipples. His rock hard penis was pressed against her leg and she could feel it pulsing with need. R.J. kissed her again, another deep kiss that turned her insides to molten lava. She knew she was wet, knew she was ready for him. She arched her pelvis up and pressed his penis against her belly. He knew exactly what she wanted.

R.J. raised up on his elbows and without thinking, Jillian spread her legs for him. He moved against her, pressing the head of his penis against her wetness. He stroked her clit with it several times, becoming more excited as each stroke caused her to thrash beneath him. She had her eyes closed and was moaning deep in her throat as he slowly slid into her. He pushed his penis all the way inside her hot, dripping pussy. The feeling was so intense he had to fight to maintain control. It was like she was made for him, a perfect fit. He began to thrust in and out of her heated core.

Jillian was writhing beneath him, unable to think a single coherent thought. Her world narrowed to the incredible spasms of pleasure each thrust created in her. R.J. felt her muscles tighten and heard her cry out as she orgasmed again and again. He felt her wetness gushing over his penis, dripping down over his balls. The idea that she was so turned on by what he was doing made him crazy. This woman was not pretending, she was not faking an orgasm.

He thrust harder and faster, her cries each time she orgasmed getting closer and closer together. Finally Jillian screamed and wrapped her legs around his waist. She pulled him deeper into her as she had a gigantic orgasm, her entire body arching into his. R.J. lost it then. His self-control flew away as he came with a force and fury he didn't know existed.

They lay entwined as their bodies relaxed and their minds slowly returned to consciousness. Finally, R.J. rolled off Jillian but he pulled her on top of him. He had to feel her skin against his. Anything else was unbearable. They dozed awhile and when they awoke, sunlight was beginning to peek into the window.

"Hey there," Jillian whispered as she poked R.J. in the shoulder.

"Hey there yourself," R.J. replied with a wicked gleam in his eyes.

"Don't get any ideas," she whispered again. "You need to leave before Kellie and Stephen get up."

"Are you sure you want me to go?" R.J. asked as his fingers began caressing her breasts.

"Oh god, don't do that," Jillian moaned. "I don't want you to go, but you have to anyway. How about a rain check for tonight?"

R.J. got up on one elbow and looked at her. She was just as beautiful in the morning as she was on the beach and at the tiki hut. He wanted her so bad it hurt.

"I have some things to do today but we are definitely on for dinner," he said running a finger over her lips, down her chin, and between her breasts. "And tonight we stay at my place. Tell Kellie not to expect you home until tomorrow afternoon at the earliest."

R.J. rose from the bed and Jillian watched as he pulled on his shorts and shirt. He was so handsome with dark hair, deep brown eyes, and a hard, chiseled body. He took her breath away as she watched him dress. When he was done, he leaned over her on the bed and kissed her. It was a soft, sweet, sensual, heart-wrenching kiss that made her want to invite him back into the bed. A noise from the outside hallway brought Jillian back to reality and she broke the kiss.

"Let me up and I'll walk you out," she gasped.

"Stay in bed, beautiful lady," he responded. "I'll let myself out. I'll pick you up here at seven o'clock, OK? Maybe go to Murrell's Inlet for dinner?"

"I'll be ready for dinner and whatever comes after that," Jillian grinned at him suggestively.

R.J. leaned down for another quick kiss and was out the door. Jillian heard the outside door open and close. A smile played across her lips as a contented sigh escaped them. This was a man she definitely wanted to see again.

CHAPTER 8

S everal hours later, Jillian was awakened by a knock at the bedroom door. She put a pillow over her head and tried to ignore it but whoever was out there wasn't giving up. Finally she peeked out and mumbled what was supposed to be "go away." At that, the door burst open, revealing a smiling Kellie.

"Come on, sleepyhead," Kellie chided. "Get your lazy butt out of bed. It's nine o'clock and I'm ready for the beach!"

"Go away," Jillian tried again, this time more forcefully.

"Oh, no you don't," Kellie grinned. "Just because you had a late date, don't think that gives you an excuse to bail out on me. I need to do more work on my tan and the weather is perfect for it."

Jillian wriggled up into a sitting position and looked at her best friend. She debated how much she should tell Kellie about her "late date." Before she could decide, Kellie spoke again.

"Get your sexy bikini on and all your beach stuff together. I went over to that little store by the causeway and I've got bagels, orange juice, and water to take to the beach with us. Stephen is fishing until late afternoon and I'm ready for some girl time. All I need now is the other half of the Dynamic Duo to get her butt out of bed," she declared.

Groaning as she threw the cover back, Jillian swung her legs over the side of the bed. She stood up but immediately dropped back down on the bed, a look of pain etched onto her face. She had forgotten the cut on the bottom of her foot.

"What's wrong?" Kellie asked with concern.

"I forgot I cut my foot last night," Jillian responded as she removed the bandage from the bottom of her heel. "It's a little bit sore today."

"How did you manage that?" Kellie inquired as she looked closely at the wound. "It doesn't look too bad actually. Just a surface cut."

"Let me get awake and into my bathing suit, Kell," Jillian answered. "I'll tell you all about it when we get to the beach. Now get out of here so I can get ready."

Kellie jumped up and saluted Jillian as she marched out the door. Jillian sat for a moment, remembering her night with the very interesting and extremely sexy R.J. Williams. She picked up the pillow he had slept on and brought it to her face. She sighed as she caught his scent and remembered his kisses. The man had the most delicious lips. He was by far the best kisser she had known in her thirty-two years. Correction, he was by far the best lover she had ever known. Something about him set her on fire, even now when all she had was a pillow that held his scent.

Limping into the bathroom so her heel did not touch the floor, Jillian took a quick, cold shower, brushed her teeth, and slipped into her bikini. She gathered her towels, sunscreen, hat, and cover-up into her beach bag. She bandaged her heel and stuck her feet into flip-flops.

Ten minutes later, Jillian and Kellie were setting up their beach chairs in the same spot as the day before. They put up the umbrella and then began slathering sunscreen over their bodies. Bagels and juice appeared on top of the cooler that was between their chairs. Jillian looked at the water glittering in the bright sunlight and smiled as she ate her bagel. A day at the beach with her best friend, beautiful blue skies, deep blue water with white-topped waves, and dinner tonight with an extremely handsome, sexy, successful man. It didn't get any better than this.

"OK, I've been as patient as I can be," Kellie blurted. "Spill it girl, right now."

"What do you mean?" Jillian giggled, then became serious when she saw Kellie's face. "OK, I'll tell you everything. Well, almost everything…."

"Almost? What does that mean?" Kellie was really curious now.

"Just sit back and listen," Jillian replied waving her hand at Kellie. "You guys left and I got really nervous. So when R.J. said he would order more drinks so we could talk, I asked him to dance instead. You know I can't drink more than two glasses of wine and we had already had that much. I was afraid I'd get drunk and say something stupid."

"Oh, smart move, Jillie," Kellie said with a nod.

"We danced almost every song until the band stopped playing," Jillian continued. "I realized it was way past midnight so he walked me home."

"Is he a good dancer?" Kellie wondered.

"Oh my god, he's an excellent dancer," Jillian declared. "I felt like I was floating when he had his arms around me. It was absolute heaven."

"Um, are we still talking about dancing?" Kellie asked, taking in the dreamy look on her friend's face.

"Of course," Jillian answered but her flustered expression said otherwise.

"Yeah, sure we are," Kellie muttered. "I'm guessing this is where 'almost everything' comes into the picture."

"He's a fabulous dancer," Jillian stated, then broke into a fit of laughter. "And he's pretty good at other things too, but you're getting ahead of the story. Let me finish."

"Carry on my friend, carry on," Kellie laughed.

"So we took our flip-flops off and walked in the sand along the water line," Jillian said. "When we got to this section of the beach, I showed him where I was staying. That's when he kissed me. We were standing right over there and he pulled me against him and kissed me."

"And?" Kellie was wide-eyed at the tone of her friend's voice. She sounded like she might swoon any minute now.

"And the man can kiss," Jillian closed her eyes and smiled. "Wow, can he kiss! I thought I was going to melt into a puddle at his feet and be carried out to sea on a wave."

"Don't stop now," Kellie was practically shouting. "What happened next?"

"We kissed a couple of times and I realized it could easily get out of hand," Jillian answered. "So I told him I needed to get back to the condo and started towards the walkway. He followed saying that he had promised you that he would see me to the door. He also said that he was afraid you would hurt him if he didn't keep his promise."

"And he was absolutely correct!" Kellie proclaimed.

"Anyway, we were headed to the walkway stairs when I stepped on something and cut my foot," Jillian said. "He helped me up to the condo and into my room. He cleaned the cut and bandaged it for me."

Jillian had stopped speaking and was looking out over the ocean. She had a look of total rapture on her face. Kellie studied her for a minute and suddenly realized that the story was far from over. She also realized that she probably wouldn't hear any additional details but decided to press on.

"So, he bandaged your foot," Kellie prompted. "Then what?"

"I believe we have reached the 'almost' part of almost everything," Jillian replied with a smile on her face.

"You did it with him, didn't you?" Kellie cried. "He stayed the night, didn't he?"

"What part of 'almost' don't you understand?" Jillian laughed.

"So not fair, Jillie!" Kellie yelled.

"Sssshhhhh, Kellie," Jillian put her fingers to her lips.

"Don't you shush me, Jillian Stanley!" Kellie responded. "I want details and I want them now!"

"OK, OK," Jillian giggled. "But I'm warning you. You're going to blush when I tell you!"

"I'll take that chance. Now spill it," Kellie declared.

"He finished bandaging my foot and began caressing my leg," Jillian said quietly. "It felt so good that I couldn't even think straight. I think he realized how it was affecting me and he said he'd better leave. I told him I thought he should stay. And he did.....oh boy did he stay...."

"There you go, getting all dreamy on me again," Kellie noted. "I'm guessing it was good."

"It was so far beyond good that I don't think there's a word to describe it," Jillian spoke so softly Kellie had to strain to hear her. "It was the most incredible sexual experience I've ever had, Kellie. I had no idea it could be like that."

"Wow," Kellie let out the breath she had been holding. "You mean that, don't you?"

"Kell, he is so sweet and gentle but when things began to heat up, oh my god," Jillian sighed. "He made me absolutely crazy. It was like we were made for each other, we fit together so perfectly."

"OK, I'm blushing now and the 'ick' factor is about to set in," Kellie replied with a grin. "I get it, he's Mr. Stud in bed."

"No, you're wrong," Jillian laughed. "Mr. Stud wishes he could be R.J."

"So where was he this morning when I came into your room?" Kellie asked. "Ewww, don't tell me he was hiding under the covers!"

"No, I sent him back to where he's staying when it started to get light out," Jillian said. "I didn't want an awkward morning after scene with Stephen. And you will NOT tell Stephen about this."

"My lips are sealed, Jillie," Kellie responded. "I know Stephen would tease you for the rest of your life if he knew. So, are you going to see him again?"

"He's picking me up at seven o'clock tonight for dinner," Jillian confided to her friend. "We're going to dinner somewhere at Murrell's Inlet. Do you mind if we don't invite you and Stephen to go with us?"

"No problem," Kellie commented. "I know how star struck Stephen is and he would monopolize the entire evening. You go and have a good time."

"Oh, one other thing," Jillian disclosed, her face taking on that dreamy look again. "R.J. said I should tell you that I won't be back here until late tomorrow afternoon."

"Whoa, sounds like you weren't the only one who had a good time! Go and have fun. That's exactly what you need girl," Kellie giggled. "And tell him I give my blessing!"

Jillian laughed with her friend. She was so happy right now that she couldn't stop smiling. As they settled in to sunbathe, her thoughts kept returning to the night before. She had spent the evening and then the night with a handsome, sexy, successful man. A man who was not only a gentleman in public, but who also made her feel desired and then totally crazed in bed. He had seemed genuinely interested in her, who she was, what she thought.

Sure they hadn't talked a lot, but every word she did say he seemed to listen to with interest. And he hadn't tried to force the situation in her bedroom. If she had told him to go last night, she had no doubt he would have gone without an argument. He was so different from both Gary and Victor. Jillian smiled again. Maybe things were finally going in a positive direction for her.

When the beach got crowded, the women headed back to the condo. Stephen came back from fishing about two o'clock, disappointed that he hadn't caught anything. However, the fishing scene was still positive for him. His father had called and was feeling better, so he was going to go back to Raleigh for a shortened version of the planned fishing weekend.

"I hope you ladies aren't too upset that I'm leaving so soon," he said as he gathered his belongings from the living room. "My dad really wants to get in some night fishing tonight. Maybe I'll have better luck on the lake."

"I'm sure we will survive," Kellie observed, rolling her eyes at Jillian. "It will be hard, but we'll muddle through."

"Of course, we'll miss your sparkling wit," Jillian noted, trying not to laugh at Kellie. "And it will be difficult only having each other to talk to."

"I get it, I get it," Stephen surrendered. "You can't wait for me to leave. But I know in my heart you will miss me."

"We'll miss you, sweetheart," Kellie murmured as she hugged him. She kissed him goodbye and pushed him toward the door as she said, "Now get going. I'll see you tomorrow night."

"Bye, Stephen," Jillian waved as he went out the door.

"I love him to death, but I'm glad he's going back," Kellie acknowledged. "Now what do you want to do this afternoon? We have girls' weekend back!"

"Whatever you want my friend," Jillian hesitated. "You know, maybe I should cancel my dinner with R.J."

"No you will not cancel dinner with a handsome, sexy man who is obviously very much into you," Kellie exclaimed. "You can invite me to go with you and then drop me off afterwards. I promise to sit quietly and let you two get to know each other."

Jillian began to laugh out loud. Kellie would be sitting quietly? That would never happen! Kellie quickly realized what she had said and joined Jillian in gut-busting laughter.

"All right, I guess I need to take that statement back," she said when she recovered her voice. "We both know I can't sit quietly. If you want to go without me, I would totally understand."

"If my best friend ever won't let me cancel my date, how could I possibly leave her alone?" Jillian asked. "You'll come with us to dinner. I'm sure R.J. will understand. I told you he's very sweet and caring. I think he would be upset if he knew you were here alone. It's decided and no arguing!"

"Thanks, Jillie," Kellie replied. "You're the best! I hope this guy is good enough for you."

"Time will tell," Jillian responded, hoping in her heart that he was too.

By seven o'clock Jillian and Kellie were dressed for dinner. Since Jillian didn't have R.J.'s cell phone number, he didn't know it would be a party of three. When Jillian told Kellie that she and R.J. had not exchanged cell phone numbers, they had debated leaving a message on his business voice mail. They had decided against it, thinking it would be interesting to see how he reacted.

They sat on the balcony having a glass of wine while they waited. It was a beautiful scene before them. The water had calmed during the day and there were no waves except for some tiny white caps. The sun was getting lower in the sky behind them, turning the few clouds they could see to pink and orange hues. This was Jillian's favorite part of the day at the beach. The time when the sky was exquisitely painted, the beach was empty except for a few people strolling at the water's edge, and a gentle breeze cut the heat and humidity of the day.

"I think this would be the ideal place to live," Jillian spoke with reverence as she watched the colors in the sky change with the setting sun.

"I don't know," Kellie said quietly. "I love it here, but I love the mountains too."

They sat in silence for a long time, watching the gulls circling as they prepared for nightfall. Finally Jillian sat up as if waking from a trance. She looked at her watch and sighed.

"It's almost seven-thirty," she murmured. "I think I've been stood up."

"Maybe he got busy taking pictures and lost track of time," Kellie suggested, her heart breaking for her friend. "Let's give him a few more minutes."

They had another glass of wine and waited some more. As the time approached eight o'clock, Jillian knew he wasn't coming. Once more she had misjudged a man's intentions. When would she learn?

"Let's go eat, Kellie," she said finally. "He's not coming."

"Oh Jillie, I'm so sorry," Kellie cried. "I can't believe he would do this. He seemed so nice last night."

"Well, we both were taken in by his apparently false façade," Jillian replied forcing a smile. "But it's OK. I had a good time last night and that's that. We had a fun vacation fling, not a relationship. Let's go to Murrell's Inlet and have some fresh fish."

"You could call the number on his card," Kellie said. "Let him know that you're disappointed he turned out to be a lying scum."

"I could," Jillian laughed. "But it's not that important to me. Let's forget about him and enjoy the rest of our girls' weekend."

"Girls only dinner in Murrell's Inlet it is!" Kellie shouted as they started toward the door.

As Kellie led the way, Jillian followed, a sad expression on her face. She was really disappointed that R.J. had thought of her as a one-night stand. He had seemed so real, so open, so honest. Once again, she wondered about her ability to see people as they were instead of as she wanted them to be. Maybe she should stick to phone friends. At least Will couldn't stand her up on a date.

At noon the next day, Jillian and Kellie began the trip back home. Kellie talked non-stop about her tan, the wonderful seafood dinner they had the night before, and how they needed to do this more often. R.J. was not mentioned and Jillian was glad. Her pride was still stinging over the missing photographer.

Arriving home about four o'clock, Jillian unpacked and then sent Will a text message.

Hey there, it's Angel. Back home and would love to talk.

She waited until ten o'clock but there was no response. Maybe he had to leave the country again, earlier than he had expected. Yeah, that must be it. Disappointment flooded Jillian as she got ready for bed. Even her phone friend was apparently off limits tonight. Jillian sighed. There had to be someone out there who would treat her right, love her for who she was, and be her partner in life. The problem was she had no idea how to find him.

CHAPTER 9

Back at work on Tuesday morning, Jillian threw herself into the project she had told her mother about. She was doing a complete financial review for a huge Raleigh-based construction and development company. They had taken a big hit when the housing market fell and were trying to get back on track. Jillian had to review their financial records for the last five years and determine the best way to cut costs and increase their return on investments.

Deep in paperwork, she ignored her constantly ringing phone as well as Allison's attempts at getting her on the intercom. If she stopped to talk, she would lose her train of thought and have to start over again on the document she was reviewing. Jillian was startled when there was a knock on her door.

"Come in," she called as she tried to keep her place on the paperwork for an intricate construction project.

"Sorry to disturb you Ms. Stanley," Allison said as she came into the office. "I've been buzzing you but you're not answering."

"That's because I'm up to my neck in the documents for Ridell Construction." Jillian replied as she waved her hand at the massive piles of paper on her desk. "I thought I told you not to disturb me. I sure hope this is important."

"Mr. Krenshaw wants to see you as soon as possible, so it must be important," Allison advised. "I think it has to do with a long time client of your father's."

"OK, tell him I'll be there is five minutes," Jillian said standing up to stretch. "I need a bathroom break anyway. While I'm in with Kent, can you order me a grilled chicken salad from Deli Delight? Oil and vinegar dressing on the side and unsweetened, iced, green tea."

"Sure, Ms. Stanley," Allison nodded. "Anything else?"

"No thanks, Allison," Jillian replied, handing Allison some money. "I'm going to be tied up with this paperwork for weeks. I'll try to do better about letting you know when I don't want to be disturbed. It's just really difficult to get back to where I was once my concentration is broken."

"Maybe you should move into one of the conference rooms so you can spread out," Allison suggested. "Your phone wouldn't bother you there. And I'll know that when you're in there, you don't want to be disturbed."

"Excellent idea!" Jillian beamed at the young receptionist. "I'll do that tonight when everyone is gone. Thanks for a really good suggestion. That's the kind of proactive approach I like to see."

Allison smiled back at Jillian and went out the door. Jillian started to follow Allison out when her iPhone buzzed with a text message. She reached for it and saw it was a text message from Will. Her day had just improved one hundred percent!

Hi Angel. Dealing with a difficult situation right now. Be in touch in a few days.

Jillian found she was very disappointed. She had missed Will's sweet, funny text messages and was really looking forward to talking to him. Get over it, she told herself. He has some kind of issue and I need to be supportive, not whiny. She typed a message for him and hit send.

Hope everything is OK. I'll be here when you can talk.

Jillian put the phone back on her desk, went out the door, and turned right to go down the hall to Kent Krenshaw's office. With her father and Andrew Wilson, Kent was one of the founding partners of Stanley, Wilson, and Krenshaw. She had grown up around Kent and Andrew and still thought of them as kindly uncles. She knocked on the open door of Kent's office and grinned when he looked up.

"Hey Kent, I hear you need to see me." Jillian smiled at the older man as he rose from his chair.

"Jillian, how are you?" Kent asked as he came around the desk and enveloped Jillian in a bear hug. "Did you get moved? How was the beach weekend? I missed all the good news while I was gone on my vacation."

"Apparently you didn't miss too much," Jillian giggled. "I'm thinking Mindy and my mom have been talking recently."

"You know my wife," Kent chuckled. "You're the daughter she never had and she revels in every story your mom has about you. I guess Barbara mentioned your move and your trip when they talked Sunday. I heard about it soon after, along with a complaint that Mindy never sees you anymore."

"I'll call Mindy and set up a weekend lunch soon," Jillian replied. "I'm up to my eyeballs in documents from Ridell Construction. I'm hoping to review all of them over the next two or three weeks. Then I can begin drafting some investment and cost cutting guidelines for Pete Ridell. I told him I would have something for him by early October."

"Good job, Jillian," Kent responded. "Just be sure there's money somewhere in their budget so they can pay us!"

"Don't worry, Kent," Jillian laughed as they sat down on the sofa against the wall. "Payment to SW&K is the number one line item on that budget. So what's up? Allison said that you needed to see me."

"Did you ever meet the owners of Big Jake's Automotive Sales?" Kent asked. "They were one of your dad's first clients well before we became partners."

"Yes, a couple of times," Jillian said thoughtfully. "After Dad died, I met Jake and his business partner. Some guy named Nick or Rick? That Rick person was concerned about whether a woman could properly handle the accounting for their car dealerships. I believe that Rick called me 'little lady' and wondered what I could possibly know about cars or making money. Now that I think about it, you were in that meeting too."

"I sure was and I was livid," Kent exclaimed. "I remember you told Rick that the State of North Carolina thought you were perfectly capable when they gave you a license and then excused yourself from the meeting. Once you left, I told Rick you were the best accountant that SW&K had ever employed. I also told him if he called you 'little lady' again, I would personally knock his head off."

Jillian laughed at the thought of Kent protecting her honor. She was glad she had a couple of honorary uncles.

"So that's why the other two or three meetings were just with Jake," she said. "Thanks for having my back, Kent. I wondered why the little worm never showed his face again. So what's up with Big Jake's?"

"I received a call earlier this morning," Kent's voice was somber now. "Jake passed away last weekend. I'll be going to his funeral tomorrow, representing the firm."

"Oh no, I'm so sorry to hear that!" Jillian cried. "Please extend my condolences to his family."

"Of course," Kent noted. "His only family is his son. His wife passed several years before your dad. I spoke to the son this morning and he is selling his father's share of the business to the 'little worm' as you so aptly called Rick. We need to do a complete accounting of the business and assist with a value for Jake's share."

"Kent, I'm really swamped right now," Jillian said. "Can't someone else take it on?"

"I'll get Eddie to do the initial review and make some recommendations," Kent replied. "But Eddie's so new and so green. I really need you to look at what he does before it's presented to Jake's son. Since your dad and Jake went way back, I think it's only reasonable that you make the presentation to Jake's son."

"That sounds like a good plan," Jillian agreed. "Have Eddie let me know when he's finished so we can go over it. Then I'll set up a meeting with the son."

"OK, but you need to do a preliminary meeting with the son before Eddie starts," Kent advised. "We need to be sure he really wants to sell everything to Rick. The business at one point was up to four or five car lots. With the economy the way it's been, they closed a couple of them in the last year.

"I want to be sure we have a proper value on what's left. I hope you don't mind, but I set up a meeting with Jake's son on Thursday morning at ten o'clock. Allison said your calendar was clear then. He said he will only be in town until Saturday, but will come back when the sale closes."

Jillian sighed. She really didn't have time to hold the hand of a client's distraught son right now. But Kent rarely asked her to do anything and Big Jake's Automotive Sales was one of her father's first clients.

"You know I can't say no to you, Kent," Jillian grinned. "I'll meet the son, reassure him we will protect his interests, and then send him on his way. Thirty minutes, tops, and I can get back to Ridell. Speaking of Ridell, I hear all those stacks of paper calling me now."

After making a promise to call Mindy for lunch soon, Jillian went back down the hall to her office. Later that evening when everything was quiet, she moved all of the paperwork for Ridell Construction to the smaller conference room. She returned to her now clean office and checked her phone for the tenth time since lunch. Nothing from Will, but then he said it would be a few days. Why was she so disappointed?

Jillian arrived at the office on Thursday morning at eight o'clock sharp. She still hadn't heard anything from Will. She made a cup of tea, started a pot of coffee for the coffee drinkers, and went to her office to check email. As she was finishing up, she heard a rap on her open office door.

"Good morning, Ms. Stanley," Allison greeted her. "How's it working out in the conference room?"

"That was a great idea!" Jillian exclaimed. "I can hide from the office small talk and the phones so I'm really getting a lot done. This is much more involved than I originally thought and I can really concentrate since it's quiet."

"I'm really glad to hear it's working out," Allison responded. "Where do you want to meet Big Jake's son when he gets here at ten?"

"Put him in my office and then let me know he's here," Jillian said. "I really don't want him to see the Ridell paperwork all over the conference room. Besides, my office makes a much better impression."

Allison went back to the reception desk and Jillian went to the conference room. She was deep in concentration when there was a knock on the door. Checking her watch, she realized it was a few minutes after ten o'clock. Allison opened the door and entered the room.

"Big Jake's son is in your office. I got him a cup of coffee and told him you would be there shortly," she advised.

"What's his name?" Jillian asked. "I don't want to call him by the wrong name."

"When he called the other day, he identified himself only as Big Jake Williams' son," Allison replied. "When I called him Mr. Williams, he didn't correct me."

"Thanks, Allison," Jillian said. "I'll be there in a minute."

Jillian sat for a moment, collecting her thoughts. Hearing the name out loud reminded her of the photographer with the same last name and how he had lied to her. Although she had tried to downplay it, being stood up had really stung. She stood, walked around the corner, and went down the hall to her office.

Jillian stopped outside the office door and took a deep breath. She wasn't good at consoling people about a death in their family. It brought back too many memories of her father's death. And R.J. Williams was now intruding on her thoughts too. She shook her head to rid it of the distracting thoughts and stepped into her office.

"Mr. Williams, I'm sorry to keep you waiting," Jillian said in a warm voice.

"No problem, Ms. Stanley," the gentleman in the chair said as he rose and turned toward her.

Jillian stopped in her tracks as the man's face came into view. What in the world was R.J. Williams doing in her office? Her mouth dropped open at the sight of him and she was speechless. Apparently R.J. was speechless too as he just stood there, staring at her. He was the first to finally find his voice.

"Well, this is certainly a surprise," he stammered. "Uh yeah, but a nice one for sure."

"What are you doing here? I mean…..um well….I mean I don't understand how you found me or know where I work," Jillian stuttered in response, her face now completely red with embarrassment. "I'm expecting a client at any moment. I can't talk now, R.J."

"I'm the client, Jillian. I'm here because my father, Big Jake, died. I'm supposed to be meeting Jesse Stanley's daughter about the sale of my dad's business," R.J. replied, his voice a little more steady now. "Honestly, I had no idea it would be you."

"It's me, Jillian Stanley," she noted, then remembered her manners. "I'm so very sorry about the loss of your father, R.J. He was one of my father's first clients. When my dad passed away a few years ago, I became the person who oversaw the work our firm did for your father."

"Oh, so you're the fiery redhead who put Rick in his place?" R.J. asked with a chuckle. "My dad laughed about that so many times I know the story by heart."

"Yes, that would be me," Jillian said with an embarrassed smile. "Rick and I didn't hit it off very well when we met that time."

"Don't worry about it," R.J. laughed. "Rick doesn't hit it off with very many women. He's a bit of a sleaze, which is why he's so good at selling used cars. My dad was the brains of the business and Rick is the sales whiz."

Jillian regained her poise and crossed the room. She sat down behind her desk and clasped her hands on the top, hoping that R.J. couldn't see how badly they were shaking. This was like a lightening bolt out of the blue and her stomach was in knots.

"First of all, I owe you an apology," R.J. said, bringing Jillian back from her thoughts. "I didn't have your cell number to call and cancel our dinner date. I kept hoping you would call my office number so I could call back and explain why I didn't show up. I guess now you know."

"You don't need to apologize, R.J." Jillian answered softly. "I was upset but now I completely understand. What happened with your father? All I know is that he passed away over the weekend and the funeral was yesterday."

"I left you Sunday morning and went back to my house," he began. "I decided to sleep for a few hours and woke up to a message on my cell phone. It was Rick telling me my dad was in Raleigh General Hospital. He had a stroke and was on life support."

R.J. drew a shaky breath and looked at Jillian. He had tears in his eyes. She wanted to go around the desk and hold him. He was in so much pain that her heart was about to break, but she told herself that she didn't have the right to do that. They had had one evening together and she didn't know if he would think she was being too familiar. Besides, he was a client now and the firm was clear that clients were off limits for personal relationships.

"Oh R.J., I'm so very sorry," she said. "It must have been terrible for you."

"I left Ocean Isle so fast it was all a blur," R.J. responded, looking down at his hands, his voice quiet. "By the time I got to Raleigh, the doctors had done a bunch of tests and they told me the stroke was so massive that he would never recover. Sunday afternoon we took him off life support and he went peacefully in just a few minutes."

Again, Jillian had a strong urge to go around the desk and pull R.J. into a comforting embrace. She stifled the urge, knowing it would be awkward for both of them. Instead she stayed silent for a few moments, giving him a chance to get himself under control. When he looked up at her, he seemed to be ready to go on.

"Oh R.J., how awful for you," Jillian spoke quietly too. "I know how hard this time is, when you can't believe someone you have known your entire life is now gone."

"My dad was an amazing person," he replied. "We had our differences but he was always there for me, always supported whatever I wanted to do. And now he's just gone. I have a thousand things in my head that I want to tell him. I had no idea it would this hard."

Jillian felt tears forming but fought them back. This sweet, handsome man was devastated and she wanted to tell him everything would be all right. However, she knew that nothing can make such a loss all right and only time can make it bearable. She decided they needed to get down to business before they both ended up bawling like babies.

"Hang in there, R.J.," she replied. "I know this sounds trite, but it does get better with time. In the meantime, let's focus on Big Jake's business holdings. Tell me what you're thinking about doing with it. I'm assuming you're his only heir and his part of the business now belongs to you."

"It's just me and I now own half of Big Jake's Automotive Sales," R.J. sighed. "Sleazy Rick owns the other half and is willing to buy me out. I'm willing to sell for the right price."

"R.J., are you sure about that? It's only been a few days, so it might be a good idea to think about it when the hurt isn't quite so fresh," Jillian said. "I would hate for you to make a rushed decision when you're still reeling from your dad's death."

"You know I travel all over the world with my job, Jillian," R.J. answered. "I don't have time to be tied to this business. I don't trust Rick to run it properly if I'm not there. He and my dad clashed constantly over Rick's penchant for promising customers the world and delivering only a used car in 'as is' condition.

"I can see Rick turning the entire operation into one of those used car places whose television commercials make you cringe. I just want out of it, but I want to make Rick pay me a fair price. I don't really need the money, but I want to do right for all the blood, sweat, and tears my dad put into the business over the years."

"I have to admit, I can see Sleazy Rick on TV now doing one of those commercials that cause me to change channels fast," Jillian laughed. "They also cause me to avoid that business like it's a contagious disease."

"Ah, so you do know Rick," R.J. said and smiled at her. "Then you certainly understand why I don't want to be involved in a business with him. The only person he ever listened to was my dad. He would cut his hands off before he would listen to anything that came out of my mouth."

"OK, let's do this," Jillian stuttered. R.J.'s smile had turned her insides to jelly. She had to focus on business before she said something stupid. "Let the firm do an inventory and a financial analysis. We have most of the information we need except for a current inventory of the cars and their Blue Book values. If you can get that for me, we can determine a fair market value for the business. Then you can decide if you are ready to sell to Rick."

"Thanks Jillian," R.J. smiled at her again. "I think that's a good idea. How long will it take? I have to leave for Europe on Saturday evening. I was supposed to be there now, but my client gave me an extension to wrap things up here."

"We'll need a couple of weeks at least," she replied, trying to keep focused on business while her heart was pounding and her body was feeling a rush of heat. "Can you get me the current inventory before you leave? That's a critical piece of information. At some point we will also need a copy of the death certificate and the will leaving his piece of the business to you. Your dad's lawyer should be able to send me the last two items."

"Sure," R.J. remarked. "I'm meeting the lawyer as soon as I leave here, so that's no problem. And I have a good relationship with the office manager. She had a crush on me when I worked there and we're good friends now. I should be able to have the current inventory for you by tomorrow."

"That's great," Jillian noted, feeling a tinge of jealousy. Now where had that come from? "If you can get her to fax it over, we can get started first thing Monday. The lawyer can messenger the other things to us next week. Wait a minute, is this the job you had after college that you hated so much? Selling used cars?"

"Oh that's right, I told you about that when we were at The Isle with your friends." R.J. smiled his killer smile again. "My dad thought it would be best if I learned the business from the ground up. So he put me at the lot where Rick spent most of his time. It was the most miserable experience of my life. I knew in two days that I could never sell cars, but my dad was adamant that I had to know everything about the business if I was going to take it over for him someday."

"How did he take it when you told him you were leaving to be a photographer," Jillian asked.

"He said he was glad I hated the car business," R.J. replied, grinning at the memory. "He put me with Rick to try and convince me to use my business degree for something besides selling cars. It certainly worked! I was so glad to get out of there.

"My dad always supported my photography and he was happy when I got an opportunity to make some money with it. When my business took off, he was the first one to suggest I open a studio in New York. I'm going to miss him so much. No matter where I was on this Earth, I always knew I could come home. Now with both my mom and dad gone, I feel so lost."

Jillian realized she was staring at R.J., mesmerized by his sexy voice. Her entire body was tingling. Her mind was screaming at her to go around her desk and kiss him, comfort him. He seemed so bereft. What was wrong with her? This man was sitting there like a lost little boy and she was thinking about kissing him. She had to get it together and get professional again, now!

"Can I ask you something?" she managed to stutter. "What does R.J. stand for?"

"I'm actually Randall Jacob Williams the third," he laughed. "My grandfather went by Randall and my dad went by Jake. When it got around to me, I ended up being R.J."

He smiled that killer smile again. Jillian was melting inside and still fighting the urge to kiss him. She had to focus so she tried again with another question.

"How long will you be in Europe?" was the best she could manage.

"Well, my assignment there will probably take three or four weeks," he said. "I never really know for sure. You can let me know when you're ready to discuss things. I should have a pretty good idea by then when I can get back here."

"Sounds good," Jillian acknowledged, handing him a sheet of paper she pulled from her desk drawer. "Fill this out so I know how to reach you via both office and cell phone. Be sure to give me the lawyer's name and the office manager's name. That way if we have any questions, we can reach out to them and not bother you."

"Jillian, hearing from you would never be a bother," R.J. smiled at her again. "And I have a suggestion."

"OK, what's on your mind?" Jillian was again drawn to his smile, his incredibly sensuous lips, his deep brown eyes.

"How about if I bring the inventory and other documents when I take you to dinner tomorrow night?" he asked. "I would take you tonight, but my dad's brother and his wife are still in town."

"I would love to have dinner with you," Jillian exclaimed. "But the firm has a strict policy about personal relationships with clients. As long as I'm working for you, I can't go out with you."

"What if we call it a business dinner? I mean, I'm delivering documents you need to do your work," R.J. said with a mischievous grin. "Can't you make an exception for that? Plus I owe you a dinner since I stood you up Sunday."

"Well, since you put it that way….sure, let's have dinner tomorrow night," Jillian laughed. "Be sure to bring those documents. I may be a partner in this firm, but I'm still held to the rules."

"Great!" R.J. cried. "This is the first good news I've had since I left your bed Sunday morning."

"Um, please don't say that to anyone here in the office," Jillian stammered. "I really should be handing you off to someone else since we've had a very personal encounter already."

"Once this business is finished, I'm firing your firm," R.J. declared. "And I hope we have a lot more 'personal encounters' in the future. Dancing with you was so much fun, but we didn't really get to talk much. I want to know everything about you, Jillian Stanley. You're smart, funny, sweet as can be, and an amazing lover. I haven't spent much time in Raleigh the last few years, but I may have a reason to change that now."

Jillian smiled a huge smile and pushed the sheet of paper across the desk. R.J. filled out the form and handed it back to her. They rose from their seats and walked toward the office door, Jillian's heart was beating so loud she was sure R.J. would hear it. He turned to her before they reached the door. He pulled her toward him and put his arms around her. Jillian was powerless to stop him or extricate herself from his embrace. They stood together, holding each other for several long minutes. Finally, R.J. looked down at her and smiled that sexy smile once again.

"Thank you, beautiful lady. I needed that," he murmured. "Now I have to get to the lawyer's office."

Without warning, he leaned forward and kissed her. His lips were soft on hers at first, burning her with the heat they produced. Then the kiss became more forceful, as if R.J. was afraid he would never kiss her again. Jillian was lost in his kiss, lost in his scent. Her body ached for him. A sharp knock on the door sent them skittering apart.

"Let me see who that is," Jillian mumbled as she strode toward the door.

She opened the door and Kent came in. He looked at her oddly and then turned toward R.J. The men shook hands and Kent began to speak.

"Mr. Williams, again let me extend the sympathies of Stanley, Wilson, and Krenshaw," he said. "We are so very sorry for your loss. Is Jillian taking care of everything to your satisfaction?"

"She is amazing," R.J. proclaimed and then looked at his watch. "I need to get going. I have an appointment at the lawyer's office and I don't want to be late."

"Well, you let us know if we can do anything else to help," Kent boomed.

"I'm sure Jillian will take good care of me," R.J. said to Kent. He then turned and winked at Jillian. "Now I really need to go. Jillian, I'll be in touch tomorrow morning about delivering those documents you need. And thanks again for everything."

R.J. turned and went out the door. Jillian felt like she might fall over....her legs were still weak from the incredible kiss she had just shared with an amazingly sexy man.

"Well he looks pretty happy for a man who just lost his father," Kent commented. "I guess you worked your charm on him. Good job, Jillian!"

"No problem, Kent," Jillian smiled a secret smile. If Kent only knew why R.J. was happy.....

CHAPTER 10

"You have got to be kidding me!" Kellie exclaimed. "It's definitely fate working here. The universe is pretty insistent you two belong together."

Jillian and Kellie were having a glass of wine at their favorite hang out, Pip's Tavern. They were sitting outside on the patio, enjoying the mild evening weather as the sun was setting. Jillian had called Kellie after R.J. had left her office and pleaded with her to meet as soon as they both finished work. She had refused to say why, hinting that Kellie would be astounded when she heard what had happened that day. Now they were seated with a glass of Chateau wine, Jillian's favorite. Jillian had just told Kellie about walking into her office and finding R.J there.

"I don't know about fate, but I almost dropped dead of a heart attack when he stood and turned around so I could see him," Jillian responded. "I swear I had to sit down so I didn't fall down."

"What else can you call it?" Kellie demanded. "A guy you think is sweet and sexy and perfect shows up in your office, grief stricken and needing to be consoled. The universe is definitely looking out for you!"

"Well, whatever it is, it was an unbelievable surprise," Jillian answered. "He was so torn up about his dad's death that all I could think of was going around my desk and hugging him."

"Did you?" Kellie asked. "Jillie, please tell me you did and that you have another date with him."

"No, I didn't Kell," Jillian replied. "He's a client now and the firm has strict rules about personal relationships with clients. I actually told him that I should really hand him off to someone else at the firm since we know each other….ummm intimately."

"OK, now that was smart. Get rid of the client status and go for hot date status. So when's the big date? He sure owes you a dinner!" Kellie, as always, was forging ahead.

"But I didn't hand him off." Jillian resumed her story. "Because then I would have to explain to Kent and Andrew why I can't handle the work for my dad's first client. I sure didn't want to have that conversation with them. So when R.J. asked me to dinner, I told him that I couldn't go out with him."

"Are you crazy?" Kellie cried. "The first good guy you've met since your divorce and you tell him you can't go out? Please tell me that you have lost your mind. Because if you say that Victor is calling you and you decided to get back with him, I'm going to take you to the nut house right now."

"No, Victor is not and will never be in my life again," Jillian proclaimed. "He calls and leaves me a message at least once a day. I listened to the first few but they were all the same. How he can't live without me, how he will never let me go, and on and on. I haven't returned any of his calls, I delete his messages without listening to them, and I don't intend to ever speak to him again. I'm done with him, Kellie. Now let me finish telling you about R.J., OK?"

"OK, get on with it," Kellie laughed.

"R.J. said that he wants me to take care of selling his dad's business to the business partner," Jillian continued. "Then he said when it's all done, he would fire the firm so he could take me out."

"Aha! He's a smart man after all," Kellie said, nodding her head yes.

"And I'm having dinner with him tomorrow night." Jillian smiled at the thought. "There are some papers I need from the business and from his dad's attorney. We're having a business dinner so he can bring them to me."

"Hope some of that business is 'monkey business'," Kellie giggled.

"Honestly Kellie, do you ever stop thinking about sex?" Jillian giggled in return. "It will be strictly accounting business until Big Jake's is sold to sleazy Rick, the business partner. And after that, well, we will see what happens."

"So let's see, business dinners for the next how many nights until you're in the clear?" Kellie contemplated with a grin. "Think you can hold out for ten, fifteen, or maybe twenty nights?"

"One business dinner tomorrow night," Jillian stated emphatically. "Then on Saturday he leaves town again for a work project. He was supposed to be there now actually. When he comes back in a few weeks, I'll help close the sale of Big Jake's. After that, I don't know what will happen."

Kellie laughed, a great, long belly laugh, thinking about her best friend's plan. She eyed Jillian for a moment and then got serious.

"I know what should happen then," she grinned again. "I hope you will give this guy a chance, Jillie. He seemed so nice when we met him and I know you had a great time. Plus I know how disappointed you were when he didn't show up for that dinner date. I have to assume you like him a lot."

"I do like him a lot Kell, but with my track record, I'm afraid to think too far ahead," Jillian replied. "Right now, I want to get the sale of Big Jake's finished. I just can't think about what might happen after that. My life feels too unsettled as it is. You know I'm not really happy at SW&K. I think I need to resolve that before I get in too deep with anyone or anything else."

"Jillian, I understand that, but don't walk away from something that could be good," Kellie counseled. "Yeah, you might get hurt, but you might find the person who is perfect for you too. You don't have to decide anything right now with R.J., so let it simmer. And let the universe do its work!"

"You and your belief in some crazy plan the universe has for me," Jillian smiled. "You know I don't really believe in all that. But if it makes you happy, then you can believe for both of us."

"I don't know why, but I just feel like this is going to be different for you." Kellie was very serious now. "All I'm saying is give him a chance. I just have this feeling….."

"OK, I get it my friend," Jillian said. "I'll give him a chance when our business dealings are finished. Now let's have another glass of Chateau before I send you home to Stephen."

Friday morning Jillian arrived at work early once again. She had a lot to do on the Ridell project and was nervous about her dinner with R.J. Her nerves had awakened her before the sun was up and pacing her condo didn't seem like a productive way to spend the early morning hours. She found herself in the conference room, reading paper after paper at seven o'clock in the morning. Finally at ten o'clock, she took a short break. As she passed the reception area, Allison called out to her.

"Ms. Stanley, Mr. Williams called earlier. He asked that you call him back about the paperwork you need from him."

"Thank you, Allison," Jillian responded. "Did he leave a number?"

"He said to call him on his cell phone," Allison advised as she handed Jillian a message slip. "He left it in case you don't have it."

"Thanks again," Jillian smiled as she looked down at the pink slip of paper.

Jillian turned and went toward her office. Allison stared after her, wondering why a message from a client brought such a big smile to her boss' face. Whatever the reason, she was glad to see Ms. Stanley smiling again.

In her office, Jillian picked up the phone and called R.J.'s cell phone. The number looked familiar but she thought it was just because she had seen it on the intake form R.J. had filled out the other day. As the phone began to ring, she looked out the window at the beautiful early fall day. Her heart was filled with positive thoughts for the first time in a long time.

"Hello, R.J. here," R.J. answered on the third ring.

"Hi, it's Jillian Stanley."

"Hello to my beautiful accountant," R.J. replied. "I sure hope we're still on for dinner tonight. I have all the paperwork you needed so we definitely have an excuse to meet."

"Of course we are," Jillian responded. "I wouldn't miss it for the world. Especially since you owe me a dinner."

"That I do," he noted. "Although it won't be fresh seafood, I intend to fulfill my obligation tonight and many more times after that too. Maybe when I get back from this project, I can take you to my house at Ocean Isle and cook fresh seafood for you."

"You have a house at Ocean Isle?" she asked in surprise. "I assumed you were just visiting like Kellie and I."

"I own a house there," R.J. answered. "It's my retreat when the insanity of New York gets too much for me. I'm really a North Carolina boy at heart, but my business demands a more upscale address. So I have my office in Manhattan with a couple of rooms in the back where I stay when I'm up there."

"I'm not sure which I like most, that you own a house at the beach or that you can cook!" Jillian declared. "But let's get Big Jake's sale completed first and then we can discuss more dinners."

"Sounds like a good plan," R.J. said. "Any favorite place you might like to go tonight? I was raised around here but haven't lived in Raleigh for years. I know things have changed tremendously since my high school years."

"One of my favorites that's been around for a long time is Louie's Steakhouse and Tavern," Jillian replied. "Have you ever been there?"

"Of course, it's fantastic!" R.J. exclaimed. "It was one of my dad's favorite places, so it's fitting for us to discuss his business there. Want me to pick you up at your office?"

"No, I'd better meet you there," Jillian decided. "It's still a business dinner plus I don't live too far from there. We can meet in the tavern at seven o'clock if that works for you. The food is just as good as the steakhouse but it's a more relaxed atmosphere."

"Perfect!" R.J. responded. "I'll see you then. And I'm looking forward to another interesting evening with the most beautiful woman I know."

"That's very sweet, R.J. I'm looking forward to seeing you too. Unfortunately, I need to get back to work now. See you at seven, OK?"

They said their goodbyes and hung up. Jillian spent several more minutes looking out the window, thinking about how much fun she had had with R. J. dancing at the beach tiki bar. She wanted to get this sale out of the way and see if just maybe they could have something together. Her reverie was disturbed by the ringing of her cell phone. She picked it and saw Victor's name on the caller ID. With a sigh, she wondered if he would ever give up. He had treated her like nothing more than a receptacle for his sperm the last time she saw him. And she had let him treat her that way, but never again. She had no intention of speaking to him or responding in any way to his calls.

The rest of the day flew by and Jillian was shocked when Allison knocked on the conference room door to say she was leaving. How did it get to be six o'clock already? Jillian hurried to her office to check her email and voice mail. There was nothing urgent, so she went to the ladies room to freshen up for her dinner with R.J. She hurried back to her office to grab her purse and headed out to the parking garage.

Walking across the garage, she noticed that her Jeep looked odd, like it was sitting at an angle. As she came up behind it, she realized that the back tire on the driver's side was flat. Oh great, she thought, now I have to get the tire changed. I'm going to be late for dinner.

When she got beside the car, Jillian saw that the front tire on the driver's side was flat too. Now, how did that happen? Had she run over something and gotten nails in both tires? She didn't think so, but it had been very early and still dark when she left home that morning.

With a sigh, Jillian went back to her office to call for a tow truck. She also called a local tire place that she had used before to make arrangements for her tires to be repaired. She grabbed the pink slip with R.J.'s cell phone number so she could let him know she might be late and went down to the first floor of the office building. There was a car service on that floor and she caught the owner as he was locking up for the night.

"Hi Miles," Jillian said.

"Hi Jillian," Miles replied. "You're certainly here late on a Friday."

"I was leaving but my car has two flat tires," she answered. "The tow truck is on the way to take it to Sebring Auto Repair. They're going to fix the tires for me tomorrow morning. I must have run over something when I came to work early this morning."

"Do you need a ride?" Miles asked. "I was just leaving and can drop you off somewhere."

"Oh Miles, that would be wonderful!" Jillian cried. "Could you drop me at Louie's Tavern? I'm meeting a client for a short business meeting."

"Of course," Miles responded. "Let's go out to the garage so we don't miss the tow truck."

Jillian and Miles went down the back hallway and into the garage. Miles went over to her Jeep and began looking at the tires. He ran his hand over back tire, then the front tire, and then a worried look appeared on his face.

"Jillian, I think the tires were deliberately cut," he said seriously. "I don't feel anything like a nail head and both of them have an odd mark on the sidewall of the tire. You need to ask the guys at Sebring to check them very closely for you."

"Of course, I will," Jillian replied, her voice full of concern now. "I can't imagine why someone would cut my tires. I'm sure I just ran over something really sharp coming to work this morning."

"I hope I'm wrong, but please have them checked," Miles stated firmly.

"I will Miles. Oh, here's the tow truck now. Let me get him situated and then we can go. I don't want to hold you up too long."

Jillian made arrangements with the tow truck to take the car to Sebring's. As her car was being hooked to the tow truck, she got in the car with Miles. She glanced at the clock on the dash and realized she was going to be late. It was already seven and they had at least a fifteen minute drive. As they pulled out of the garage, she fished her cell phone and the slip of paper with R.J.'s phone number out of her purse.

"Miles, I need to call my client and let him know I'm going to be late," Jillian said as she began dialing R.J.'s number.

When she finished punching in the number, she looked at the screen and saw Will's name pop up. Well, that was odd. Jillian wondered if Will was trying to call her and she had hit the wrong button. She hit the button to terminate the call. Will had said he would call her when his "difficult situation" was resolved and she didn't want to bother him. She decided she must have dialed incorrectly and tried again. Again, Will's name popped up on the screen. What in the world was wrong with her phone?

"Something the matter?" Miles asked when he saw the perplexed look on Jillian's face.

"My phone isn't dialing right," she responded. "I'm dialing my client's number, but a friend's number is what my phone is actually calling. This makes no sense. Looks like there may be new tires and a new phone in my immediate future."

"Here, use my phone," Miles said as he pulled his cell phone from his pocket.

Jillian called R.J., successfully this time, and told him she was running late. She said she was having car troubles but was now on the way. He said he would get a table and order a bottle of wine while he waited for her. Smiling, she hung up and handed the phone back to Miles.

Twenty minutes later, they arrived at Louie's Tavern. Miles was concerned with how Jillian would get home but she assured him it was a short cab ride to her new condo. She headed into the restaurant and quickly found R.J. waiting at a table.

"I'm so sorry!" she exclaimed as she reached the table. "I had car trouble and had to call a tow truck."

"No problem," R.J. smiled at Jillian, causing her heart to skip a beat. "I would wait all night for you if I had to. I'm having dinner with the most beautiful, interesting woman in the city of Raleigh. Why wouldn't I wait?"

"That's very sweet, R.J." Jillian beamed at him. "I just hope you aren't starving while you're waiting."

"Not at all. As a matter of fact, here's our appetizer now," R.J. pointed to a waiter who put a plate of Thai shrimp skewers down on the table. As the waiter poured a glass of Chateau wine for Jillian, R.J. said, "Thank you. Can you give us a few minutes to look at the menu?"

The waiter left the table and R.J. turned his attention to Jillian. She was absolutely beautiful but he didn't think she realized exactly how gorgeous she was. He took in a sharp breath as she smiled at him. Smart, pretty, unpretentious, sweet as can be.....could he really be lucky enough to have someone like that in his life? His track record wasn't very good thanks to his constant traveling. He could hardly wait to finish his current assignment, get back to Raleigh, and complete the sale of the business so he could find out.

"Did you get your car taken care of?" he asked. "What happened?"

"It's been towed to have the tires fixed or replaced," Jillian related. "I went out to the parking garage and both tires on the driver's side were flat. I must have driven over something on my way to work this morning."

"That's really odd that both tires would be flat," R.J. speculated. "I can't imagine what you would have run over that would flatten both of them. Did you find a nail or anything in them?"

"Miles, the owner of the car service on the first floor of our building, looked at them for me but didn't find anything," Jillian explained. "He said there weren't any nails or anything protruding out of them. I'm sure the tire place will be able to tell me what happened."

Just then, Jillian's cell phone began to ring. She apologized to R.J., saying that she needed to check and see if it was the Sebring's calling. When she saw that it was Vincent, she sent the call to voice mail.

They tackled the shrimp skewers and chatted about what to order for dinner. The waiter appeared and took their order, pouring more wine before he left. As the waiter walked away, Jillian's phone rang again and this time it was Sebring's. Jillian took the call. R.J. watched her as she listened to the man and then her face went deathly pale. When she hung up, she sat quietly for a moment.

"What's wrong?" he asked. "You look scared out of your mind."

"That was my mechanic friend," Jillian whispered. "He said both of my tires were deliberately slashed, most likely with a knife. I can't believe this is happening."

"He said what? How?" R.J. was staring at her wide-eyed.

"He said someone stuck a knife or something extremely sharp in the sidewall of both tires," Jillian muttered. "Why would someone do that to me?"

"I think you better call the police, Jillian," R.J. stated firmly. "It takes a sick mind to do something like that."

At that moment, her phone rang again. And again it was Victor. This time, after Jillian sent the call to voice mail, she turned the phone off. She had enough to deal with and didn't need a continuing interruption from Victor. She looked up at R.J. and saw the concern in his eyes.

"I will, R.J.," she promised. "I'll go over to get my car in the morning, get a statement from the tire shop, and then go to the police station afterwards."

"Please do, Jillian," R.J.'s tone was very serious now. "It's probably nothing more than a random act, but just in case, you need to make a report."

"I will tomorrow, I promise," she replied as she sat up straight and looked deep into his eyes. "Now let's enjoy our dinner and forget about this mess tonight."

"I like your attitude, beautiful lady," R.J. said raising his glass in a toast. "Here's to finishing our business and moving forward to new things."

"To finished business and new things," Jillian smiled as she touched her glass to R.J.'s glass.

In a few minutes, dinner arrived and they talked about the sale of Big Jake's as they ate. R.J. told her stories about his dad, their fishing and camping trips, and his time working at the car lot. She could see that being able to talk about his dad was very therapeutic for him. Several times he had tears in his eyes and it was all she could do to stay in her seat. Her heart wanted to hold him and tell him everything would be all right.

When they finished their entrees, R.J. insisted on ordering dessert too since he had stood her up at the beach. When they had finally eaten every last bite of the cheesecake he had ordered, it was late. Jillian was having such a good time that she had completely forgotten about her car. R.J. paid the bill and they went out the door of the restaurant. At that moment, Jillian realized she didn't have a way home.

"Oh, I need to go back inside and see if they have the number of a cab company," she exclaimed. "I completely forgot that I don't have any transportation tonight."

"No need," R.J. responded. "I'll take you home."

"R.J., that's really not necessary," Jillian said. "I'll just call a cab. I'm sure you have packing and things to do at your Dad's house before you leave town tomorrow."

"I won't take no for an answer Jillian," R.J. was adamant. "It worries me that someone slashed your tires. I want to be sure you get home safe and sound. Besides, I left Ocean Isle so fast that all I really have here are some clothes."

"But what about your Dad's things?" she asked. "Don't you have to take care of that before you leave tomorrow night?"

"I can't do it right now," he murmured. "I decided to wait until I get back. I'll just lock up the house and deal with it in a few weeks."

"I think it makes a lot of sense to wait," Jillian agreed. "You can decide what to do with things when the whole situation isn't so fresh in your mind. So if you really don't mind, I'll take that ride home."

CHAPTER 11

They piled into R.J.'s car and headed to Jillian's new condo. When they arrived, R.J. insisted on walking her to the door. She tried to argue, but in reality, she was still shaken over the slashed tires and appreciated his company. When they got to her door, she turned to look at him. His eyes sent a bolt of electricity through her body. And his lips looked so good she longed to lean over and lick them. Before she knew what she was doing, she spoke.

"Why don't you come in for a nightcap? I have some very good brandy."

"Now this is a surprise," he drawled, his amazing eyes looking deep into hers. "But I guess I do need to show you those papers you need for the sale of the business."

"Umm, yes, that's right," Jillian stuttered. "We didn't have a chance to talk about that at dinner."

R.J. continued to stare into her eyes as he chuckled at her stuttering. Without warning, he leaned forward and placed his lips against hers. Jillian thought she would melt on the spot. That simple act sent heat waves throughout her body. Without thinking, she put her arms around his neck and leaned into his body. She felt him relax as the kiss deepened and their tongues began to play. Finally, he pulled back and looked at her again.

"Do you think maybe we should take this inside?" he asked with a wicked, sexy grin. "I would hate for the neighbors to get jealous."

Jillian giggled and turned to put the key in the door. As the door opened to her new home, she turned on the lights and swept her hand out in invitation for R.J. to join her. She took him on a quick tour, describing how she had sold her large house and moved into this small condo until she decided what she wanted to do next. Ten minutes later, they were settled on the living room sofa, sipping glasses of brandy.

Jillian and R.J. chatted briefly about the paperwork from Big Jake's. When that was done, they began talking about Ocean Isle Beach and other vacation spots from their childhoods. Jillian brought up the subject to try and keep things on neutral ground. She realized she had let her body take control over her mind at the front door. With the SW&K policy about no personal relationships with clients, she had to get back in control. She had to make sure R.J. understood he could not stay the night no matter how much they both might want it.

"Although I love the beach, we spent a lot of time in the mountains when I was growing up," Jillian related. "My family has a cabin up in the mountains outside of Asheboro. It's so much cooler up there in the summer that we used to go at least one weekend a month."

"I totally understand," R.J. noted. "I already told you I spent a lot of time in the mountains too. Usually on summer breaks. The other thing that I realize now is that Ocean Isle is really crazy in the summer time. It wasn't quite so bad fifteen years ago, but now I sometimes wish I had a place in the mountains to go during the summer. But I really love the beach the rest of the year."

"My mom moved back to Asheboro after my dad died, but she never goes to the cabin," Jillian said, her voice a little sad. "I think it just reminds her too much of my dad. But I still like going there when I need to think or want to be totally alone. It's peaceful, quiet, and no cell phone service!"

"That sounds wonderful," R.J. cried. "As much as I love what I do, sometimes I like to shut everyone and everything out. Total relaxation with nothing more than a good bed and my favorite camera."

Jillian was about to respond when a loud, long knock on her front door startled both of them. She jumped up but stopped there, concerned about who would be at her door this late at night. The knocking began again, this time followed by a booming male voice shouting her name. Jillian cringed when she realized it was Victor.

"Are you expecting someone?" R.J. asked.

"No, and the person out there is not someone I want to talk to," Jillian replied. "But I guess I'd better see what he wants before my neighbors call the police."

"Want me to go instead?" R.J. suggested.

"That's very nice to offer but I need to take care of this now and for good," Jillian responded as she walked across the room.

Opening the door, Jillian saw Victor standing on her small front stoop. She gave him an angry look as she crossed her arms over her chest. He returned her look with an insolent grin.

"Hey babe," he began. "How about a kiss? I've missed you so much. You haven't returned any of my calls and I can't stand being away from you. I didn't even know where you had moved to until I followed you home last week. How can you be so cold to me?"

"Go away Victor," Jillian replied in a steely voice. "The last time I saw you, I told you that we were done. Leave me alone, don't call, don't text, and don't you ever appear at my door again."

"Now babe, you know that's not what you really want," Victor whined. "You know you want me. What do I need to do? I'll apologize if that's what you want, even though I have nothing to apologize for. So, I'm sorry for whatever it is you think I did wrong. How's that?"

"Get out of my life, Victor," Jillian replied. "Go home to your wife. Do NOT contact me again or I'll have you arrested for stalking. Do you understand?"

"I understand that you're nothing but a slut!" Victor shouted. "My wife left me because she found out I was fucking you, you little slut. You owe me, bitch!"

Victor stepped forward and reached toward Jillian. Before he could touch her, R.J. flew across the room and stepped in front of her. As Jillian retreated, R.J. pushed Victor backward and watched as he lost his balance and fell to his knees.

"See what I mean! You're such a slut that you're already fucking someone else," Victor screamed, enraged now as he looked up at R.J. "She's a good fuck, but don't think she will ever care about you. She has no heart. She only wants to be someone's whore!"

"I think it's best that you leave now," R.J. said quietly, his eyes boring into Victor's. "If you don't, Jillian will be forced to call the police."

"Oh, I'm leaving alright," Victor yelled as he got to his feet. "But this isn't over, Jillian. Either you come to your senses or I'll be forced to make you come to your senses. Tires aren't the only thing that can be cut, you know."

Victor turned and went back down the walkway toward the parking lot. R.J. stood in the doorway, watching him go.

He didn't move until he saw Victor get in the car and saw the car leave the parking lot. When it looked like Victor was gone, R.J. slowly stepped back in the room and closed the door. When he turned and looked at Jillian, he saw she had gone completely white at Victor's last rant.

"Oh my god," Jillian whispered. "Victor slashed my tires today. Why would he do that?"

"He's obviously crazy and sounds like he's obsessed with you, too," R.J. said.

"But I don't understand," she responded, her voice breaking and tears very close to spilling from her eyes. "We had a fling, nothing serious. He's married and made sure I knew it after he seduced me. I really don't understand."

With that, Jillian dropped to the sofa as if her legs could no longer hold her. R.J. could see that she was shaking with fear and he wanted to hold her, tell her everything would be all right. He crossed the room and sat beside her. He wanted to reach out but something told him now was not the time. Jillian was too shocked right now to think clearly. Her head was bowed and she kept shaking it in disbelief.

"Jillian, take a deep breath," R.J. murmured. "It's going to be O.K. He's gone now."

"But what if he comes back?" Jillian uttered in terror. "He threatened me! And he slashed my tires. And he apparently followed me home after I moved here. I'm so scared, R.J."

"First thing tomorrow morning, you and I are going to the police," R.J. said quietly. "You are going to report your tires being slashed and that he showed up tonight making threats. I'm going with you to give a witness statement. With documentation from the tire place and a witness to his confession, they should be able to arrest him for vandalism."

"You're also going to swear out a restraining order against him," R.J. continued. "That way, if he shows up again, you call the police and they can arrest him for stalking."

"But you're busy and leaving town tomorrow," Jillian's head was down and her voice was quiet with fear. "I can't ask you to get involved in my problem. We barely know each other."

"Jillian, look at me," R.J. declared, lifting her chin with his fingertips and looking into her eyes. "You didn't ask me to get involved, I offered. And even though we barely know each other, I want to do this for you. I know that you don't deserve the things that man said about you. You're a sweet, intelligent, wonderful woman. He's obviously become unbalanced since his wife left him and he holds you responsible. You have to do something about that before he does something worse."

Looking into R.J.'s eyes, Jillian knew he was absolutely right. If she and R.J. were ever going to have a chance, she had to get Victor out of her life for good. She was surprised that he wasn't running for the door as most men would. She smiled as she remembered what Kellie had said about fate. Maybe the universe did have a plan for her.

"Now, that's better," R.J. murmured, his fingers gently stroking her cheek. "When you smile like that your whole face lights up. You're so beautiful Jillian, but when you smile, there's a whole other level to your beauty. You glow from the inside out."

Jillian smiled shyly at R.J. Now that Victor was gone and the adrenalin rush was over, she was both exhausted and embarrassed. He must think she was crazy to have had a fling with a married man.

"R.J., I'm sorry you had to meet my past in such a horrible way," she said, her face turning red with embarrassment.

"I know what you must think of me, having an affair with a married man. It's not something I'm very proud of."

"I think you made a poor decision," R.J. replied. "And you're not alone. We all make poor decisions sometimes. It's called being human, Jillian. It doesn't change the person you are inside. You're still an amazing person, one I want to get to know better. Don't let the past come between us before we have a chance to see what the future holds.

"As I've so recently learned, life is too short. We need to find what makes us happy and hold on to it. You make me happy Jillian. There's an old Native American saying that I love. 'Many things will catch your eye, but hold close only those that catch your heart.' You've already caught more than just my eye. Put the past in the past and give us a chance. Please."

Jillian looked deep into R.J.'s eyes and saw only truth in them. He didn't think she was a bad person. He thought she was amazing just as he had said. Then his eyes got dark, almost black, and she saw desire in them. She reached over and touched his face, setting off a searing heat that traveled through her fingertips and down her arms. As the heat spread through the rest of her body, R.J. leaned forward and gently pressed his lips to hers.

The kiss was so soft, so sensual, that Jillian didn't want it to ever end. This sweet, undeniably sexy man could kiss like no one she had ever known. R.J.'s hands moved up to caress her cheeks and then slowly slid down her neck to her shoulders. His lips parted and her tongue was in his mouth before she realized what she was doing. For several minutes, they explored each other's mouths, their tongues dancing back and forth. Finally, Jillian broke away, sighed, and looked into his eyes once again.

"As much as I am enjoying this, I need to send you home," she whispered. "You're still my client."

"I'll sleep on the sofa, but I'm not leaving," R.J. stated firmly. "Until the police are notified, he may come back. I won't leave you alone tonight. I just can't do it."

"I'll be fine," Jillian said but her shaky voice told a different story.

"Jillian, I just lost my dad," R.J. murmured. "I can't bear the thought of losing someone else that I care about. If something happened to you because I went home, I would never forgive myself. I couldn't live with myself."

"Ah, pulling the sympathy card are you?" Jillian grinned at him. "That's not fair, but you win. I really would feel better if I wasn't here alone."

"And I'll feel better knowing you're not alone," R.J. said seriously, then he smiled. "I think I'll fix both of us another glass of brandy. It's great for calming the nerves."

They enjoyed another drink and talked some more about their childhoods. After wine with dinner and two glasses of brandy, Jillian was feeling a little sleepy and slightly tipsy. She decided it was time to fix R.J. a bed on the sofa. She rose and picked up the glasses to take them to the kitchen. He stood too and their fingers touched as he reached to take them from her. An electric current jolted both of them and all thoughts of R.J.'s client status vanished from Jillian's head. She turned as he went to the kitchen and shut off the lights in the living area.

"I'm going to need some light to make up the sofa to sleep on," he stated, a little puzzled at what she was doing.

Without speaking, Jillian walked to the kitchen and took his hand. Then she led him to the bedroom. When they reached the bed, R.J. pulled her close and kissed her softly. Then he leaned back slightly so he could look at her.

"We don't have to do this tonight," he murmured as his hands gently caressed her back. "I never want you to do anything that you don't want to do. Really, baby, it's OK if you want me to sleep out there."

In reply, Jillian pulled him close against her body and kissed him again. It was a sweet, slow kiss at first that soon turned into a white-hot flame consuming both of their bodies. She began unbuttoning his shirt and when it was open down the front, she kissed and licked his neck and chest as she pushed the shirt off his shoulders. He smelled and tasted so good that she felt intense heat and wetness forming between her legs.

R.J. was in heaven. When he had come to Raleigh and left Jillian in Ocean Isle Beach, he was sure he would never see her again. She had made such an impression on him as a beautiful, thoughtful, considerate woman that he had wanted to share his sorrow with her. But that wasn't to be....he didn't know her full name, had no cell phone number, and no way to reach her to explain missing their date. And now this incredible woman was back in his life, removing his clothing, taking him into her bed. He knew his dad was grinning from ear to ear at being the reason they were together again.

R.J. felt her fingers at his waist as Jillian unbuckled his belt and unzipped his pants. She pushed his jeans down until they fell to the floor. His already hard penis was quickly captured by her hands and she stroked him as her lips traveled up to meet his. They kissed again but this time it was a kiss filled with passion and urgent need.

His fingers found the zipper in the back of her dress and pulled it all the way down. Jillian shivered as R.J. slipped the dress off her shoulders and pushed it to the floor. She heard him groan as his hands slid over her red lace bra and began caressing her breasts. Her nipples were hard little nubs, pushing against the lace and his demanding fingers. She heard a moan and realized it had come from her own throat. The feel of his fingers as they lightly pinched her nipples through the lace was sending shock waves to the rest of her highly sensitized body.

Moving his hands to her back, R.J. unhooked her bra and watched as she removed it. Her breasts were perfect....round, firm, and swollen with heat and desire. He reached out and covered each one with a hand, his fingers unhurriedly caressing them until Jillian was moaning out loud. When he could stand it no longer, he moved his hands down to the elastic band of her sheer, lace panties. He slid them over her hips and pushed them down.

Jillian was so aroused her knees were weak. R.J.'s fingers and hands were burning her skin with every touch, every caress. As she stepped out of the panties around her ankles, he pulled her against him. Oh god, his hard, pulsing penis pressed against her stomach as her engorged breasts pressed to his chest. Every inch of skin on her body was flushed with need and desire. She had never wanted anyone the way she wanted R.J. right this minute.

Sensing her intense excitement, R.J. lifted her and laid her on the bed. Jillian was gorgeous with her deep red hair fanned over the sheet, her body practically writhing with anticipation. He climbed onto the bed and positioned himself between her legs. He leaned over and took one nipple into his mouth, while his fingers found the other one. He sucked and fondled her breasts, listening to her breathing becoming more and more ragged with each moment. He moved his hips closer to her and lightly rubbed his rock hard penis against her clit.

Her mind had shut down and all Jillian could do was feel the incredible sensation of R.J.'s mouth suckling her breast. She felt him move slightly and then her body arched up as his penis came in contact with her swollen clit. With a cry, Jillian came in a huge crashing wave. He continued to caress her with the head of his penis and she was lost as wave after wave of pleasure swirled through her body.

Suddenly, R.J. raised his head and whispered that he needed to taste her. He moved down her body, his lips searing her skin with hot kisses on her stomach. He caressed her inner thighs as he pushed her legs wider apart. He groaned again when he saw the wetness glistening in her neatly trimmed pubic hair. Just like the other time, her response to him was so passionate, so natural, so real.

R.J. lowered his head and let his tongue lap up her juices. Jillian writhed on the bed as she felt him lick and suck her dripping wet pussy. Over and over his tongue slid in and out of her, assaulted her extremely sensitive clit, and then licked up the wetness rushing out of her. Her world was a non-stop orgasm for what seemed like hours, building and building until she could no longer breathe. She arched up against his mouth and he cupped his hands around her butt cheeks, pressing her pubis into his face. She came once more with a scream of pure, total pleasure, covering his face with her juices.

Needing to be inside her, R.J. moved slowly up the length of Jillian's body, giving her a moment to catch her breath. Her skin was hot to the touch and that inflamed him even more. His mind couldn't focus on anything except being wrapped in her heat. He kissed her hard, his lips bruising hers as she pulled his body to her. He felt an almost frantic need radiating from her.

"I need you inside me," Jillian whispered. "Please, now."

R.J. was gone. Knowing that she needed him as much as he needed her, hearing her say it out loud, sent him over the edge. He took her then, his hard penis disappearing into her heat and wetness. This had to be the most incredible feeling in the world was the last thought he was able to complete. His hips began moving of their own accord. His hard penis was thrusting in and out of her in a rhythm that had her moaning again in seconds. Somewhere in the haze in his brain, he felt her pussy begin to spasm and clench his penis. She screamed again and he lost all control. As she came, he came too in a blinding explosion of uninhibited ecstasy.

He wrapped Jillian in his arms, holding her until she was breathing normally again. R.J. knew this was different from any other relationship he had ever had. He had to feel her skin against his. He had to hold her until she was asleep. He had to find a way to have this amazing woman in his life permanently. He felt her breathing deeply and realized she had fallen asleep. But R.J. lay awake for a long time wondering how he had ever survived without Jillian in his life.

CHAPTER 12

The next morning, after a repeat of the previous night's intimacy, Jillian and R.J. sat at a little table on the balcony, which was just off the kitchen. Jillian had made them hot tea while R.J. insisted on fixing them veggie omelets and toast for breakfast. They were both ravenous and ate with gusto.

"This is so nice out here," R.J. began. "I like how it backs up to park land. It's a quiet and private oasis in the middle of a condo complex. That's certainly unusual."

"That's part of the reason I decided to rent this one," Jillian said. "Since this is an end unit, the floor plan is a little different. Most of the units have the balcony off the bedroom and the neighbor's balcony is right next to your own. This one has the balcony off the kitchen and there are no neighbors. I always liked that about my house. It backed up to a wooded area too."

"It's really nice having breakfast in the cool morning air. And it's nice to see a woman who doesn't eat like a sparrow," R.J. grinned at Jillian as she put a forkful of eggs in her mouth. "It amazes me how some women will order the most expensive thing on a menu and then pick at it instead of really enjoying it."

"I love good food and this is definitely good!" she replied. "You're quite a cook."

"I just try to cook fresh, healthy foods," he said. "Nothing fancy or complicated. Unfortunately, I spend so much time on the road that I end up eating way too much fast food. So when I get the chance, I go to the farmer's market and the fish market and fix something that won't clog my arteries. You had a good selection of vegetables to choose from in the fridge."

"I cook simple and clean most of the time, too," Jillian advised and then laughed. "If I don't, my hips start expanding."

"I think your hips are perfect just the way they are," R.J. laughed, and then became serious. "And if they expand, it wouldn't matter to me. You're so beautiful that I wouldn't even notice. And your beauty isn't just about how you look on the outside, Jillian. You're intelligent, sweet, and a very caring, considerate person. Your inner beauty is even more attractive to me than your outer beauty."

"Oh, R.J., that's such a nice thing to say," she cried. "After those horrible things Victor said last night, I really needed to hear that. I look at him now and wonder what I ever saw in him. And I wonder what I was thinking when I got involved with a married man. I guess I was more lonely that I realized."

"We all make mistakes, baby," R.J. suggested. "Especially if we're lonely or hurt or depressed."

Jillian's heart skipped a beat. R.J. had just called her baby. She hoped it wasn't a nickname he used with every woman he went out with. He had said last night that he wanted to spend more time with her and get to know her better. She felt such a strong connection with him. It was almost like she knew him from somewhere. Did he feel it too?

"Earth to Jillian," R.J. intoned. "Are you in there?"

"What? Oh, sorry," Jillian murmured. "I was just thinking how it feels like I know you from somewhere. But I'm sure we never met before."

"I know what you mean. I feel a real connection between us but I'm sure we haven't met," R.J. said looking directly into her eyes. "I could never forget someone as sweet and lovely as you."

"Now you're making me blush," she said quietly. "But I really do appreciate the compliment."

"I believe in complimenting someone who deserves it and you deserve it. I'm a very honest person, Jillian. I don't say things just because I think you want to hear it," R.J. noted and then got quiet for a moment. "I guess I value honesty and being open with each other most in any relationship. I'm realizing that you know a lot about me, but I don't know much about you except what you do for a living. And I also know you have excellent taste in furnishing a home. This place is gorgeous!"

"Well, let's start your education about me with this condo," Jillian responded. "I moved in here a few days before Labor Day."

"Wow! I'm impressed at what you've done in such a short time," he exclaimed. "You moved, decorated your home, and still had time for a vacation at the beach. Did I miss the Superwoman costume in your closet?"

"I can't claim to be Superwoman," she giggled. "And I can't claim to be an amazing decorator. Actually this place was furnished when I moved in. I'm renting for awhile until I figure out what I want to do."

"What do you mean?" R.J. was puzzled. "Figure out what you want to do about what? I think I'm missing part of the story of Jillian."

"I guess I better back up a bit," Jillian replied. "I got married right out of college and went to work for my dad's accounting firm. Gary and I had been married for about eight years when we realized we weren't really well suited for each other. We were good friends, and are still good friends, but there really wasn't the deep passionate love we both wanted in a life partner. We decided to get divorced."

"I don't want to sound cold," she continued. "But it was the best thing for both of us. I didn't want to end up hating him for a bad marriage. So we filed for divorce and looked into selling our house. The market had gone downhill pretty fast in this area and we couldn't sell the house without taking a big loss. Gary moved out when we filed, so it only made sense for me to stay in the house until we could sell it."

"So an amicable divorce is actually possible?" R.J. questioned.

"Only if you realize early enough that the marriage will never work," Jillian answered. "We get along really well now and, honestly, I think of him now as the brother I never had."

"There are no bad feelings or animosity between you?" R.J. was astounded.

"Like I said, I didn't want to end up hating him," Jillian responded. "We sat down and talked about where we were and where we wanted to go in the future. After eight years we had both changed a lot and grown and wanted very different things for our future. It was apparent to both of us that divorce was a likely ending so we decided to end it while we could remain friends."

"That's really rare and a very mature way to handle the whole thing," he said. "I'm impressed."

"Well hang on, the immaturity is still to come," Jillian chuckled. "Anyway, I stayed in the house while we waited for the housing market to stabilize. I guess I should tell you that a few months before Gary and I decided to divorce, my father died. It was the worst time of my entire life. I was a 'daddy's girl' from day one. My parents had a difficult time conceiving and I'm an only child. My dad doted on me and his dream was for me to be an accountant and join his firm."

"So you really do understand about the relationship between me and my dad," R.J. commented. "And you understand the loss I'm feeling right now."

"Yes I do," she responded sympathetically. "My mother is still alive, but shortly after my dad's death, she moved back to Asheboro. That's where she grew up and where my parents met. She was so lost and depressed. I think she needed to go back to the beginning in order to work through her feelings. But to me, it felt like both my parents had died. My dad was gone and my mom withdrew from the world. And then Gary and I split up. I felt so completely alone."

"Oh, Jillian, how awful for you," R.J. sighed. "At least I had a few years in between my mom's death and my dad's death. I hope your mom gets better soon."

"Actually, she began dating last month," Jillian confided. "I'm so happy for her! She is finally moving on with her life."

"What about you? Are you moving on?" R.J. asked.

"I'm trying, R.J., really trying" she said. "It was terribly difficult at first and I was so lonely and depressed. When the housing market started to look up, we put the house up for sale. Victor was the realtor Gary chose. I didn't meet him until the house had been up for sale for about three months. He stopped by one day to talk about bringing the asking price down.

"To make a long story short, we ended up going to dinner one night and that began the affair. He didn't tell me right away that he was married. By the time he did tell me, I couldn't seem to tell him to go away. It was nice to have someone tell me I was beautiful and sexy. It was nice to have someone call and text me everyday."

"Based on last night, I'm guessing you finally got tired of him," R.J. noted.

"By the time the house sold, I was tired of his lies, tired of being second all the time," Jillian disclosed sadly. "I began wondering why I was putting up with him. I decided that I would rather be alone than be used that way. So I told him we were over."

"He apparently didn't take that well," R.J. said.

"He called day and night, leaving messages and begging me to take him back. At first I listened to them but didn't respond. Kellie threatened to take my phone away and lock me up if I even thought about responding. After a few weeks, I just stopped listening to the messages. I hoped that he would get tired and leave me alone. I realize now that his messages must have escalated to threats of violence. Sometimes I still can't believe I was so stupid. See, I told you there was immaturity."

Jillian tried to smile at her last remark, but the smile faltered. R.J. felt a stab in his heart when he saw how sad and lost she looked. He stood up and walked around the table. He took her hand and pulled her to her feet. When she was standing directly in front of him, he looked deep into her eyes.

"You are not stupid," he said forcefully but quietly. "Don't ever say that again. You had a tragic loss of your father, a divorce, and you felt alone. We all make poor decisions at some point in our life, especially when we're lonely or sad. That bastard took advantage of you when you were feeling down. And then he turned into a stalker. He's bad news and now you realize it. And, even more important, you realize it's time to move on."

"Yes, it is time to move on," Jillian replied. "That's part of the reason I chose to rent this furnished condo."

"Ah, so we're back to the condo," R.J. smiled at her as they sat back down.

Jillian's heart skipped a beat again. No one had ever smiled at her like that. She felt his smile envelope her heart and she knew she could fall deeply for this man.

"So here's the rest of the Jillian Stanley story," she smiled back at R.J. "I chose accounting because of my dad's dream that I would work with him at his firm. It was something that he talked about from the time I was a little girl. It just seemed like the natural thing to do."

"I can certainly understand that," R.J. responded. "However, I'm sensing that you may have changed your mind."

"Now that Dad is gone, I've realized that this isn't really what I want to do," Jillian confessed. "So I decided to wait to buy a house until I decide what to do about my career."

"What other options do you have?" R.J. asked. "Is there another field you are interested in?"

"I've always wanted to travel and write," she answered. "I did some writing for the school newspaper in high school and college. The professor that sponsored the college paper tried to get me to change my major to journalism. He said my writing was excellent and he thought I would have no problem getting a job with a newspaper."

"Maybe you should look into going back to school," R.J. suggested.

"Reporting the news is not really what I want to do," Jillian replied. "I want to travel and write about what I see, who I meet, and how life is in other places."

"Then you should do it!" R.J. exclaimed.

"That's what Kellie keeps telling me too," she disclosed. "But then Kellie isn't very good at managing her money.

Stephen handles their finances and she has no idea how much it takes to support yourself."

"You do have a point. It could take awhile to make enough money to support yourself," R.J. counseled. "I don't mean to pry, but do you have the means to live until you find people who will pay for your writing?"

"I'm an Accountant and financial management is what I do, R.J.," Jillian chuckled. "Between my investments, my share of the house sale, and what I would get from selling my share of the firm, I would be financially set for a long time."

"OK, who's stupid now?" R.J. snorted. "Here I am asking an accountant if she has invested her money wisely. Let me take that question back and ask one that's not quite so ridiculous. What's stopping you?"

"Honestly, nothing more than my fear of failure," she said thoughtfully.

"I don't see that you have anything to lose, baby," R.J. spoke softly now. "If you're unhappy with your current situation then it must be time for a change. How will your mom take the news if you decide to leave your father's firm?"

"She told me a few weeks ago that I should do what makes me happy. She said my dad would understand and support me if he was here."

Jillian was speaking, but her mind was stuck back on the fact that R.J. had called her baby again. That was the second time this morning. Was she reading too much into it? Did he mean it as an endearment or did he say that without thinking?

"I can't tell you what to do, Jillian," R.J. interrupted her thoughts. "But you need to live your life for yourself, not anyone else. It's scary as hell venturing out on your own, but it's also extremely rewarding. I love being my own boss. I take the jobs I want and decline the ones I don't want. I'm not rich by any means but I'm comfortable and truly love photography."

"Do you ever want to do something different?" she asked.

"Remember when I came up to you on the beach, asking to take your picture?" he questioned in return. "That wasn't a line to get to talk to you. I really am photographing people and things I find interesting wherever my work takes me. At some point I plan to take off work for awhile and put them all together in a book."

"Maybe after you fire my firm, you can show me the pictures you have so far," Jillian replied. "I'd love to see them sometime."

"Of course!" R.J. exclaimed. "And I'd still like to take some candid shots of you, if you will let me."

"Let me think about that one," she said with a warm smile. "I'm not really sure I want my picture in a book."

"Fair enough," R.J. responded. "I'm glad you were honest with me and didn't say yes just to please me. I really do value honesty most in any relationship. For me, honesty can make or break the relationship.

"Jillian, I'm really enjoying getting to know you, but we need to get to the police station. I have to drive back to Ocean Isle today to pack and close up my house. I have a flight from Myrtle Beach to New York in the morning. Then I have to do a couple of things at my studio before my flight to Berlin tomorrow evening."

"Oh R.J., I'm so sorry," Jillian cried and jumped up from the table. "I'm not thinking straight this morning. Let's go get my Jeep and then we can make a quick trip to the police station."

"Jillian, slow down," R.J. said as he stood and took her hands in his. "We need to get moving but we don't need to rush. I want to make sure we have plenty of time at the police station so you will be safe from Victor. Now come here."

R.J. folded Jillian into a warm embrace. He held her tight, breathing in the scent of her shampoo and perfume. When he heard that his father was gone, he had felt so alone and so deeply sad. When he was with Jillian, he didn't feel alone anymore and his heart felt light and happy. For the first time in a very long time, he was leaving for a job with thoughts of getting back home as fast as possible.

As R.J. embraced her, Jillian put her head on his shoulder and sighed. Never before had she felt so connected to someone. With all her heart, she wished the sale of Big Jake's was complete and she was free to pursue something more with this amazing man. Her problems with Victor and her unhappiness with work vanished when R.J. held her.

Jillian lifted her head and looked into R.J.'s eyes. The connection she felt intensified as he stared back at her. She was sure he could see into her mind and her soul because she knew she was seeing his. This was her future staring back at her. Jillian knew that with every fiber of her being.

"You feel it, don't you," he whispered.

"Yes, I do," was her hushed response.

R.J. leaned forward and kissed her. It was a soft, gentle kiss full of promise. His lips pressed against hers and then his tongue lightly grazed them in a sensual movement. His arms were still holding her tightly and she felt her entire body go white hot against his. Jillian was shocked that such a simple act could cause intense heat from her head to her toes. She opened her mouth slightly and his tongue slid inside. For several minutes, they remained locked in an increasingly smoldering embrace, bodies melting into each other, tongues dancing together. Finally, R.J. broke the kiss and sighed loudly.

"If only we could stay like that forever," he murmured as he looked into her eyes again. "I would be the happiest man on the planet."

"I know what you mean," Jillian said wistfully as she took a step back. "But we have to get going now or there's a good chance you will miss your flight tomorrow. If you kiss me again like that, I can't be held responsible for my actions."

R.J. smiled at her as he released her from his arms. "Be forewarned that I intend to continue this when I get back."

"As soon as the sale of Big Jake's completes," she reminded him with a grin. "Then watch out mister!"

They cleared the breakfast dishes and headed to Sebring's to get Jillian's car. The mechanic told them there was no doubt the tires had been slashed. R.J. convinced him to write that conclusion on the invoice and got the man's name in case the police wanted to talk to him. From the garage, they took separate vehicles to the police station. With the documentation from the garage and their individual accounts of Victor's threats the night before, the police officer told them Jillian could obtain a restraining order against Victor. However, without a witness to the actual event or some other evidence, he could not be arrested for slashing the tires.

Jillian completed the paperwork so the restraining order could be served on Victor as soon as possible. Once served, Victor was not permitted to be within one hundred yards of Jillian's home or work or he would be arrested. It would also cover phone calls, text messages, emails, and any other form of contact. The officer said the paperwork would be served on Victor within a few days. Until then, if he appeared at Jillian's home or work, she should call 911 right away.

With the restraining order completed, Jillian and R.J. left the police station. They walked to the parking lot and stood by Jillian's car. She was suddenly nervous about saying goodbye to R.J. She realized she didn't want him to leave. She didn't want to be alone again, but she had no right to ask him to stay. Jillian looked at R.J. and saw in his eyes that he was feeling the same thing. He spoke first.

"I hate having to leave you right now. I want to stay and make sure you're safe."

"It's OK," she responded. "I'll be careful. Just go so you can get back here soon."

"Have someone walk you to your car in the garage at work, please," R.J. pleaded. "And make sure you look around before you get out of it in the parking lot at home. If you see anything strange, call the police to escort you inside. Damn it, Jillian, I'm going to worry about you."

"R.J., I'll be all right," Jillian said as she smiled at him. "I'll be careful and aware of my surroundings. If anything at all happens, I'll call the police. I'm not going to try to deal with Victor by myself."

"Just take care of yourself, baby," R.J. replied. "I have a lot to do today and tomorrow before I fly out. I'll try to call you before I leave but I can't promise. However, I'll definitely call you once I get to Berlin. Since it's six hours later there, I guess I should call your office. But you call my cell right away if you need me to come back."

"You take care of yourself too," Jillian said with a heavy heart. "And get back here soon. Now go and we'll talk on Monday."

They kissed again, another slow, sweet kiss. R.J. stepped away to go to his car and suddenly turned back. He pulled Jillian to him and kissed her with so much passion that she was left breathless. When he let her go, she was flushed and gasping for breath. He flashed her a sexy smile.

"That's so you won't forget me," he said and then turned to get into his car.

Jillian leaned against her car door as she watched him pull out. He waved and she returned the wave, smiling with all her heart. Her knees were weak from the last kiss and her heart was beating wildly. Oh wow, she thought, I never expected this. When her legs would hold her again, she got into her car and immediately called Kellie.

CHAPTER 13

"Hi Jillie, how was your dinner last night with the handsome photographer?" Kellie answered her phone with a question, a common occurrence.

"You will never believe what happened, Kell!" Jillian was practically shouting.

"Does it begin with 's' and end with 'ex'?" Kellie laughed. "I sure hope so!"

"Of course that's where your mind goes," Jillian giggled in return. "I had a totally unexpected adventure last night. Want to meet for lunch so I can tell you all about it?"

"I guess that answers one question," Kellie replied. "He's obviously not with you now if you want to spend time with me."

"So, lunch?" Jillian asked impatiently.

"Where and when? And don't make me wait too long or I might have a stroke trying to figure out what happened," Kellie exclaimed.

"How about Soups & Salads near your house?" Jillian responded. "I have a couple of errands to run in those shopping centers around there. Maybe one o'clock?"

"I'll be there!" Kellie cried. "Be ready to get deep into the details my friend, because I want all of them."

Laughing, the ladies said their goodbyes and hung up. Jillian stopped at The Big Wine Shop to replenish her stock of Chateau wine. Then she went to the mall for a couple of throw rugs since the ones she brought from the old house clashed with the colors in the condo. She also purchased a coffee maker. Gary had taken the one they had since he drank coffee and she didn't. For some odd reason, the furnished condo didn't have one. R.J. had asked for coffee but settled for tea when she told him she didn't have a coffee maker. If he truly meant to spend time with her, she wanted him to have coffee in the mornings.

With her errands finally done, she met Kellie at Soups & Salads. They ordered salads and iced tea and found a table in the corner. As they dug into their lunch, Kellie was eyeing Jillian with great interest. When she was about half way finished, she put her fork down.

"I cannot take one more minute of silence," Kellie was adamant. "You obviously had sex with the man last night, but something else happened too. So spill it girl!"

"What makes you think I slept with him?" Jillian asked in an innocent voice.

"Jillie, who are you talking to here? I know you better than anyone else in the world." Kellie was sure now. This was typical Jillian behavior!

"Oh, all right," Jillian conceded. "Yes he stayed over last night. And I slept with him and it was spectacular! Last night and again this morning…..oh my God he was incredible!!"

"I knew it!" Kellie crowed. "You have that extremely satisfied look on your face and you can't stop smiling. But there's something else, isn't there?"

"There's a lot more, but let's finish eating and then I'll tell you the rest," Jillian replied.

When they were done eating, Jillian told Kellie about the flat tires, towing the car, and having R.J. take her home. Kellie was wide-eyed at all that had happened. She took a drink of her tea and began asking questions.

"How could both of your tires be flat?" she asked. "I can't believe you just ran over a nail that popped both tires at the same time. Do you think they were just bad tires? I don't understand."

"I didn't run over anything," Jillian responded. "They were cut with a knife."

"What?" Kellie choked on her tea as her mouth dropped open.

"The guys at Sebring's said both had been cut in the sidewall with a knife," Jillian noted.

"Who in the world would want to slash your tires, Jillie?" Kellie was astonished.

"Victor did it," she answered.

"What? How do you know?" Kellie had a dozen questions running in her head, but these were the only ones she could get out.

"If you will give me ten minutes of quiet, I'll tell you." Jillian smiled. "Think you can do that?"

Kellie made a big production of pretending to zip her lips. Then she nodded to Jillian to continue.

"OK, here's the rest," Jillian began. "R.J. took me home after dinner. We ended up kissing at the door and I invited him in for a brandy."

"Jillie, the tires! What happened?" Kellie was about to explode from curiosity and concern for her best friend.

"I'm getting there, Miss Impatience," Jillian replied. "R.J. and I were having a brandy when someone knocked on the door. It was Victor. He said he followed me home one day to find out where I was living now. When I didn't respond to his calls or texts, he decided to do something that would really get my attention. So, he cut my tires sometime yesterday afternoon and then he showed up at the door while R.J. was there."

"Yikes, awkward!" Kellie giggled.

"Actually, I was glad R.J. was there," Jillian said. "Victor was really scary. He called me a slut and a whore and was screaming at me, totally out of control. He even admitted to slashing my tires! He was threatening me and reached out to grab me. R.J. came flying across to the front door and knocked him on his butt!"

"Oh my god!" Kellie shouted, drawing looks from those sitting at tables near their booth. She continued a little more quietly. "Jillian, he's crazy!! I knew he was bad news. You need to call the police first and his wife second."

"R.J. and I went to the police station this morning after we picked up my Jeep," Jillian responded. "I have a restraining order in place now so he will be arrested if he comes within one hundred feet of me or if he calls or texts. And trust me, if he comes near, I'll call the police without a second thought.

"R.J. tried to get them to arrest Victor for slashing my tires, but our statements that he said he did it aren't enough proof. At least the statements are on record with the restraining order so if anything else happens, the police will know it's not the first time. R.J. didn't want to leave, but I promised to be extra careful until he is back in town."

"Ah, R.J. to the rescue," Kellie smiled. "I'm liking this guy more and more. What about Victor's wife? Do you think you should call her? Or maybe the real estate agency he works for?"

"Part of Victor's issue is that his wife found out he was seeing me," Jillian informed her. "Apparently she threw him out and now he thinks that I'm responsible for his marriage collapsing. I suggested to the police officer that they serve the restraining order on him at his office since I have no idea where he is living. So I think the agency will soon know he's in trouble."

"I want you to come and stay at our place," Kellie demanded. "I'm afraid for you to be alone with that nut case stalking you!"

"Kellie, I so appreciate the offer but I need to be in my own home," Jillian advised. "I will not let that idiot send me into hiding. If I catch even a glimpse of him, I'll call the police.

"I'll also let security in our building at work know about my car. And I'll make sure Kent and Andrew know about it too. Oh man, I am not looking forward to that conversation! You know those two are like uncles to me and they are going to hit the roof. What an embarrassing discussion that's going to be."

"They will be so worried about you and so ready to come to your defense that I might just have some pity for Victor if they find him," Kellie noted. "NOT! I will never have any pity for that disgusting man."

"The evening wasn't a total loss, Kell," Jillian continued. "R.J. insisted on staying last night. He even offered to sleep on the sofa."

"Yeah, right. Like that would happen!" Kellie giggled. "Oh wait, with you it could I guess. But from what you said earlier, I'm guessing you made him welcome and comfortable in your bed."

"I was scared and really upset," Jillian smiled in reply. "No way was I letting him sleep on the sofa! If Kent and Andrew found out, I'd be in big trouble, but at least I'd have a good excuse for violating company policy."

"Good move, my friend," Kellie said. "And my lips are sealed. They won't hear it from me! So what's going on with R.J?"

"After the police station, he headed home to Ocean Isle," Jillian answered. "He owns a house there and needed to close it up since he's going to be gone for several weeks. He will be flying to New York early in the morning and then to Berlin later in the day."

"That's all nice Jillie, but what's going on with you and him?" Kellie asked, growing impatient.

"We talked a lot this morning, getting to know each other better," Jillian responded. "He's such a nice person and was so sweet and gentle with me after Victor was so nasty. We definitely have some chemistry. And it's odd but I feel like I know him already."

"Oh Jillie, I'm so happy for you!" Kellie cried. "How long will he be gone? You're going to see him when he gets back, right?"

"Of course I'm going to see him!" Jillian smiled happily. "I really like him Kell, and once we finish the sale of his dad's business, we plan to see where this might go. He said he feels like he knows me too. It's so weird but it all feels so right."

Jillian's phone buzzed with a text message. She pulled it from her purse and grinned.

"Oh, finally, a text from my phone friend Will," she noted. "I hope everything is OK with him. I haven't heard from him in several days."

Hi Angel. Hope you are OK. Major life changes for me. I can't text or talk with you anymore. Sorry, but I don't want to lead you on when I know I can't be there for you.

Jillian read the text in confusion. She wondered briefly what was going on that prevented Will from talking to her or texting. Seeing the strange look on her friend's face, Kellie spoke.

"What's going on? You look upset."

"I don't know what's going on except that Will says he can't talk to me anymore," Jillian replied. "That's really odd."

"I guess that solves your problem of how to tell him you're not Angel," Kellie opined. "But does it really matter anyway now that you have R.J.?"

"He's a really nice guy and I like him, but I guess you're right," Jillian said. "It's too bad. I think he would be a good person to be friends with."

"From what you told me, I don't think friends is what he really wanted," Kellie noted. "I think he was going along with you hoping it would go further."

"Well, now it doesn't matter anyway." Jillian shook her head sadly, then looked up at Kellie. "It probably would have ended when I told him I wasn't Angel. At least with R.J., everything is out in the open."

The ladies cleared their table and walked outside. As they walked toward their respective cars, they discussed what the rest of the weekend would hold. They made plans for dinner at Kellie's the next evening. Kellie turned to get into her car and then turned back toward Jillian.

"Do not hesitate to call me if you need anything, Jillie," she exclaimed. "If you get scared or if Victor shows up, call the police and then call me. Stephen and I will be there in minutes if you need us."

"Thanks, Kell," Jillian responded as she stepped forward to hug her best friend. "I'll be OK. If he shows up, I'll call you for sure."

They parted ways and each got into her vehicle. Jillian completed her errands for the day and headed home. As she pulled into the parking lot, she scanned the area for Victor or his car. Seeing neither, she took her purchases inside and made herself dinner. After eating, she thought about calling R.J. but decided not to disturb him. He said he had a lot to do and would call her once he got to Berlin. Feeling a little lonely, Jillian settled onto the sofa with a glass of wine and watched television until she went to bed.

At Ocean Isle Beach, R.J. was feeling lonely too. He couldn't believe how much he missed Jillian. He really didn't want to go to Berlin, didn't want to go anywhere if she wasn't with him. How had this woman burrowed so deep into his soul in such a short time? He didn't know how that had happened, but he did know that he wanted nothing more than to spend as much time as possible with her. He couldn't wait to get back, complete the sale of Big Jake's, and see where this relationship might go.

CHAPTER 14

On Monday morning, Jillian arrived at work ready to tackle the remaining paperwork on the Ridell Construction reorganization. She had found a number of ways the company could save money and was sure there were more lurking in the papers still stacked all over the conference room table. She was not, however, looking forward to her discussion with Kent and Andrew concerning Victor. When Jillian walked in, she saw that Allison was already seated at her desk.

"Good morning, Miss Stanley," Allison called out as Jillian walked into the reception area. "Did you have a good weekend?

"It had both good parts and bad parts," Jillian replied with a smile. "Do you have a minute? I need to talk to you about something before anyone else shows up."

"Of course," Allison answered. "Uh, I'm not in trouble am I?"

"No, Allison. Come on in and I'll tell you what it's about," Jillian advised.

Once Allison was seated across from her, Jillian tried to think of the best way to tell her about the trouble with Victor. Realizing there was no good way, she forged ahead as best she could.

"Do you remember the guy who came in one day and said he was my real estate agent?" Jillian asked.

"Yes, I remember him," Allison said. "He was really pushy and not very nice to me. I guess you have to be pushy to sell real estate."

"Well, now that my house is sold, he has turned into a stalker," Jillian noted solemnly. "And he slashed my tires on Friday."

"What? Why would he do that?" Allison cried.

"I quit responding to his calls once the sale of the house closed," Jillian began. "He wanted me to go out with him but I told him I wasn't interested. To make a long story short, he's apparently unbalanced and now he's stalking me."

"We need to call the police right now," Allison exclaimed rising from her chair.

"Already taken care of, Allison," Jillian responded. "Sit down and let me finish. I swore out a restraining order against him on Saturday. The reason I'm telling you this is because I want you to be aware of what is going on. If he shows up here, let me know immediately and then call the police. Don't challenge him or engage him in any way. Let him come back here if that's what he wants and then 911."

"Oh my god," Allison murmured, close to tears. "Do you think he might try to hurt me?"

Jillian rose and walked around her desk. She sat in the chair next to Allison and reached for her hand. She gave the girl a few moments to compose herself and then spoke again.

"Allison, I honestly don't believe you are in any danger," she said quietly. "He is obsessed with me for some reason. I really think that once he realizes he can be arrested for coming near me, he will back off. Are you going to be OK with this?"

"I'm OK," Allison sniffled. "I'm sorry to be such a baby but I've never been around a stalker. I don't know what to do."

"You just keep doing your job and it will be all right," Jillian answered. "I really don't think he will show up here. He's a coward and a bully but he's not stupid. Like I said, if he does appear, you buzz me and then call the police. If you feel at all unsafe, go straight to Kent or Andrew. They will know what is going on as soon as I can get with them this morning."

"OK, Miss Stanley," Allison said. "Do you want me to set up a meeting with Mr. Krenshaw and Mr. Wilson?"

"Thank you, but I'll get with them personally when they come in," Jillian advised. "Can you let me know when either of them arrives, please?"

"Sure," Allison agreed. "And Miss Stanley, I'm so sorry this is happening to you. You're a good person and you don't deserve so many bad things happening."

"Oh Allison, that's such a sweet thing to say," Jillian cried. "I know I haven't been the nicest person lately. I've been cranky and unreasonable and I'm sorry. Now let's get busy and leave all the unpleasantness behind us."

Allison returned to her desk while Jillian went through email. When Kent and Andrew arrived, she had similar conversations with them. Jillian refrained from telling them she had had an affair with Victor but she told them all the details of the continuous phone calls and the tire-slashing incident. As expected, they were irate at Victor and worried for Jillian. Reassuring them that she had done everything possible, they all got down to business for the day.

As Jillian was thinking about what to have for lunch, the intercom on the conference room phone buzzed. She picked it up and heard Allison say that Mr. Williams was on the phone and wanted to speak to her about the sale of Big Jake's.

"I tried to take a message Miss Stanley or put him back to your voice mail," Allison confided. "But he said he is out of the country and it would be difficult to reach him."

"No problem, Allison," Jillian replied. "I'll take the call. By the way, let me know anytime he calls. I'm trying to tie up the details so the sale can be completed when he gets back home. I don't want to miss a call from him."

"OK, I'll find you when he calls," Allison continued. "He's holding on line three right now."

Jillian thanked the receptionist and hit the button for line three.

"Hi there. How's Germany?" she asked.

"Hi yourself, beautiful lady," R.J. responded. "Germany is wonderful but the nights are so cold since I'm all alone in my big bed."

"Is that so?" Jillian laughed. "Do you mean there aren't any beautiful, blonde German ladies in Berlin who want to keep a handsome man warm at night?"

"Actually I'm in Hamburg now. I drove from Berlin to Hamburg this morning and met with my client," R.J. advised. "Now I'm at a very German bed and breakfast on the outskirts of Hamburg not far from the client's estate. And I'm all alone in an amazing king-sized feather bed."

"Are you avoiding my question about blondes?" Jillian giggled.

"I'm sure I could find a cute, willing, blonde if I wanted one," R.J. chuckled and then his tone turned serious. "However, the only woman I want in this bed with me is a fiery redhead who, unfortunately, happens to be four thousand miles away."

"That's very sweet, R.J." Jillian sighed as her heart skipped a beat. "I wish I was there too, but I'm back here slaving away so we can get Big Jake's sold."

"That damn sale needs to get finished in a big hurry," R.J. huffed. "I want to be back in Raleigh or Ocean Isle and free to find out everything there is to know about Jillian Stanley."

"Somebody's feeling cranky today," Jillian teased. "I guess I can ignore it since you're probably jet-lagged."

"I am a little jet-lagged and I'm sorry to be a grouch," R.J. murmured. "But I miss you so much, baby. My head is full of pictures of you in Ocean Isle…..sitting on the beach in that incredible bikini, dancing at the tiki bar, walking along the beach, the way you look when you're sleeping. Damn I can't wait to take you back there!"

Jillian's heart did a little dance this time. She could not stop thinking about R.J. either….the way his gorgeous eyes crinkled at the corners when he smiled at her, his full sensuous lips, the sound of his voice whispering in her ear when they made love. She felt connected to him in a way she never had with any other man in her life.

"Hey handsome, it's OK to be a little cranky when you've flown half way around the world," she said softly. "Do your job over there and then this sale will be finished before we know it. We have years ahead of us to discover everything there is to know about each other."

"Hmmm, I think I like it when you call me handsome." R.J. was laughing now. "I know I like it when you talk about us having years ahead of us to be together."

"Any idea yet how long you might be there?" she asked. "I want everything ready for you to sign once you arrive back in the states."

"I think I should be able to wrap this up in two weeks," he replied. "The client owns one of the largest collections of vintage German automobiles in the world. He's getting old and can't drive well anymore. Since he has no children or family of any kind, he wants to sell them at top dollar and donate the proceeds to the orphanage where he was raised. I'll be taking photos of them and then helping him decide which ones to provide for the auction catalogue."

"That sounds like fun!" Jillian exclaimed. "But it's really not fair. Here I am sitting with piles and piles of paper while you wander around beautiful cars in a foreign country."

"Some day, I'll bring you here," R.J. promised. "Berlin is a big, bustling city and I don't really like it. Hamburg, however, is an exciting place. It's a maritime town with an amazing waterfront, a beautiful port, big brick warehouses set on wooden pilings in the water, canals and waterways you can travel via boat, and seventeenth century architecture that is absolutely astounding. I think you would really like it."

"It sounds fabulous! I'm going to hold you to that promise," Jillian responded. "I've always wanted to travel the world, but haven't made it any farther than the islands of the Caribbean."

"Anything you want, beautiful lady," R.J. said with a smile. "I would take you to the moon and back if I could."

"R.J. you're so good to me." Jillian was smiling ear to ear. "I hate to end this call, but I don't want to run up your phone bill. It must cost a fortune to call from there."

"I don't care what it costs as long as I get to hear your voice," he replied. "But I do have to get ready to have dinner with my client. Do you have everything you need for Big Jake's? I don't want anything to hold the sale up."

"I think we have everything," she said. "If I need anything, I'll get in touch with the lawyers or the office manager. You just concentrate on those pictures and getting your seriously sexy butt back here."

"So you think my butt is seriously sexy?" R.J. asked mischievously.

"Did I say that?" Jillian was giggling again. "Must be a bad connection on this line."

"Uh huh, some bad connection," R.J. laughed. "But I do need to go now baby. I think I'm having one of those heavy German meals with foods that have names I can't pronounce. And I was told it was formal dress. So I'm guessing in a few hours I'll be stuffed with Wiener Schnitzel and ready to pop the buttons on my jacket."

"Poor R.J.," Jillian cooed and then burst out laughing.

"I see how it is," R.J. chuckled. "No sympathy for the poor sleep-deprived, jet lagged, overstuffed photographer. I'll make you pay for that when I get back."

"Oh, that sounds very interesting, Mr. Williams. I'm looking forward to it!" Jillian chuckled too. "Now go and we can talk again soon."

"Is it OK if I call you around this same time in a day or two? I'm trying to keep the six-hour time difference in mind, but I'm still worried about you. Anything new from Victor?"

"The time is perfect, R.J. and not a word from Victor," Jillian responded. "I told Allison to put you through to me anytime you called. I'm spending most of the day in the conference room with my mountain of papers. Lunch is about the only break I take these days."

"If you need anything at any time baby, call my cell phone," R.J. said quietly. "I don't care if it's the middle of the night. I want you safe and happy. Goodbye, sweet Jillian. Take care of yourself."

"You too, R.J.," Jillian murmured as her heart skipped another beat. "Talk to you soon."

Jillian hung up the telephone, her heart soaring and her face alight with a huge smile. It felt good to know that R.J.

cared about her, wanted her safe and happy. She could barely wait for the two weeks to be over and feel his arms around her again. She sighed and turned back to the papers strewn across the conference table with renewed determination.

The next ten days were long and busy for Jillian. She immersed herself in the Ridell reorganization plan to meet the early October deadline she had given them. She also worked closely with Eddie on the valuation of Big Jake's Automotive Sales. She wanted to be sure she had determined a fair market price for R.J. when it was time to complete the sale. She was working ten and twelve hour days, as both projects were tedious and time consuming.

R.J. called her office nearly every day around her lunchtime since that was close to his dinnertime. He always asked how things were coming along with Big Jake's and if the lawyers were being cooperative. Once that was out of the way, they chatted about anything and everything. Although the phone calls were short, Jillian was amazed at how easy he was to talk to. Sometimes, their conversations reminded her of the one phone call she had with Will. He had been easy to talk to also.

They had discovered that they both loved the ocean, the mountains, and traveling. Of course, his travels had taken him to places she had only dreamed of. He told her again and again that he wanted to take her to some of his favorite cities, show her the sights, and make love to her in hotels all over the world. She firmly believed that he would indeed take her someday and this knowledge made her disquiet with her job bearable.

On his tenth day in Hamburg, R.J. called at his usual time and Allison put the call through to the conference room. Jillian smiled as she answered the phone. She had just been thinking that she would see R.J. in four short days and, hopefully, her work for Big Jake's would be complete.

"Hi there, handsome," Jillian said when she picked up the receiver.

"Hi, baby, how's your day so far?" R.J. asked in reply.

"Busy and crazy but better now that I'm talking to you," she answered. "Did you make your reservations to come back yet?"

"Well, there's been a slight snag," R.J. responded sadly. "After looking at hundreds of photos, my client has decided that he wants to include some pictures of the cars in motion and at night. It looks like I'll probably be another week. I'll be working with his driver to photograph some of the cars as they move down the autobahn. And then we'll be taking them out at night to brightly lit local sights to take some staged photos. If the money wasn't so good, I'd tell him I have a beautiful, sexy woman waiting for me at home that I need to get back to."

"Oh R.J., I'm so sorry," Jillian cried. "I know you were anxious to get back and get your dad's business finished."

"I'm even more anxious to see you and know you're all right," he replied. "Have you seen or heard anything from Victor?"

"Not a peep," she said. "I think he must have realized what he was jeopardizing if he continued to bother me. Honestly R.J., I'm fine. I'm still staying alert and aware of my surroundings."

"That's my girl," R.J. beamed. "I really can't wait to see you and hold you. I go to bed at night thinking about you and wake up every morning thinking about you. I miss you so much, Jillian."

"I know, I miss you too," Jillian smiled too. "Am I really your girl?"

"Do you want to be?" he asked. "Because I really want you to be."

"I guess that settles it then. Once my work for Big Jake's is done, I'm officially you're girl," Jillian was ecstatic. "Until then, I'll have to be you're girl unofficially."

"That's just more reason to get this job done and get my seriously sexy butt back to North Carolina," R.J. said with a chuckle.

"Am I ever going to hear the end of my sexy butt comment?" she giggled. "I think you brought that up in almost every conversation we've had!"

"Nope, you will never hear the end of it because it's true," he chuckled. "I have a seriously sexy butt. Besides, it turns me on that you think my butt is sexy."

"OK, let's talk about something else before I end up in trouble," Jillian declared with a grin. "Back to business, buster. Eddie and I are finished with our review of Big Jake's. We should have a formal valuation for you by Monday of next week. I think your share is going to end up being close to two million."

"That much? Really?" R.J. was flabbergasted. "I had no idea it was worth that much. I thought they were struggling the last few years."

"A few years ago, the business was worth probably twice as much," Jillian noted. "Your dad and Rick closed several less profitable locations. But the remaining locations and inventory are worth over four million. So your dad's half is going to be close to two after you pay taxes."

"Wow, that changes everything Jillian," R.J.'s mind was spinning. "With that much money I could take some time off and work on the book I told you about. Oh man, I need to do some very heavy thinking."

"R.J. that would be so fantastic if you could spend time on your book," Jillian cried. "You definitely should think about it since you would have the financial means."

"I will, trust me, baby," R.J. confirmed. "I don't think I'll be able to think about anything else…..except you."

They discussed some small financial details and then ended the call. Jillian was smiling when she hung up the phone. She was happy that R.J. would be financially set for life. But she had an even bigger reason for her smile. If R.J. took time off to work on his book, maybe he wouldn't have to travel all the time. Maybe they could have a real relationship. With that thought in mind, Jillian dove back into the Ridell paperwork. She couldn't remember the last time she felt so good!

CHAPTER 15

On a Tuesday in the middle of October, R.J finally got back to Raleigh. He had been gone just over three weeks and Jillian had missed him more as each day went by. He had called her at work almost everyday and they had grown closer and closer as they chatted. Jillian realized that she was falling in love with R.J. She felt so connected to him, even though he had been four thousand miles away for most of the time she had known him.

R.J. was feeling the same thing. He had fallen for Jillian hard. He had soon realized that not only was she beautiful, but she was also very intelligent, funny, and perceptive. He couldn't wait to see her and decided to call her as soon as his plane landed in Raleigh. It was almost eight o'clock and he wondered if she would still be at work. With the time difference, he had called her office phone while he was gone and he had number stored in his phone.

R.J. thought that she was likely gone for the day and calling her office would be a waste of time. He was disappointed that he would have to wait until the next day to talk to her and made a mental note to get her cell phone number. Then R.J. remembered that he had her cell phone number from when she was late for their dinner. He dialed the number that had been stored on his incoming call list as he was walking through the terminal. He was very surprised when a man answered saying Satellite Car Service.

"Hi, this is R.J. Williams," he began. "I'm trying to reach Jillian Stanley."

"Hello, Mr. Williams," the man responded. "This is Miles, from Satellite Car Service. I know Jillian, our businesses are in the same building, but I don't know why you're calling my work phone."

"Jillian called me from this number last month when we met for a business dinner," R.J. advised. "She was running late for our appointment due to some car trouble. I didn't realize she wasn't calling from her own phone."

"Oh, right, I remember," Miles replied. "I gave her a ride to Louie's Tavern after her tires were flattened. She was having trouble with her cell phone too and called you from my phone."

"Would you have her cell phone number, sir?" R.J. asked. "I really need to reach her."

"I'm sorry Mr. Williams, but I don't have it," Miles responded. "If her firm needs my car service, they normally call from the business phone."

"Thank you, sir," R.J. said. "I'm sorry to have bothered you."

R.J. hung up and dialed Jillian's direct number at Stanley, Wilson, and Krenshaw. He listened as the phone began to ring. Sadly, he realized he would probably have to leave Jillian a message.

Jillian, however, was still at work. She was finishing up the final recommendations for the Ridell Construction project. The meeting with the client was in a few days and she was glad she would soon be done with the whole thing. While it had been tedious work, she had completed her review and recommendations right on time. She knew the client would be happy with both her ideas and the fact that he could implement them quickly. She had also realized how much she wanted to do something different with her life. Jillian no longer derived pleasure from her job and she knew she had to make some changes.

Jillian went back to her desk, wondering if R.J. had arrived in Raleigh yet. She could hardly wait for the sale of Big Jake's to complete so she and R.J. could begin a real relationship. As she walked into her office, her phone was ringing. It stopped before she could answer and the caller ID showed a New York number. She was sure it was R.J. calling, so she quickly picked up the phone and called him back.

"Hey there, handsome," Jillian said when he answered. "You have no idea how glad I am that you're back. You are back, right?"

"Getting a taxi as soon as I get my bags, then heading towards my dad's house," R.J. remarked. "But I can change course to wherever you're going to be this evening, beautiful lady. Looks like you're still at work if my caller ID is right. Have you had dinner yet?"

"Not yet," Jillian acknowledged. "I was finishing up another project for a client that I'm meeting on Thursday."

"I'm dead tired but starving," R.J. began. "Want to get something quick somewhere? I really would like to see you, Jillian, even more than I want to eat or sleep."

"How about I pick you up at the airport? We can get something to eat and then I'll take you home," Jillian suggested.

"Sounds good to me," R.J. responded. "I'll be in front of the United pick up area in about fifteen minutes."

"Don't rush," Jillian said. "It will take me at least twenty-five minutes to get there. I'll be driving my red Jeep."

"Fire engine red car for a fiery redhead?" R.J. cracked. "Sounds perfect! I'll be looking for you, baby."

Excited, Jillian shut down her computer, grabbed her purse, turned off the lights, and headed out the door. She couldn't wait to see R.J.! On Thursday, she would go with him in the morning to complete the sale of Big Jake's. In the afternoon, she would make her presentation to Pete Ridell. After that, she would take time off. She was hoping she and R.J. could spend a few days together before his next project. Then she needed to decide what she wanted to do with her life.

Jillian was not looking forward to telling Kent and Andrew that she was leaving SW&K. Just that morning, she had scheduled a meeting with them for the following afternoon. As she had toiled over both Big Jake's and Ridell during the last weeks, she had come to the firm conclusion that she wanted out. Seeing how much money R.J. would make selling Big Jake's had convinced her she could be financially independent for awhile if Kent and Andrew would agree to buy out her shares of the company. She knew the firm was doing well and was pretty sure they would agree. While the sale was being set up, she would spend time transferring her clients to other capable accountants in the firm.

Thinking back to her conversation with her mother on Sunday, Jillian smiled. She had been terrified to tell her mom that she was going to talk to Kent and Andrew about selling her share of the business. When her dad died, his one-third share had been split between his wife and his daughter. Barbara received a good income each month from her part and Jillian's business equity had continued to grow. When Jillian told her mother that the projects she had been working on had convinced her it was time to move on, Barbara had been very supportive.

"My darling daughter," Barbara had begun. "I want you to be happy. Your dad would want the same thing. You do what you need to do. You will always have a share of your dad's business because my part goes to you when I'm gone. If selling your share now will allow you to spend time finding a career you really want, then that's what you should do."

"It's time for both of us to move forward," Barbara had continued. "Your dad wouldn't want our lives to go on hold just because he is gone. I've already wasted too much time grieving for the love of my life. I'm moving forward and enjoying Thomas' company. He will never replace your dad in my heart, but I know your dad would approve of him and our relationship. Don't stay at SW&K simply for Dad's sake. If he was here, he would tell you to sell and go do what you want to do."

"Oh Mom," Jillian had said with tears in her eyes. "Your support means so much to me! And I'm so happy you found someone to spend time with. I promise to come for a visit in the next few weeks. We'll talk about my ideas for a new career and you can introduce me to Thomas."

All of this thinking had made the trip to the airport fly by and now Jillian was coming into the maze of roads that circled the terminal. Watching for signs for United Airlines arrivals in the darkness, Jillian's elation grew. She could barely wait to pick up R.J. and give him a kiss that would banish his fatigue. A plan for the evening formed in her mind as she rounded the terminal to the arrival gates. Then she saw him and her heart skipped a beat. Oh wow, she thought, I'm head over heels in love in a way I've never been before.

Seeing a red Jeep come around the bend, R.J. felt his heartbeat speed up. He was so excited to see Jillian, he no longer felt tired or hungry. R.J. was feeling only one thing when he saw that car—a deep, pure love. He wanted to be with this beautiful, smart, funny woman. Of that he was certain. And he was equally certain she wanted to be with him. How had he gotten so lucky?

Jillian pulled up at the curb and jumped out to open the back hatch. R.J. stepped over to the Jeep and threw his bags into the back. Then he pulled Jillian to him and embraced her. His arms wrapped around her back and he pressed her body as close to his as he could. He smelled her hair and her unique scent and sighed. This was absolute heaven.

"I am so glad to see you," he whispered in her ear. "This is the best welcome home I've ever received."

Then R.J. kissed her. A long, slow, sensual kiss that made them both forget everything else. They were lost in the sensation of lips and tongues touching when a car horn began to blare. Jillian stepped back and giggled.

"I guess someone is in a hurry and we're blocking the curb," she said as R.J. shut the back hatch.

"Or maybe someone is jealous they aren't being kissed by a gorgeous redhead?" R.J. remarked with a huge smile. "Too bad for them. I'm not letting anyone else kiss you tonight."

"Come on, let's get in the car before this turns into road rage," Jillian smiled back at him. "We can continue that kiss when I get you home."

As they left the airport, R.J. made several suggestions on where to have dinner. He also told her where his father's house was. Jillian murmured something non-committal to each comment and continued driving. When they passed the exit to his father's house, R.J. wondered what she was up to. Finally he could stand it no longer.

"You're being very mysterious," he noted. "What's up?"

"Nothing," Jillian replied and kept driving.

"You do realize don't you that you missed the exit to my dad's house?" R.J. asked.

"Yep, sure do," she responded.

"OK, so where are we going?" R.J. was really curious now.

"Just hang tight and be patient," Jillian advised.

They chatted about his trip and the pending sale of Big Jake's. When they finally got off the interstate, R.J. realized they were close to Jillian's condo. He smiled in the darkness. He was being kidnapped and he didn't care. Spending the night alone in his dad's house had seemed gloomy and depressing. It certainly wasn't his first choice for what to do that night. Now it looked like he was going to get his first choice – a night at Jillian's.

"Am I being kidnapped?" he asked playfully.

"Yes," was all Jillian said but he could see her smiling in the dark car.

"Oh, does that mean you're going to tie me up and have your way with me?" R.J. was grinning now.

"It might," Jillian giggled. "What would you like from the Chinese place? I'm calling an order in now."

"Anything as long as it's quick," he said. "And then we can get to the part where you take advantage of me."

Jillian took out her cell phone and dialed the Chinese restaurant not far from her condo. She placed an order for delivery. They soon reached her parking lot and R.J. took one of his bags from the back. When they were inside, he dropped it to the floor and pulled Jillian to him.

"How long before the food arrives?" R.J. wanted to know as he kissed her neck. "I'm not sure I'm hungry anymore baby. At least not for Chinese."

"Ten minutes, tops," she murmured as heat roared through her body. "You need to eat because I plan to keep you awake for awhile yet. I want to be sure you have plenty of strength."

"Oh my god," R.J. moaned as his hand slid over Jillian's butt and pulled her even closer. "I dreamed about this every night for the last three weeks. I swear baby, sometimes I could smell your scent and it just about drove me insane."

Jillian's reply was cut off by a kiss that rocked her to the soles of her feet. R.J. pressed his lips to hers and very slowly slid his tongue into her mouth. His other hand snaked tighter around her waist, pressing her entire body against his. He could feel the heat radiating from her body, feel her nipples hard against his chest. His tongue did a sensuous dance with hers as her hands locked around his neck.

They remained entwined at the front door, neither wanting to let go of the other. The kiss continued, becoming deeper and setting both of them on fire. Jillian's knees went weak with longing, her body crying out to be naked against his. She felt his erection pressing against her abdomen, hard and throbbing. She had never wanted a man the way she wanted R.J. at that moment. They finally broke apart at the sound of a knock at the door.

"I hope this is dinner," R.J. said. "Because if it isn't, I don't think we will be having dinner tonight."

Jillian opened the door and accepted the food from the deliveryman. She and R.J. headed into the kitchen with the bags of food. She removed plates, wine glasses, and silverware from the cupboards, opened the door to the balcony, and set the outside table. She lit the big candle sitting in the middle of the table. In the meantime, R.J. found a bottle of wine and opened it. He brought the wine and the food out to the table. Jillian reached in to turn off the kitchen lights and they sat down to eat.

"Thank you for rescuing me from a lonely evening." R.J. raised his glass in a toast after he had filled their wine glasses.

"May this be the first of many, many evenings spent together. To our future!"

Jillian raised her glass too and smiled a thousand watt smile at R.J. She could not remember the last time she had been this happy. Her mother was right, it was time to move forward with her life. And just maybe, R.J. would be a very big part of her future.

As they ate, they chatted about what would happen the rest of the week. Jillian outlined how the sale of Big Jake's would take place. Then she asked R.J. what he would do once it was complete.

"I really need to check on my house in Ocean Isle," he replied. "I was hoping that you would come down with me for the weekend. Then next week I guess I'll come back to Raleigh and clean out Dad's house. I need to get it ready to sell. What do you think? A weekend trip to the beach?"

"I'm always up for a weekend trip to the beach," Jillian answered. "Sounds heavenly! But I will have to get back to work on Monday to begin transferring my clients to my colleagues."

"Transferring your clients? What does that mean?" R.J. was perplexed. What was this woman who had so captured him up to?

"I've decided to leave SW&K, sell my part of the business," she confessed. "I have a meeting with Kent and Andrew tomorrow to tell them. I don't know what I'm going to do yet, but I know I don't want to be an accountant anymore."

"Jillian, that's fantastic!" R.J. cried, then became serious. "Are you really sure this is what you want to do? Would it be better to maybe take a leave of absence for awhile?"

"I'm absolutely certain, R.J.," she confirmed. "I've been thinking about this for a long, long time. The last six weeks have settled it in my mind. I need to do something different and I need to do it now."

"I'm excited for you, baby. And I'll help you in any way that I can," R.J. responded. "If you want to hang out at the beach while you think, I would love to have you."

"That's such a sweet offer and I might just take you up on it," Jillian said with a huge smile. "Where better to get my head on straight than by the ocean? The water always calms me and clears my head. How long will it be before you have to leave again?"

"Actually, I did a lot of thinking while I was in Germany," R.J. confided. "With the money I make from Big Jake's and what I already have, I can take off for a long time. I only have one more shoot scheduled right now. I called a photographer friend of mine yesterday and asked him if he would do it for me. He agreed as long as the client agrees."

"Are you going to work on your book?" Jillian asked excitedly. "I would love to look at the pictures you took for it."

"If the client will let my friend do the job, then I'm going to work on my book," he replied. "I have calls to make tomorrow and, hopefully, I'll know for sure by the end of this week."

"Oh R.J., I'm so happy for you!" Jillian exclaimed. "I know how much you want to do this. I can see it in your eyes when you talk about it."

R.J. beamed a smile at Jillian in the candlelight and she smiled back at him. They stared into each other's eyes for a full minute, neither wanting to look away.

CHAPTER 16

A ringing from the kitchen broke the spell. Jillian rose from the table and opened the sliding glass door. She turned to R.J.

"It's after nine so that's either Kellie or my mom. No one else calls me this late," she said. "If I don't answer, my cell phone will start ringing next. And neither of them give up until they find me."

Jillian went back into the kitchen and picked up the phone. As she had thought, it was Kellie. Jillian quickly told her friend that she and R.J. were just finishing dinner at her condo. She explained how she had picked him up at the airport and kidnapped him.

"Well now," Kellie laughed. "Someone is certainly getting bold! It's about time too. You should tie him up and take advantage of him just like he said."

"I was just getting to that when the phone rang," Jillian giggled. "So let me hang up and get back to business!"

"Wait a minute. I have a great idea. Why don't we all go out to dinner tomorrow night?" Kellie asked.

"Do you really think you can get Stephen to leave the house on a weeknight?" Jillian burst out laughing. "That's one of the things I like about him. You and I can go out on a weeknight and he wouldn't go with us if we paid him."

"To be able to swap fishing stories with R.J., I think he would," Kellie responded. "He can't stop talking about the pictures he saw in that magazine. He tells everyone he knows that he met a famous photographer."

At that moment, R.J. came through the French doors. He carried dirty plates, empty food boxes, and an empty wine bottle. He looked up at Jillian as he put the plates into the sink.

"Hang on, Kell," she said as she covered the mouthpiece of the phone with one hand. "Kellie wants to know if we would like to go out to dinner tomorrow night with her and Stephen."

"Sounds like fun," R.J. said. "I would love to see them again."

"Are you sure?" Jillian asked. "Stephen seems to be quite excited that he met you. He might drive you crazy with questions."

"Baby, these are your friends," he murmured as he kissed her cheek. "Your best friend and her husband. If I'm going to spend time with you, I know I'll be spending time with them too. They're a big part of your life. So let's go and have a good time."

"You are absolutely amazing," she whispered. She kissed him lightly on the lips and went back to the phone. "Kell, dinner tomorrow night is on. How about Romeo's at seven o'clock?"

"Ah, now you're talking," Kellie smiled at her friend's ingenious idea. "Stephen's favorite restaurant with his new favorite guy friend. No way he can resist that!"

"My thoughts exactly," Jillian acknowledged. "See you there?"

"For sure, Jillie. Now go tie that man up and enjoy your night!"

Kellie hung up, leaving Jillian smiling at an empty phone line. She turned to R.J. who was standing at the door. He was looking directly at her, a look of such intensity it made her shiver.

"Let's go outside and finish our wine," he said simply. "You can tell me about Romeo's."

Jillian plugged her cell phone into the charger on the counter and turned it off. They want back to the balcony, sat, and sipped their wine. She explained to R.J. that Romeo's was Stephen's favorite restaurant and had excellent Italian food. She also explained that Stephen normally wouldn't go out on a weeknight, but the combination of Romeo's and R.J. would prove hard to resist. She then learned that R.J. loved Italian food too and was happy with the choice. When their glasses were empty, he stood, took her hand, and pulled her to her feet. As his arms went around her body, she felt an electric frisson pass between them.

"This must be what life is supposed to be all about," he sighed as he nuzzled her neck. "Good wine and a beautiful woman that I absolutely adore together in a peaceful outdoor setting. It can't get any better than this."

"Aren't you tired?" she asked with little conviction. "Your body must think it's the middle of the night."

"Let me show you just how tired I am, baby," R.J. growled as his lips moved from her neck to her mouth.

He kissed her softly at first, his lips whispering across hers. Jillian put her arms around his waist and pulled him tight to her. His arms tightened around her back as his tongue slid into her mouth. The feeling of R.J.'s tongue touching hers while his fingers trailed up her spine made Jillian shiver. Heat began to bloom inside her. As the kiss deepened and became more demanding, the heat exploded into a roaring flame.

R.J. was far from tired. His entire body was awake and engulfed in flames just as Jillian's was. No woman had ever made him feel this kind of heat before. No woman had ever made him feel so good that all thought left him.....all thought except how he could give her pleasure until she begged not to cum again. He felt his penis becoming erect, hardening like a steel rod. Oh god he wanted her.

"Let's go inside," Jillian murmured against his lips. "I need to feel your skin touching mine."

"In a minute," he whispered as he broke the kiss. "Turn around and look out at the sky."

Jillian did as instructed, wondering what R.J. was up to. She looked toward the full moon but didn't really see it. Her brain had stopped working when R.J.'s lips had pressed hard against hers, forcing her every sense to full alert. His arms came around her from behind and, this time, his fingers trailed across her breasts. He took one breast in each hand, squeezing, caressing, urging them to swell with desire. They responded as commanded.....sensitive, swollen, with nipples becoming as hard as little pebbles in a matter of seconds. Jillian moaned as the sensation in her breasts rushed another flame straight to her now wet pussy.

Hearing her moan with pleasure was R.J.'s greatest reward. He wanted only to give this incredible woman the sexual thrill and satisfaction she so deserved. His gratification came from taking her body to heights she didn't know existed. As his hands moved down to Jillian's stomach, he wondered briefly why he had never felt this extreme need to give unending pleasure before. But the groan she emitted when he pushed her skirt down and slid his fingers under her thong banished all thought once again.

R.J. pulled her closer to him with the hand still around her waist. He wanted her to feel his hardness pressing against her, wanted her to know just how erotic this giving of pleasure was for him. He felt the heat of her pussy before his fingers reached it and he knew she was already wet for him. He growled deep in his throat as his fingers slid between Jillian's legs. She was on fire, on fire with desire for him.

"Spread your legs just a little, baby," he breathed into her ear as his fingers slipped deeper into her heat. "Oh baby, so hot, so wet."

The first jolt of electricity went straight through Jillian when R.J.'s fingers skimmed over her clit. Her body arched but he held her firmly against him, his erection pressing hard and throbbing into the curves of her butt. When his fingers found her now dripping pussy and pushed up inside her, she went white hot all over. She threw her arms up and back, wrapping them around his neck, thrusting her swollen breasts out until they strained against her blouse.

R.J.'s head moved forward until he was breathing on her cheek. As his fingers moved inside her, his thumb found her swollen clit. He rubbed the engorged knob of nerves causing her to arch up again. Holding her tight to him, R.J. stroked her inside with his fingers and outside with his thumb. Jillian moaned and he felt her muscles tighten as she began to cum. She pulled against the back of his neck as the orgasm rolled over her body.

"Yeah baby, cum for me," he crooned and kissed her cheek. Another orgasm followed immediately on the heels of the first. "Oh yeah, that's my sexy, hot baby. Let go and feel it baby. I'll hold you up…..you just feel it!"

R.J.'s voice quietly registered in Jillian's swirling head. He was urging her to let go and feel his tender but demanding touches. She could do nothing else. His fingers were stroking her inside, caressing a spot that sent shock waves through her body. His thumb was grinding against her clit, increasing the voltage of the electricity coursing inside her. She had a succession of orgasms, each stronger that the last, until finally she could take no more.

Sensing that Jillian had reached her limit, R.J. slowly pulled his fingers from her now dripping pussy. His hand was wet with her juices and he raised it to his face. He licked her cum from his fingers, feeling her chest move as she fought for breath. She surprised him when she removed her arms from his neck and grabbed his hand. She put the fingers that had been inside her pussy into her mouth and sucked her own cum from them.

"Do you have any idea what that does to me?" he asked breathlessly. "Oh my god….."

Jillian turned in R.J.'s arms until she was face to face with him. She looked directly into his eyes. Seeing the raw passion and need, she took his face in her hands. She kissed him gently, then licked her own taste from his lips.

"See what you do to me?" she murmured. "Now we go inside."

Taking R.J. by the hand, Jillian blew out the flickering candle, opened the French doors and slipped inside. R.J. pulled the door closed behind him and locked the deadbolt. He made no sound as Jillian led him into her bedroom. They reached the bed and she turned to him. She took his face in her hands again and softly kissed his lips, both cheeks, and then his chin. She slowly unbuttoned his rumpled white shirt and licked his chest as she pushed it off his shoulders and down his arms. Her hands moved to his pants, unzipping them and pushing them quickly to the floor.

Jillian caught her breath as R.J.'s hard penis sprung from his pants, begging for her attention. She had an overwhelming desire to run her tongue from the top to the bottom. She motioned for R.J. to lie down on the bed and then slowly removed her blouse, bra, and panties. She watched his face as her fully naked body came into view. The combination of appreciation and raw lust she saw inflamed her once again. She wanted him to feel the same exquisite pleasure he had give her on the balcony.

"Get comfortable, my love," she said as she climbed onto the bed. "This time it's your turn to feel."

R.J. settled back onto the pillows and spread his legs to allow Jillian to kneel between them. She leaned over and let her hard nipples rub against his throbbing penis. He groaned at the sensation and closed his eyes. She sat back, put his legs over hers, leaned forward, and gave in to her desire to lick him. Her tongue flicked out and made a lazy circle around his balls. She slid it up the length of his shaft until she reached the head. She rubbed the tip of her tongue over the purple tip of his fully erect penis and felt him tense at the jolt of pleasure it caused.

Again and again, Jillian licked him from bottom to top. Each pass of her tongue was excruciatingly wonderful torture, causing R.J. to moan and rock upward. His eyes remained closed as he savored the sensations she caused throughout his body. Finally, Jillian took him in her mouth and sucked gently. Her lips were firmly around him as her head moved up and down, sucking him to delirium. R.J. was beginning to thrash about on the bed. His hands gripped the sheets as she took him close to the edge without allowing him to crash over.

When he could stand it no longer, R.J. opened his eyes and looked down at Jillian. Her silky red hair was splayed over his thighs as her incredible mouth teased him. The sight was almost more than he could bear.

"Baby, I want to be inside you when I cum," he managed to croak.

Jillian looked up at him and slid her luscious lips up the length of R.J.'s penis one more time. Then she leaned forward and slid her entire body over his hard shaft as she moved on top of him. She spread her legs and he immediately felt her heat and wetness cover him. She slowly moved her hips, getting him wet with her juices and ready to enter her.

Without warning, Jillian raised her hips and slipped his pulsing penis deep into her heated core. R.J. gasped at how hot, wet, and tight she was. She sat up and grabbed his hands, pulling them to her breasts. In seconds, he felt her stiffen and her muscles tighten as she had a massive orgasm. Her head fell back in ecstasy and her breasts swelled in his hands.

Again, the sight was almost more than R.J. could bear in his extraordinarily aroused state. When her orgasm subsided, Jillian fell forward until she was pressed against his chest. He unconsciously began to move his hips, thrusting deeper and deeper into her. Her hips responded to his rhythm and when she began to cum again, he thrust harder and harder until he crashed over the edge, his orgasm more intense than he thought possible.

For several minutes, they lay entwined together, enjoying the high. Eventually, their breathing returned almost to normal. Jillian rolled off of R.J. and felt suddenly chilled. She wanted to feel his skin, feel his heat. R.J. reached over and pulled her head onto his shoulder. He needed to feel her heat too. He had one arm around her and held her hand with his free hand. She pulled a blanket over them and sighed, a deep sigh of pure bliss. In the darkness, R.J. smiled a smile of total contentment. His last thought as he fell asleep was that he never wanted to leave Jillian again.

CHAPTER 17

Wednesday morning was sunny, bright, and crisp. Fall was definitely in the air in Raleigh, N.C. Jillian woke to sound of her alarm clock and the smell of coffee brewing. As she shut off the alarm, she was disoriented for a moment by the smell of coffee in her house. Then she remembered that she had purchased a coffee pot so R.J. could have his morning coffee. She got out of bed and made a quick trip to the bathroom. With freshly brushed teeth, she slipped on a robe and padded into the kitchen.

A smile lit up Jillian's face when she saw R.J. standing at the kitchen counter in his boxers, pouring a cup of coffee. His dark hair and broad, lightly muscled shoulders made her mouth go dry. He looked so good she entertained the thought of having him for breakfast instead of her normal bowl of oatmeal. She stopped in the doorway and watched him as he put a few drops of milk into the coffee.

When R.J. turned and saw Jillian standing in the doorway, his heart almost stopped. She was breathtakingly beautiful with her red hair wild around her head and her eyes full of lust. He wanted to scoop her up and take her directly back to the bedroom. From the look on her face, he didn't think she would say no.

"Good morning, beautiful," R.J. said with a mischievous grin. "I hope I didn't wake you but I seem to still be on German time."

"No, my alarm woke me," she grinned in return. "Have you been up long?"

"About an hour. I hope you don't mind that I made coffee," he responded. "I needed some caffeine to get the cobwebs out of my head. I came in to make tea but then saw the Mr. Coffee. I thought you didn't have a coffee pot."

"I bought that while you were gone," Jillian replied. "I was hoping you would be spending more mornings here."

R.J. crossed the kitchen and took Jillian in his arms. He looked into her eyes and then kissed her soundly. A smile played across his lips when he finished kissing her.

"I'm hoping I'll be spending more time here too," he said. "A lot more time."

He kissed her again and slipped one hand inside her bathrobe. Her nipple was already hard when his finger grazed across it. He cupped her breast and squeezed gently. He felt his penis stir and suddenly it was partially erect.

"R.J., this feels incredibly good," Jillian began, luxuriating in the feel of his hand as it moved to the other breast. "Unfortunately, I have to be at work in an hour."

"Uh huh," R.J. murmured as his hand continue to caress her.

"Really, I have to get ready for work," she breathed, fervently wishing she didn't have meetings this morning. "Oh god, that feels good."

"Uh huh," he murmured again.

"Um, can I get a rain check for tonight?" Jillian stuttered as R.J. finally removed his hand.

"Baby, you can get a rain check for anytime you want it," R.J. exclaimed softly as he stepped back. "I just hope there's time for me to take a cold shower before we leave. When we walk to your car, I don't want to scare any women or children with the huge bulge that's now in my pants."

"Oh, crap," Jillian muttered. "I'm not going to have time to take you home before my first client will be in."

"Don't worry about it," he replied. "I'll take a cab to Dad's house. I have his car there."

"Why don't you just take my Jeep?" she asked. "We're going out with Kellie and Stephen tonight anyway. You can pick me up from work and we can sort out the car situation later."

"Yeah, that probably makes more sense," R.J. noted as the tea-kettle began to whistle. "Now how about I fix you a cup of tea while you shower?"

"That sounds heavenly. And you can shower while I get ready," Jillian responded with a wicked grin. "I'll be sure to use up all the hot water so you have a nice, cold shower. Wouldn't want to hear screaming when we go out the door."

R.J. gave her the evil eye and then burst out laughing. Giggling, Jillian turned and scooted back to the bedroom. After she was showered and dressed, she sat down at the kitchen table to eat her oatmeal. R.J. was just finishing his shower when she put her bowl in the sink and turned on her cell phone. The phone beeped that she had new voice mail messages.

Jillian dialed the voice mail number and started to listen to the first message. When R.J. entered the kitchen, he saw her drop the phone like it was burning her hand. She looked up at him, her face a mask of terror.

"What is it, Jillian?" he asked as he hurriedly sat down beside her. "You look like you just heard from a ghost."

"Victor," she shuddered and pointed to the phone. "Listen, go ahead, pick it up and listen."

R.J. picked up the phone but the message was almost over. He pressed two to repeat the message. His face grew taut and dark as he listened. He listened to two more messages, each worse than the last. He carefully saved each one, then looked at Jillian.

"Has Victor been bothering you while I was gone?" he questioned, his face a grim mask. "I thought you said you hadn't heard from him."

"I haven't heard anything from him until now," Jillian cried, tears threatening to spill from her green eyes. "I swear, nothing until now."

"Apparently he's been watching you, baby," R.J. said, his face softening at the fear in her voice. "He said he saw me come in last night according to the first message. And in the second message, he said he saw us on the balcony."

"What? How could he see us on the balcony?" she asked, both furious and frightened out of her mind. "Oh my god, was he hiding in the woods? He's crazy, R.J.!"

"He didn't say where he was but you're right, he's crazy," he replied. "We need to report this to the police."

"I'm scared, R.J., really, really scared," Jillian said softly. "I've never heard him sound like that. He doesn't sound like the person I knew. How could he do that?"

"Jillian, he made threats in the last message. But I won't let him hurt you," R.J. uttered in a quiet voice as he reached for her hand. "Not now and not ever. Hopefully threats on voice mail will be enough for the police to pick him up. Until they do, I'll be with you every moment."

"Thank you," she murmured, her eyes full of love as they looked at each other. "You have no idea how much that means to me."

"You have no idea how much you mean to me," he replied, his eyes also full of love. "Now let's get you to work on time. You can call the police from there and have them come to the office if they need to see you. I'll hang around all day just to be safe."

"Oh R.J., that's asking too much and I really don't think it's necessary," Jillian exclaimed. "He hasn't come to the office and I don't think he will. There are too many people there. Go do what you need to do today at your dad's house. I won't leave the building until you come back to get me."

"I guess that makes sense," R.J. conceded. "Maybe it's a good thing that I'll have your car. He might think you were too scared to come to work."

Jillian got her jacket and purse while R.J. waited. He decided to leave his overnight bag there. He had no intention of leaving Jillian alone while Victor was on the loose. As they left the condo, R.J.'s head swiveled back and forth, looking for any sign of trouble. They reached the Jeep and Jillian handed him the keys.

The drive to Jillian's office was quiet. Her mind was in turmoil, wondering why Victor was doing this to her. R.J.'s mind was in overdrive thinking about what he needed to do to keep Jillian safe. There was no way he was going to let that insane man scare her like this again.

When they reached the building housing Stanley, Wilson, and Krenshaw, Jillian directed R.J. to the parking garage. He pulled up to the door that went directly to the lobby. Jillian turned to him and saw concern all over his face.

"I'm going to be OK," she said. "I'll call the police and let them deal with it. And I promise not to leave until you get here this evening. Please don't look so worried, R.J."

"I'm sure you will be fine, but don't ask me to not worry," he responded. "That's something I can't help. The only thing I ever really worry about are the people I care deeply for."

"If it will make you feel better, call me later," Jillian advised, her heart beating wildly from his statement. "I have meetings off and on today, but I'll tell Allison to find me when you call."

"Good luck with the meeting with your partners," R.J. murmured as he put his hands to her face. "I hope it goes exactly the way you want it to."

Jillian leaned closer too him and softly kissed him. When she leaned back, he looked directly into her eyes. She saw such emotion in them her heart fluttered even harder.

"I have to go," she whispered, never breaking eye contact. "And R.J., I care very deeply about you too."

R.J. kissed her again and then Jillian got out of the Jeep. He watched until she was inside the door and out of sight. He was terrified for her safety. She hadn't heard the horrible threats Victor had made on her voice mail. He debated whether to go to his dad's house or simply sit outside the building all day. Finally logic overcame emotion and he pulled out of the parking garage.

Jillian was smiling as she took the elevator to the offices of SW&K. She knew she should be scared but that was completely overshadowed by the knowledge that R.J. obviously felt for her what she felt for him. Maybe this relationship had a good chance after the sale of Big Jake's was completed tomorrow.

When she reached her office, Jillian heard a beep from her cell phone. When she pulled the phone from her purse and looked it, she realized she had missed another call from Victor while she was in the elevator. She didn't bother to listen to it. Instead, she pulled out the business card from the police detective she had spoken to when her tires were slashed. She dialed his number and they set up an appointment at her office for later in the day. He told her not to answer any call from Victor or respond to any voice mail or text message. Jillian advised Allison that there would be a police detective arriving late in the afternoon. She also told the receptionist that if Victor happened to show up in the office, she should call 911 immediately.

The day progressed in a blur of client meetings and paperwork. At lunchtime, Jillian checked her phone again and saw more missed calls from Victor. She also had several text messages from him. She didn't listen to the voice mail or read the text messages. She didn't want to know what this crazy, scary man was threatening to do. As she ate her lunch at her desk, her office phone rang and she saw it was R.J.

"Hi there, handsome," Jillian answered. "How's it going at your dad's house?"

"Hi there, beautiful, sexy lady," R.J. replied. "This will be a long process, but I'm making slow progress. How's it going with you? Anything more from Victor?"

"He's still leaving voice mails and now he's added text messages," she said. "The police detective will be here at three o'clock. I'm not answering my phone or responding in any way until after I talk to the detective."

"That's my girl," he smiled as he spoke. "Did you have your meeting with the partners yet?"

"I'm meeting with them in about half an hour," Jillian responded. "I want them to know about what's going on with Victor before the police show up."

"I think that's a good idea," R.J. remarked. "They should know in case Victor decides to show up there."

"Let's change the subject," she declared. "I talked to Kellie a little while ago and Stephen is excited about having dinner with you tonight. He kept her up half the night talking about how cool it will be to hear your stories about fishing lakes. I think I'm just extra baggage that he has to put up with."

"You will never be extra baggage to me," R.J. laughed. "Gee, I hope he doesn't have a man crush on me!"

"If he does, that's too bad for him," Jillian giggled. "I'm not sharing you with my best friend's husband."

"Don't worry, baby," R.J. proclaimed. "I'm going home with you tonight. Stephen will just have to deal with the let down."

They spoke for a few minutes more, R.J. explaining what he had done so far at the house. He was a little overwhelmed by the amount of things he had to deal with, but he was moving forward. Jillian promised to help him when they came back from their weekend in Ocean Isle. She knew how heartbreaking this exercise could be. She had helped her mom clean out the home she had grown up in after her dad died. She also knew it was a necessary task so R.J. could say a final goodbye to his dad. Just before they hung up, they decided on a time that R.J. would be in the garage to pick Jillian up for their dinner with Kellie and Stephen. They were both wearing huge smiles when the call ended.

At two o'clock, Jillian met with Kent and Andrew in Kent's office. She was feeling nervous about the whole thing, but was also anxious to find out how they would react to her desire to leave the business. First, however, she needed to tell them about Victor.

"So what's on your mind that required a formal meeting with both of us?" Kent inquired. "It must be pretty serious."

"Actually, there are two things I want to talk about," Jillian squirmed uncomfortably in her seat. "Remember our conversation several weeks back about the man who slashed my tires?"

"Of course," Andrew responded. "But the last several times I asked you about it, you said you hadn't heard anything more from him."

"Is he bothering you again?" Kent asked with a serious expression on his face. "Just tell me where to find him and he's history."

"And I'm right there with Kent," Andrew exclaimed. "He won't want to even think your name when we finish with him."

"Guys, I so appreciate the thought, but slow down for a minute," Jillian cried. "I didn't hear from Victor for almost a month. Then last night he started calling and leaving me nasty voice mail messages. My phone was off so I didn't know until this morning. Then today, he's been leaving voice mail and text messages."

"Where do I find him," Kent yelled as he rose to his feet. "He's not getting away with this!"

"Kent, let me finish, OK?" Jillian smiled at her honorary uncles and their desire to defend her. "The police detective who helped with the restraining order will be here at three o'clock. I spoke to him this morning and he says the messages are a violation of the order. After he hears them and has them transcribed, he can arrest Victor."

"Good, that's what I want to hear," Kent said as he sat back down. "I wonder what caused him to suddenly start up again?"

"Yeah, that is kind of odd," Andrew noted. "A month of quiet and now he's making an ass of himself."

"Well, apparently he's been following me all this time," Jillian began, feeling slightly uncomfortable that she might have to tell them about R.J. "I guess he was content with that until last night. See, I started seeing someone around the time of the first incident. The man I'm seeing was out of town for a few weeks and just came back. Victor's first message was that he saw us go into my condo last night."

"You're seeing someone?" Kent questioned. "How come Mindy didn't tell me? Who is this guy anyway? You know I need to meet him."

"Kent, calm down," Jillian laughed. "Mindy didn't tell you because she doesn't know. She doesn't know because Mom doesn't know either. I've kind of kept things quiet until I see where the relationship is going. I'm going to see Mom in a few weeks and I'll tell her then, maybe even take him with me. After that, I'll be glad to introduce you."

Jillian winced at the small lie she had just told. Kent would be shocked when he realized he already knew her new beau, but that was how it had to be right now. She couldn't risk telling Kent or Andrew until after Big Jake's sale was completed. And her mother had to be the first person she told or she would never hear the end of it.

"I guess I'll have to accept that since you are legally an adult," Kent conceded. "But just let this guy know he will have to withstand my scrutiny at some point. If I don't like him, he's out. Understand, young lady?"

"I understand, Uncle Kent," Jillian said seriously as a hint of a smile played at her lips.

"And he has to pass muster with me, too," Andrew put in. "He's not getting a free pass just because Kent likes him."

"I understand that too, Uncle Andrew," Jillian agreed as she tried not to laugh. "You're the best uncles a girl could ever ask for and I want both of you to like him."

Jillian took a deep breath and decided to plunge ahead with the next topic of discussion. She was dreading this even more than the first one. She knew beforehand how they would react to Victor's antics but she had no idea how they would react to her wanting to leave the firm.

"So guys, there is something else I need to talk to you about," she began. "I'm not sure if you noticed but for the last six months or so, my heart hasn't really been in my work."

"Jillian, you've had a really difficult time the last few years," Kent acknowledged. "With your dad's death and your divorce, we knew you were struggling. If you're worried that your job is in any kind of jeopardy, it isn't."

"We understand that it's been trying for you," Andrew continued. "We've tried not to overwhelm you with new clients or let you get too inundated with work. The work you've been doing is excellent and, as always, you go above and beyond for you clients. When you're ready, we'll put you back into the rotation for new business. Just say the word."

"You're right, I have been struggling," Jillian admitted. "Part of that struggle was working through my grief for dad and my marriage, but there's more too it than that. That's what I want to talk about."

"Whatever you need to get back on your feet," Kent stated. "You're family and we will help you anyway we can."

"Here's the thing," Jillian said nervously. "Since Dad died, I don't seem to enjoy my work as much as I did. Part of the allure of the job was getting to work with my father. I've done a lot of thinking and I've decided that I'm going to resign from the firm. It's time for me to do something different, something that makes me happy."

Kent and Andrew sat in stunned silence for several moments. They looked at each other and then at Jillian. Jillian was becoming uneasy and started to speak. Before she got two words out, Kent seemed to come out of his shock.

"Jillian, are you sure? That's a major, life changing decision," he cried. "Maybe a leave of absence would be better. It's not so final, dear. You can take time to rest and relax and, when you're ready, come back to work."

"Listen to him, Jillian," Andrew exclaimed. "A leave of absence is fine with me. And what about your mom? What will Barbara think if you leave the firm?"

"I've already talked to my mom," Jillian confided. "She supports me totally. She realizes that Dad would not want me to be here if I'm unhappy. But there's more to this than just quitting my job."

"More? Oh lord, what more can there be?" Andrew stood up and began pacing the room. He wasn't a person who embraced change.

"Before I tell you, please understand that Mom and I talked about this too," Jillian disclosed. "She supports this next part too. And she said she is sure Dad would agree if he was alive."

"It must be dire," Andrew noted as he sat back down.

"I want to sell my part of the business to the two of you," Jillian stated quickly, afraid she would lose her nerve if she hesitated. "I want to have the freedom to begin a career as a writer. If I have money from the sale of my part of the firm, I'll be financially sound for several years while I get started."

The room was extremely quiet and Jillian felt like the air had been sucked out of it. She looked from Kent to Andrew and back again, trying to read their faces. They exchanged several looks but she couldn't tell what messages passed between them. Then Kent stood up.

"Andrew, let's step into my conference room for a quick chat," Kent said quietly and then turned to look at Jillian. "Wait here for a few minutes please, Jillian."

The two men Jillian had known her entire life stood and went into the small conference room that was an extension of Kent's office. They closed the door, leaving her a mass of nerves huddled in a chair. So many thoughts were careening through her head, she felt dizzy. Would they agree to buy her out? Did they think she was crazy from the last few years of personal stress? What would they offer if they wouldn't let her sell? The only thought that really stood out was her absolute knowledge that this was the right decision for her future. Finally, the conference room door opened and Kent and Andrew returned to their seats.

"We have known you your whole life, Jillian," Kent began. "You're like a daughter to both of us and we want you to be happy. If your work doesn't make you happy anymore, then maybe you do need to do something else."

"We discussed buying your shares of the business," Andrew continued. "We're not sure that's the best thing for you to do right now with the economy the way it is."

Jillian's heart sank and her thoughts spiraled out of control. They weren't going to let her sell. Without the money for her part of the business, she would only be able to stay afloat for a year at most. How could she become an established writer in just a year?

"So we have a proposition for you," Kent advised. "What if we give you an advance on what your proceeds would be? After a year or two, if you still want to sell, then we will draw up the papers. The economy should be on the road to recovery by then and your share will be worth more. However, if you change your mind, then you can come back to work at SW&K and pay the advance back."

"You two are absolutely the best!" Jillian exclaimed as she flew over to hug both men. "That's the best idea I've heard in ages. I love you both so much for doing this for me!"

Kent and Andrew stood and hugged Jillian in return. They chatted about Jillian's future plans and agreed to have the paperwork for the advance completed by the end of the month. Jillian told them of her ideas to transition her clients to other SW&K associates. She also promised to help get her clients over the hurdle of becoming comfortable with a new accountant. With that done, she practically floated back to her office.

At three o'clock, Allison advised that the police detective was there. Jillian met him in the reception area and took him back to her office. She outlined for Detective Oliver what had happened when she turned her cell phone on that morning. She told him about the calls and text messages that had been coming in from Victor all day. She also told him that R.J. was just back from Europe and she thought his return may have caused Victor to be more aggressive than he had been before. Then she handed the phone to the detective so he could listen to and read the messages.

"Mr. Henderson has definitely violated the terms of the restraining order," Detective Oliver confirmed. "We can pick him up and charge him. However, you need to understand that he can be bailed out. We can't keep him in jail indefinitely so be on the lookout. Obviously, he is upset about your new relationship, so Mr. Williams should be careful too."

"What if he keeps leaving messages?" Jillian asked.

"He will until we pick him up," the detective said. "I have no doubt about that. I need you to come down to the station so we can record the messages. You will also need to sign the paperwork so we can get a court order to obtain legal copies of them. Be sure you save every single message he leaves."

"I don't plan to even listen to them so they will be right there," Jillian noted. "When do you want me to come to the station? Tomorrow afternoon would be best if that's all right. I'm kind of swamped today prepping for two big meetings that I have tomorrow. Can I come tomorrow around four-thirty?"

"That's perfect, Miss Stanley. I have some paperwork to do also to have things ready for you to sign," Detective Oliver replied. "In the meantime, be extra careful and keep someone with you at all times. I'm sure Mr. Williams will be glad to stay with you. He seemed pretty taken with you when you were at the station last month."

"R.J. already told me he will be staying with me until this is over with Victor," Jillian disclosed. "We're planning to leave for a weekend trip to his house in Ocean Isle on Friday. Hopefully you will have Victor in custody by then."

The detective left and Jillian sat thinking for a moment. While the threat from Victor was scary, she couldn't stay scared for long. Thoughts of R.J. and his obvious feelings for her surfaced and made her smile. The fact that the detective commented on how R.J. must feel about her made her smile even more. And tonight, he would be with her for dinner with her best friends. Yes, this relationship just might have a chance.

Jillian spent the next two hours preparing for her meetings with R.J.'s lawyers and Pete Ridell. She was excited to complete both projects and get busy on the transition of her other clients. Allison came in at five-thirty to see if Jillian needed anything before she left for the day.

"Thanks for asking, Allison," Jillian said. "I'm ready for both meetings tomorrow. I appreciate everything you have done to help me on both of them. Once we get them finalized, you and I will go for a victory lunch celebration."

"Miss Stanley, that's so nice of you!" Allison cried. "You worked so hard on both of them and it's really cool that they will both complete on the same day."

"I couldn't have done it without your suggestion to take the Ridell paperwork to the conference room," Jillian commented. "That was a life saver."

"Miss Stanley, can I tell you something?" Allison asked nervously.

"Sure, Allison. What's on your mind?" Jillian replied.

"Well, it seems like you have been so much happier lately," the receptionist remarked. "I don't know why, but I'm glad things are finally going well for you. You had so much turmoil in your life the last couple of years. It's nice to see you smiling and happy again."

Jillian rose from her seat and came around to the front of the desk where Allison was standing. She hugged the girl and then stepped back. She smiled the biggest smile of the day.

"Thank you, Allison," Jillian said. "I am happier these days. There are some changes happening in my personal life that are really positive. Next week, we will go to lunch and talk about what's going on."

"I'd like that," Allison replied and turned to leave. "Have a good evening."

"And Allison," Jillian spoke before Allison got to the door. "Thank you for putting up with me being such a bear for so long. It's been a difficult time but things are definitely looking up. You have a good evening, too."

CHAPTER 18

S hortly after six o'clock, Jillian's work phone rang. It was R.J. and he was waiting outside for her. Jillian shut her computer down and bounded out to the garage. It felt good to know a man who really cared for her was waiting for her after work. She thought she could get used to this.

When she got in the Jeep, R.J. was smiling a huge smile too. His heart did a flip when Jillian had come through the lobby door. Apparently things had gone well with her partners as she was grinning from ear to ear. She leaned over and gave him a big kiss as soon as she sat down.

"Wow, someone is feeling good this evening," he teased her. "Does that mean things went well today?"

"Get this vehicle moving and I'll tell you all about it," Jillian commanded as he put the car in gear.

They rode to Romeo's Italian Restaurant with Jillian providing a non-stop commentary on her day. R.J. was thrilled that Kent and Andrew had offered her an alternative to selling out right away. He wanted her to have a back up plan in case the writing thing didn't work out. And he was happy that Victor was going to be arrested. When they reached the parking lot, he turned and took Jillian's face in his hands. Looking into her eyes, he felt a surge of love like he had never known for any other woman.

"It sounds like your future plans are taking shape in a good way," he said as his eyes devoured hers. "I hope that I can be part of those plans."

"I want you to be part of my future, R.J." Jillian murmured, feeling her heart swell with love. "I want that more than anything else. No matter what happens with my writing career or any other future plans, you will definitely be part of my life for as long as you want to be."

R.J. kissed her then with such passion that Jillian's entire body began to tingle. His lips caressed her lips and his tongue made slow circles with her tongue. It was the sweetest kiss she had ever experienced....sweet with a strong sensual undertone that now had her on fire.

They were lost in the kiss until a sharp rapping occurred on the car window. They looked up to see Stephen grinning at them. R.J. dropped his hands and looked at Jillian.

"Looks like my man crush is here," he said with a sly smile. "Let's go have some dinner."

Dinner was a huge success. R.J. felt totally accepted by Jillian's two friends. Stephen and R.J. hit it off and talked incessantly about nearby fishing spots as both had grown up in the Raleigh area. It turned out they even had some common acquaintances during their college years. Jillian was beaming the entire evening as she watched her friends get to know the man she had fallen totally in love with. She felt like her life was finally going in the right direction once again. After dessert was served, she raised her wine glass and asked the others for their attention.

"I have a couple of things to say, so please listen up," she began. "First, thanks to all three of you for one of the best nights of my life. It fills my heart to see my two oldest and dearest friends enjoying dinner with the man who has brought such happiness and love into my life. I didn't think I could ever be this happy again and it's because of the three of you. I love all of you. Thank you from the bottom of my heart!"

They clinked their glasses together and each had a sip of wine. All four had big smiles on their faces. Jillian set her glass down and looked around the table.

"Next, I have an announcement to make," she continued. "I'm leaving my job in a few weeks. I've decided to try to make a career of writing. I spoke to Dad's partners today at SW&K and we worked out an arrangement that will give me an income for several years. I'm counting on emotional support from all three of you when the rejection letters start coming in."

Kellie and Stephen both began speaking at once. Congratulations and questions were flying faster that Jillian could keep up. She looked at R.J. and he grinned at her as he shrugged his shoulders. She grinned back and felt her heart soar. The love in his eyes was as obvious as the grin on his face.

"OK, you two. Slow down, please," Jillian said over her friends' chatter. "Thank you for the good words. I'm so excited about this I can barely sit still and I appreciate your excitement for me. I don't know exactly what I'm going to write yet, but I'll figure it out. Once my SW&K clients are moved to new associates, then I'll decide how to proceed."

Kellie jumped out of her seat and came around to Jillian. She pulled Jillian to her feet and gave her best friend a giant hug. Tears were streaming down her face.

"Jillie, I'm so, so, so happy for you," she crowed. "I've watched you struggle for the last few years and it broke my heart. You're such a good-hearted person and I thought you didn't deserve so many awful things happening to you. But all that is behind you now and your life is just beginning again. You have an amazing man in your life and a new career of your choice. The sky is the limit and I wish you all the love, happiness, and success you deserve."

When Kellie stepped back, Stephen was standing there. He threw his arms around Jillian in a big bear hug. He smiled when he released her and cleared his throat before trying to speak.

"You're my wife's best friend and you've been a good friend to me for many years," he mumbled, clearly fighting tears. He continued in a loud but hoarse voice. "I wish you the best, you know that. And I'm happy you finally found a man who fishes!"

They all broke out laughing at Stephen's final comment. Before Jillian could sit back down, R.J. was on his feet. He took her hands in his and gazed into her eyes.

"I'm new to this little group, but I can see that you are well loved by these wonderful people," he said seriously. "I'm honored to be a part of such a supportive group of friends. I've spent many years traveling the world and being alone. Since I met you, I realized that I don't want to be alone anymore. I want to be with you. I want a family. I want to be surrounded by people that love me and care about me. I want your future to be our future, Jillian."

Jillian was overcome with tears this time. She looked into R.J.'s eyes and knew he was being totally honest with her. With tears streaming down her face, she nodded her head because she couldn't speak. R.J. enveloped her in a hug that was strong but tender. He held her tightly for a short time and then she pushed back slightly.

"Yes," she whispered. "It's our future, R.J."

At that moment, the waiter appeared with a bottle of champagne and four glasses. He watched as the group of friends sat back down at the table. With great ceremony, he popped the cork and poured champagne in each glass once they were seated.

"Mr. Bartella, the owner of Romeo's, would like for you to commemorate this occasion you are celebrating with some champagne on the house," he announced. "Please enjoy!"

Stephen raised his glass and turned toward the long mahogany bar at the other side of the room. He nodded to Mr. Bartella, who was standing at the end of it. The others did the same and then toasted Jillian's news. Questions were asked and answered, stories were shared, and they all enjoyed the remaining time at the restaurant.

Finally, the other tables were emptying out and the evening was drawing to a close. As R.J. and Stephen argued over the bill, Jillian and Kellie went to the ladies room. They would join the men at the front door when they were finished.

"Oh Jillie, I'm so happy for you! R.J. is amazing and he's obviously head over heels for you," Kellie cried. "And to be able to try your hand at writing is so fantastic! I remember Professor Amsden trying so hard to get you to change your major in college. I know you're going to be famous!"

"Thanks Kell, I really appreciate your support," Jillian beamed. "I don't know about famous, but I'm definitely going to give it a shot."

"Everything's finally going your way, Jillie!" Kellie whooped. "Nothing can stop you now!"

"There is one little fly in the ointment, Kell," Jillian noted. "Victor has been calling and texting me all day. Apparently he's been watching my place and he saw R.J. with me last night."

"But he can't do that, can he? Not with the restraining order in place," Kellie was alarmed.

"He's not supposed to but he is. I met with Detective Oliver today and he's going to track Victor down," Jillian replied. "Victor will be arrested and charged with harassment and stalking. He might go to jail but I really don't know for sure what will happen."

"Well, I can't imagine you will be alone for a minute with R.J. in the picture," Kellie responded. "Are you two still planning a long weekend at his place in Ocean Isle?"

"We sure are! We're leaving Friday morning and coming back Monday," Jillian smiled at the thought. "I can't wait to relax and have time to enjoy some leisurely days with R.J."

"That reminds me," Kellie grinned a wicked grin back at Jillian. "I just read a book that you have to read. It will really spice up your sex life!"

"Oh no, what are you reading now?" Jillian asked with a laugh as she and Kellie left the ladies room. Kellie was always reading books from new or little known authors. She was constantly giving Jillian suggestions on good books she found on Amazon.

"This is kind of different, Jillie. It's a romance novel written by a man!" Kellie advised. "And he wrote two versions of the same book!"

"Written by a man? Really? That's pretty unusual isn't it?" Jillian was curious now.

"The author's name is James Johnson and there is a picture of him on Amazon," Kellie said with excitement. "So, I'm pretty sure a man wrote it. And the book is WOW!"

"Wow? That good?" Jillian laughed at her friend's wide-eyed excitement. "What's so wow about it?"

"He wrote two versions of the same book. One is the regular romance novel without any graphic sex," Kellie continued. "The other is so super hot that I was ready to jump all over Stephen every time I put my Kindle down. I actually read a couple of passages to him and he got all crazy sexy too!"

"Stephen listened while you read a book out loud?" Jillian asked in astonishment. "Now that has to be a first. If it doesn't have pictures of fishing, hunting, or sports, I didn't think Stephen could maintain an interest after the first three or four words!"

"Oh, it held his interest all right," Kellie confided. "He asked me on the way here to read some more to him tonight. That is a first for him, trust me."

"I'm impressed, Kell. That must be some book," Jillian exclaimed. "What's it called?"

"*Primal Impulse* by James Johnson," Kellie replied. "There's the regular romance version and then one called the Xtreme Edition. Definitely get the Xtreme Edition. If you recommend it to your mom, tell her to get the regular version. The Xtreme Edition will probably give her a heart attack."

"I'll get it and keep your advice in mind," Jillian giggled as they went out the front door of the restaurant.

"Keep what advice in mind, beautiful lady?" R.J. asked as the women reached him and Stephen.

"None of your business, mister," Jillian muttered with a smile. "That was woman talk and you'd best learn there are some things I only share with my best girlfriend."

"Get used to it, my man," Stephen said as he rolled his eyes. "These two are always up to something, but they're usually pretty harmless."

Everybody laughed and hugs were given all around. Plans were made to get together the following week and goodbyes were said. As they headed toward their respective cars, Jillian turned back towards Kellie. She called out to her friend to wait up for a minute.

"I almost forgot to tell you," she advised. "I'm keeping my cell phone on silent right now and not answering it until all this other mess is resolved. Tomorrow you can reach me at work, but I guess I'll have to check in with you over the weekend."

"Don't worry, baby," R.J. told her. "Stephen and I exchanged cell phone numbers so we can plan a fishing trip when I get back to Raleigh. He can give my number to Kellie and she can call you anytime she wants."

"Are you sure that's OK?" Jillian felt warm inside knowing that R.J. had accepted Stephen as a friend. "I can always call her."

"Not a problem," R.J. answered before turning to Kellie. "You call anytime you want. I would never try to keep Jillian from her friends. I hope that you, Stephen, and I will be good enough friends that we can call and talk too."

"R.J., you are one special guy," Kellie said as she hugged him for the second time. "You take good care of Jillie and you and I will be good friends too. As for Stephen, go fishing with him once and he will be your friend for life."

"That's going to happen very soon," R.J. replied as he hugged Kellie back. "I'm looking forward to a long friendship with both of you."

Kellie scooted back across the parking lot. As Jillian got in her Jeep, Kellie shouted across the parking lot at her.

"Don't forget to check Amazon!" she yelled.

"I won't, Kell!" Jillian shouted back. "I'll tell you how it goes afterwards!!"

"Check Amazon for what?" R.J. asked as they pulled out of the parking lot.

"So many questions," Jillian stated. "Be patient my love and you will find out. And trust me, you will like it when you do."

CHAPTER 19

The next morning, Jillian woke to find R.J. still sleeping. It was early, so she lay quietly just looking at him. They had known each other for barely two months, but she felt like she had known him forever. She had always felt a little shy with men and Gary had been her only long-term relationship. She wondered if maybe she was moving too fast with R.J., but it felt so right that she banished that thought. The connection she had with him was like nothing else she had ever known. And the love she felt deep inside could not be denied. She was smiling when R.J. opened his eyes.

"Good morning, beautiful," he murmured as he looked up at her. "What's that smile all about?"

"I was just watching you sleep and thinking I must be the luckiest woman in the world," she replied.

"That's funny," he said. "I went to sleep last night thinking I was the luckiest man in the world. I guess we were made for each other."

R.J. then reached for Jillian and began to stroke her naked breast. She sighed at the heat that began to roll through her. A simple touch from this incredible man gave her such pleasure. He rolled onto his side so he was looking directly into her eyes. The intense desire she saw in them caused another surge of heat to envelop her entire body.

Suddenly, he rolled her onto her back and his hands began caressing her all over. He fondled her breasts as his mouth began to graze down her neck. His thumbs rubbed across her nipples, bringing them fully erect. His hands moved down her torso while his tongue kept her nipples hard and sensitive. She groaned softly at the exquisite sensations that were now suffusing her body.

"Oh baby, I love it when you make that noise," he whispered as he raised his head to look at Jillian. "I know it means you're enjoying what I'm doing to you. Don't ever stop telling me how I make you feel. Knowing that I'm giving you pleasure is the biggest turn on for me."

With that said, R.J. took her breast in his mouth as his hands moved even further down Jillian's body. When his left hand reached her pubic hair, she instinctively spread her legs. Her body was demanding that he touch her in the most intimate way. R.J.'s fingers slid between her legs, touching her gently at first, then with more force as her moans grew louder. Once more R.J. lifted his mouth from her breasts to look at Jillian's face. As he looked up, he could see that she was gripping the sheets in her hands as her head fell back. He knew her well enough now to know she was about to orgasm.

"Yeah baby, cum for me," he crooned. "Enjoy the pleasure, cum baby, cum."

Hearing R.J.'s voice sent Jillian over the edge. She moaned louder than before and her pelvis arched up as the first orgasm raged through her body. R.J. kept his fingers on her clit, making circles over and over while Jillian had a second and then a third orgasm. Watching her face as she moaned and arched, he felt his penis swell until it was hard as a rock. He wanted to be inside her, feel her heat and wetness.

But that would wait until he was sure her need was beyond sated. As if she heard his thoughts, Jillian spoke softly in a voice ragged with passion.

"Inside me, oh god, please. I want you inside me right now."

R.J. moved on top of her in a split second. He felt the heat emanating from her body, felt the wetness that was pooled between her legs. He had a brief thought that he might die if he wasn't inside her immediately. He looked down and saw her watching him, her eyes huge and full of desire. In one swift motion, he entered her and knew heaven on Earth. His hips began thrusting with no conscious thought as he was incapable of any thought at that point. All he could do was feel the tight, hot, wetness that was surrounding his throbbing penis. He continued to thrust until he heard Jillian moan loudly. He felt her muscles clench around him as she orgasmed yet again and he was lost. With a growl of all consuming passion, he came. His body rocked hers with a final thrust as he filled her with his hot cum.

They lay spent, R.J. on top of Jillian. Neither could speak for several minutes but it didn't matter. They were both content to simply feel the delicious high of total sexual satisfaction. Finally R.J. rolled onto his back. He reached across and pulled Jillian onto his shoulder, cuddling her against him. He knew then that he wanted this to be a permanent thing. He couldn't imagine a life that didn't include waking up in the morning or going to bed at night without her next to him. He was almost asleep when the alarm went off with a piercing jolt. Jillian reached over to silence it then looked back at R.J.

"Time to rise and shine, my love," she said with a smile that warmed his heart. "We have an exciting, busy day ahead."

"Nothing that happens today will be as exciting as what just happened," he responded quietly.

"There's always tonight," she answered as she ran her hand over his now shrunken penis. "Hmmm, looks like some body parts agree that things might get even more exciting tonight."

Jillian leaned over and ran the tip of her tongue over his penis. It responded with a slight twitch and she smiled. She sat back up and looked at R.J. with such passion his heart was in danger of stopping. Where in the world had this amazing woman been his whole life? All he knew was that he was inordinately happy to have her in his life now. Jillian saw the love in his eyes, a mirror of her own feelings. She touched her fingers to her lips and then put them to his lips.

"You have ten minutes to snooze while I shower," she warned, her eyes taking on a mischievous glint. "After that, it's ice cubes in delicate regions, mister."

"I'm up, I'm up," R.J. declared as he sat up.

An hour and a half later, Jillian and R.J. were at her office. Jillian was gathering the files she thought she might need for the closing at the lawyer's office. She didn't want anything to get in the way of the sale of Big Jake's. R.J. was depending on her to make him a rich man and she was determined to do just that. She didn't trust that little weasel Rick. She was sure if he could somehow cheat R.J. out of some of the money, he would.

R.J. was in the reception area charming Allison with tales of his various photo shoots. She was listening with rapt attention to a story about a celebrity when Jillian came into the room carrying a box of file folders.

"Here, let me take that," R.J. said as he rushed to her side and grabbed the box. "Are you sure we're going to need all of this? It seems like a lot of paper to me."

"I'm not leaving anything to chance when Rick is involved," Jillian responded. "With this, I should be able to answer any questions he might have. I want this to go smoothly at the price we already agreed on."

"For a moment, I forgot who we were dealing with," R.J. quipped with a grin. "That slimy, weasel would gyp his mother out of her Social Security check if he could. So, are you sure this is enough? If we need more files, I can make a second trip to the car."

"We're good, R.J.," Jillian replied with a smile. "Let's get going so we can make you a rich man."

The meeting at the attorney's office went well. As expected, Rick tried to get away with a few things but Jillian had all the documentation necessary to get back on track. After two hours, the sale was completed and R.J. was holding a cashiers check for almost two million dollars. On the way back to Jillian's office, they stopped at the bank and made a deposit. When R.J. came out of the bank he was beaming.

"I never thought I would have that much money sitting in a bank account with my name on it," he commented to Jillian. "It still doesn't seem real to me that I'm in a position to take some time off and work on my book. That's been my dream for at least ten years and now I can actually do it."

"R.J., I'm so happy you finally get to realize your dream," she gushed. "I know how exciting it is to see something you want finally within reach!"

"And I have you to thank for that, beautiful lady," R.J. noted. "Without your advice and hard work, it wouldn't be possible. So how about I take you to lunch before your next big meeting?"

"A quick lunch if you don't mind," Jillian replied. "I need to get set up for my two o'clock meeting with my other client."

"A quickie? Oh I like that thought, so a quickie it is," he said with a leer. "This weekend, however, there will be no quickies. I'll spend a long, long time showing you just how grateful I am. And trust me, I'm very, very grateful."

Jillian laughed as R.J. wiggled his eyebrows but the laugh was quickly stifled when he leaned over and put his lips to hers. He kissed her softly, but the kiss was full of passion and love. She sighed at how good his lips felt and how right this whole relationship felt.

An hour later, they pulled into the parking garage of Jillian's office building. They had decided at lunch that R.J. would come back after meeting with his father's attorney about the estate. He also planned to call his remaining client to see if he had decided on the proposal to let another photographer do the photo shoot scheduled for the next week. Jillian asked him to be back in time to take her to the meeting with Detective Oliver at four-thirty. She felt that R.J. needed to be part of the discussion since he was acting as her protector.

"I'll be right here to pick you up at four-fifteen," he told her as he stopped at the lobby door. "I'll call to let you know I'm out here. Please stay inside until you hear from me, baby. I don't want you to take any chances."

"I won't, my love," Jillian agreed. "Call my office phone like you did before. I have my cell on silent and I'm not answering it."

"That reminds me, I don't have your cell number," R.J. noted. "But I guess it doesn't matter right now anyway."

"Oh that's right," she remembered. "I totally forgot to give it to you with all this craziness. Remind me later and I'll make sure you have it in your phone."

They kissed goodbye and Jillian got out of the car. She was excited to get the Ridell Construction meeting completed.

Finishing that project would signal the beginning of a new chapter in her life too. She knew exactly how R.J. felt about the chance to follow a dream. It was something that didn't happen to most people and she was indebted to Kent and Andrew for giving her that opportunity. Jillian was all smiles when she entered the office.

At three forty-five, Jillian was showing a very happy Pete Ridell and several of his business partners out of the conference room. Her presentation had gone very well and Ridell was now anxious to move forward with her suggestions. Ian, the SW&K associate who specialized in cost cutting measures, had been introduced to the client and had taken part in the meeting. He would take over at this point to implement Jillian's plans for Ridell Construction. He had worked with Jillian as the project had progressed and she knew he would do a good job for the client.

Pete Ridell was a little upset at first that Jillian was going to leave SW&K. She let him know that she would be available to Ian at anytime during the implementation of the project deliverables. She also made sure he understood that Ian would have taken over whether she was there or not. This was Ian's area of expertise and Ridell Construction was in very capable hands.

"Mr. Ridell seems very happy," Allison noted once the elevator doors shut. "I think you made two clients very happy today, Ms. Stanley. Mr. Williams certainly had a lot of good things to say about you."

"He did?" Jillian asked as a blush spread over her freckled cheeks. "Anything you want to share, Allison?"

"Well, we were just talking and he told me what a good job you were doing with Big Jake's," Allison stuttered, wondering if she had said something wrong. "But you know, I think he really likes you. You know, in a romantic kind of way."

"Did he say that?" Jillian wondered if she was in trouble now.

"Oh no! He didn't say anything personal," Allison exclaimed. "It was more the way he looked when he talked about you. Kind of dreamy eyed, if you know what I mean."

"Good….I mean, OK…..ummm, I better get back to my office," Jillian was the one stuttering now. "Any messages for me?"

"Nothing, Ms. Stanley," Allison murmured, trying to hide a smile.

Back in her office, Jillian took a few minutes to look out the window and relax. The trees in the park were beginning to show their beautiful fall colors. The leaves were turning yellow and orange. Soon winter would arrive in Raleigh and Jillian wondered if she would still be there when it did. Maybe this year, instead of cold rain, sleet, and occasional snow, she would spend her winter some place warm and sunny. And maybe R.J. would be there with her.

With that thought bringing a huge smile to her face, Jillian turned back to her computer and began to go through her email. Fifteen minutes later, she shut down her email and began the task of documenting the quirks and special things that applied to each of her clients. She wanted to make the transition to a new SW&K associate as seamless as possible for both the client and the associate.

CHAPTER 20

J illian was deep in thought when her office door suddenly burst open. She looked up in horror as Victor slammed the door shut and locked it. A scream formed in her throat, but died when she saw the maniacal look on his face.

"Well, well, well, you are here," he sneered. "I guess you thought you could fool me by letting your boyfriend take your car. But I'm not that stupid. I've been following you, you little whore. I know he's been driving you around and I know he's gone now because your car is gone. So it's just you and me…..the betrayed man and the slut who caused all his problems."

"Victor, you need to go," Jillian stammered. "I have a restraining order against you and if the police know you're here, they will arrest you."

"I know all about that, whore," he said menacingly. "I know you already talked to them about my phone calls."

"Victor, you need to go." Jillian tried again, but Victor cut her off.

"Shut up, slut! Stop lying to me. I know you called them. They went by my house and harassed my wife trying to find out where I'm staying."

Victor was pacing around the room now. His face was wild with anger and he looked insane to Jillian. She had never seen anyone look so out of control and crazed. And she had never been so afraid of anyone as she was at that moment. She sat silently and let him rage on.

"The bitch called me, yelling and screaming like it was all my fault. She said she went to a lawyer and is filing for divorce. She said she was taking the house and everything in it. The only things I get are my clothes and personal possessions.

"Then she told me she threw all of my clothes and things into the garbage and I needed to pick them up before the garbage men come again. It's your fault, whore! You did this to me. You turned my wife against me, you cost me my job, and now the police are looking for me."

"Victor, please calm down," Jillian whispered, but again Victor cut her off.

"I said SHUT UP SLUT! Are you deaf? Shut up before I do to you what I did to her!"

"Oh Victor, what did you do?" Jillian murmured, filled with fear.

"I fixed the bitch. I fixed her good," he cackled like a fiend. "I went by to get my clothes out of the trash and I fixed her right up. I told her we needed to talk but she wouldn't let me in. The bitch had changed the locks so I showed her who's the boss. I broke down the door and let myself in.

"When she started screaming at me to leave, I shut her up with a good hard punch in the face. She hit the floor like a sack of potatoes, blood pouring out of her stupid mouth. Fucking bitch deserved worse than that so I gave her a couple of good kicks to the ribs. That finally shut her up. And all those precious things of mine she planned to keep, I fixed them too. I broke every piece of furniture, every picture, every dish, every fucking thing in that fucking house. Now she has nothing but fucking crap to keep!"

The phone on Jillian's desk began to ring. That seemed to bring Victor back to the present and he turned to look at her. His face was twisted with a murderous rage so intense she shuddered. He looked at the phone as it stopped ringing and then back at Jillian.

"Don't even think about answering it if it rings again," he threatened. "It's your turn now to get what you deserve. The little whore who fucks men on her balcony will get exactly what she likes."

The phone began to ring again and Jillian knew it was R.J. He must be in the parking garage. She closed her eyes and willed him to come inside looking for her. She also said a silent plea to Allison to call the police. When she looked up again, Victor was standing in front of her desk.

"Stand up, slut," he commanded and Jillian complied. "Now take that prissy shirt off. I want to see your tits."

"Victor, please," she begged. "Don't make this any worse than it already is. Go and I won't tell anyone you were here."

Victor reached across the desk and slapped Jillian across the face. She reeled backward in shock and pain and ended up falling to the floor. In three steps, he was around the desk and had her by the arm. As he dragged her to her feet, he began screaming at her again. His face was next to hers and she could see the veins in his neck popping out.

"I said shut up! Don't even think about speaking to me, you whore! This mess is your fault and you will pay for the pain you caused me. And when I'm done with you here, you're going with me to pay again and again. You're going to do everything I tell you or you'll regret it. The things I did to my bitch wife will seem like child's play compared to what I'm going to do to you."

Victor pushed Jillian onto the desk and ripped her shirt off. He grabbed her breast and viciously squeezed it. She winced in pain but otherwise kept quiet. He reached down to the waistband of her skirt and was preparing to pull her skirt off when he heard a noise at the door. As he looked up, the door flew open, the door-jamb splintering as the lock was forced open.

R.J. bounded into the room, his eyes wide with fear for Jillian. He glanced at her briefly, confirming she was unhurt. Then he looked at Victor. Victor looked back, murder in his eyes.

"So now we have the boyfriend, come to rescue his whore," he sneered again. "Too late, you little pussy. She's going with me. She needs a real man and you aren't up to the job."

Seeing that Victor was distracted by R.J., Jillian jumped off the desk and ran to the far side of the room. She screamed in terror as Victor pulled a switchblade knife from his pocket and flicked it open. He stepped from behind the desk and advanced on R.J. They moved in a macabre dance around the office as Victor repeatedly swiped the knife at R.J. Suddenly Allison appeared in the doorway, grabbing the broken door-jamb as she too screamed in terror.

"I called the police!" she shouted as they heard sirens approaching the building.

Victor took one last swipe at R.J. and fled out the door. Luckily, he had failed to even knick R.J. with the knife. R.J. ran to Jillian and pulled her to him. She was shaking with fear and shock at what had just happened. He turned to look at Allison and began giving orders.

"Go back out to the front desk and show the police where we are," he shouted. "And call an ambulance. I'm afraid Jillian is going into shock and I want the EMTs to check her out. Get the other partners in here so they will know what's going on. Now, go!"

Allison ran out the door just as Kent came flying down the hall. She pointed him to Jillian's office and continued to the reception area. Just as she picked up the phone, four police officers came flying off the elevator. She showed them where to go and told them she was calling for an ambulance. One of the officers used his radio to ask for an ambulance and then told Allison to have everyone else in the office gather in a conference room.

An hour later, Jillian sat in the conference room with R.J., Kent, Andrew, and Detective Oliver. Allison had given a statement to the officers and was back at the reception desk, setting up an empty office for Jillian. Jillian's office was being processed as a crime scene and the officers had said it was off limits to everyone for a day or two.

R.J. had given his statement and was now glued to Jillian's side. Everyone else who had been in the office had been interviewed and sent home. Jillian wore a hospital gown to replace her ripped blouse and had been given a clean bill of health by the EMTs. Her nerves had calmed somewhat, but she had a death grip on R.J.'s hand and would not let go of it.

"Ms. Stanley, are you OK to talk about what happened?" Detective Oliver asked. "I need to get a statement from you."

"I'll be fine. Let's get this over with," Jillian hesitated. "But I need to ask something first."

"Go ahead and ask," the detective replied.

"Did Victor really beat up his wife and trash their house?" Jillian questioned.

"Yes, he did," Detective Oliver responded. "We had a call from her about thirty minutes before your receptionist called 911."

"Is she going to be all right?" Jillian felt somehow responsible for the woman's fate.

"She's bruised and had a bloody nose, but nothing was broken," he answered. "She's filing charges against him too, so I expect he will spend a long time in jail once we find him. Now tell me in your own words what happened."

Jillian quietly related her encounter with Victor, her head down and her fingernails digging into R.J.'s hand. When she reached the part where he had threatened to do worse to her than he had done to his wife, tears began to stream down her face. R.J. put an arm around her and drew her close to him. This raised the eyebrows of Andrew and Kent but they remained quiet. When she finally completed her recitation, she drew a deep breath and looked up at the detective.

"Detective Oliver, do you have any idea at all where to find him?" she asked in a shaky voice.

"To be blunt, Ms. Stanley, we have absolutely no idea right now. He managed to get out of the parking garage before my officers got back downstairs," the detective admitted. "We are interviewing his wife to see if she knows where he has been staying or where he might be hiding now. We have an APB out on him too, but it may take a little time to find him. For your sake, it would be best if you took a few days off work and left town. Is there someplace you can go for the weekend?"

"I'll take her to my place in Ocean Isle Beach," R.J. jumped in before Jillian could speak. "We were planning a long weekend there anyway. We can stay until you have that maniac off the streets. And trust me, I won't let Jillian out of my sight until that happens."

This statement raised the eyebrows of the senior partners of SW&K even further. Jillian looked up and noticed her honorary uncles looking at her. She smiled weakly at them.

"I'll bring you up to speed later, guys," she said. "Let's get through this first, then I'll answer all the questions you have."

Detective Oliver had Jillian sign papers permitting the police department access to all of her cell phone records, including text messages. They agreed that she would leave her cell phone with him also so he could access any more voice mail messages Victor left. The detective took R.J.'s phone number down so he could reach them in Ocean Isle once Victor was in custody. He gave R.J. his business card with his cell phone number on it.

"Ms. Stanley and Mr. Williams, stay vigilant and call me if you notice anything at all out of the ordinary," Detective Oliver advised. "But first call the local police if you see Mr. Henderson or feel threatened in any way. As soon as we have him in custody, I'll call you. There will be more paperwork to fill out when we're ready to make formal complaints against Mr. Henderson."

R.J. stood and removed his hand from Jillian's. He told her he would walk the detective out while she talked to Kent and Andrew. R.J. knew that she needed to explain their relationship and he felt it would go better if he wasn't there. He gave her a smile, a quick kiss on the cheek, and whispered that it was going to be OK. R.J. and Detective Oliver shook hands with Kent and Andrew and left the room.

Jillian looked up at her two honorary uncles and wondered where to begin. She took a deep breath and straightened her back. She would tell them the truth and take her punishment. Before she could speak, however, Andrew spoke up.

"I believe you have an admirer, Jillian," he said with a smile. "You know we have a policy of no personal relationships with our clients."

"I'm so sorry, Uncle Andrew," Jillian began.

"Nothing to be sorry about," Kent chimed in. "Mr. Williams called us earlier this afternoon to tell us what a great job you did for him. He was an extremely happy client."

"Was being the operative word, honey," Andrew continued. "After he sang your praises, he fired us. We still have Big Jake's as our client but not R.J. Williams III."

"And after he fired us, he told us he intends to pursue a romantic relationship with you," Kent finished. "He wanted our permission as your honorary uncles."

Jillian looked at both of them in surprise. A huge smile lit up her face as they looked back at her with love. She was so taken aback by this turn of events that she didn't know what to say.

"Of course we told him if he does anything to hurt you, he's going to be in the biggest trouble of his life," Andrew interjected. "If he's anything like his father, and we think he is, we couldn't ask for a better man to look out for you while you're working on your new career."

Jumping from her seat, Jillian flew into the waiting arms of her two uncles. Even with all the drama Victor was bringing into their lives, she still felt like the luckiest woman in the world. She hugged them with all her strength and then stepped back.

"I'm so sorry to bring all this craziness into the office," she began. "I never thought Victor would go off the deep end because I rejected him."

"Jillian, honey, don't beat yourself up," Kent declared. "The man is not stable. You are absolutely not responsible for him or what he did. I don't even want to think of the hell he would have put you through if you were with him. You did exactly the right thing."

"When we spoke to the detective, he said something about some evidence they have that this person is into drugs,"

Andrew related. "Hell doesn't even come close to describing what he would have put you through."

"Thank you again, Uncle Kent and Uncle Andrew," Jillian said as tears threatened. "I don't know what I would do without you two and I don't want to ever find out. If you ever need anything, I owe both of you big time."

"There are two things you need to do for us right now" Kent advised. "First, call your mother and tell her what's going on. I'll be telling Mindy when I get home and your mother will be livid if she finds out from Mindy instead of you. Make sure she has R.J.'s phone number so she can reach you if she needs to.

"While you're gone, we will get a new phone with a new phone number for you. Second, go home, pack some clothes, and go to Ocean Isle with R.J. That man obviously has some very deep feelings for you and, unless I'm mistaken, you reciprocate those feelings."

"Uncle Kent, my mother will be the first call I make," Jillian cried. "And yes, I do have some strong feelings for R.J. It wasn't something I planned to happen but it isn't something I can ignore either."

"Jillian, when you were born, we promised your father that we would look after you if anything ever happened to him," Andrew said quietly. "We take that responsibility very seriously. We want you to be happy and we have a gut feeling that R.J. is just the man to make you happy. His father was one of the best men we have ever known....honest, trustworthy, and loyal to his family and friends. R.J. was raised in that atmosphere and, unless my instincts are totally wrong, he's almost a clone of his father."

"Thank you both again for everything!" Jillian murmured as she hugged each of her uncles in turn. "I'll let you know when I hear from Detective Oliver that Victor is in custody.

And then I'll be back to ensure the transition of my clients goes smoothly."

"Good!" Kent beamed at her. "Now get out of here. Don't keep that fine young man waiting any longer."

Jillian left the conference room and found R.J. in the reception area regaling Allison with more tales of his photo shoots. This time it was a different celebrity who hired him to take pictures of her dogs. When he saw Jillian emerge from the conference room, his heart soared. She was smiling and, even with a bruise on her face and wearing a hospital gown, she looked more beautiful than she ever had. Jillian walked over to him, took him by the hand, and led him to the office Allison has so efficiently set up for her. While Jillian was with the detective, Allison had obtained her purse and jacket from the crime scene techs who were processing the evidence of Victor's rampage. She had placed them in the temporary office for Jillian.

When she closed the door, Jillian fell into R.J.'s waiting arms. In his strong embrace, she felt safe, secure, and deeply loved. After a moment, she looked up at him and saw the love shining in his eyes. He stared into her eyes and then kissed her. When she winced slightly, he broke the kiss to make sure she was all right.

"It's OK, my love," she said in reply to the question in his eyes. "Just a little tender where Victor slapped me."

"If I ever get the chance, that pig will know what it feels like to be slapped, too," R.J. growled with anger. "To raise a hand to a woman is the lowest a man can get."

"Don't let him ruin this moment, love," Jillian whispered. "He's not going to control my life. And he's not going have any part in our life together. Now kiss me again."

This time, R.J. kissed her with such passion she felt dizzy. He held her tightly against him, his tongue dancing with hers until they both were consumed by the passion. When they finally broke apart, she looked up at him and chuckled.

"Now you think my kisses are funny?" he asked in confusion. "You are the most perplexing woman I know."

"No, I don't think your kisses are funny," she replied as she placed another kiss on his lips. "I think you're funny."

"May I ask why?" R.J. couldn't quite grasp where this conversation was going.

"I hear you fired Stanley, Wilson, and Krenshaw this afternoon," Jillian revealed.

"Oh, well, yeah, I did," he agreed sheepishly. "But why is that funny?"

"Because after you fired me, I hear you asked for permission to date me," she chuckled louder this time. "That was a stroke of genius. Getting Kent and Andrew on your side today of all days."

"To be fair, I had no idea what was going to transpire this afternoon," R.J. admitted. "I was actually thinking that if I asked now, then we could make our relationship known to them later. However, I guess that didn't work out as planned since they obviously know there's something between us already. Are you in trouble?"

"Not at all!" Jillian declared. "I think they know that we've been seeing each other but they never said a word. They were both very impressed with the fact that you fired the firm first and then asked for permission to pursue me. It's all good, my love."

"I'm glad, baby. Wait a minute!" R.J. cried as he stepped back from her slightly. "I just realized you called me a genius! I'm glad you finally realize who you're dealing with."

"Um no, I think I said it was a stroke of genius," she giggled. "But since you rescued me from Victor and from trouble with Kent and Andrew, I won't argue the point."

"So what now? Are you ready to head to my house?" he asked.

"Let me call my mother and tell her what happened. I need to give her your phone number in case she needs to reach me," Jillian said. "And I'd better call Kellie too. If I don't, I'll never hear the end of it."

"When you're done, we can drop by your condo and pack a bag," R.J. decided. "Then we'll take off for Ocean Isle. It will be late when we get there, but I don't want you to be anywhere near Raleigh for a long time."

Jillian called her mother, explained what had happened that afternoon, and told her about R.J. Barbara was worried about her daughter, but that was tempered by her excitement over the relationship with R.J. Jillian provided R.J.'s phone number and agreed to check in with her mom every day until the Victor situation was resolved. She also made plans to go and see her mom once she finished up at SW&K.

The next call was to Kellie. Jillian did her best to make it brief and promised to call in a day or so for a longer conversation. She gave Kellie R.J.'s phone number too, even though Stephen already had it. Kellie agreed to tell Stephen that the fishing trip was postponed until Jillian and R.J. could return to Raleigh.

With the most important people notified, Jillian put down the phone and looked at R.J. Her heart swelled until she was sure it would explode with love. She was very thankful that he wasn't running from her due to Victor. She wouldn't blame him if he did, but he showed no inclination that he had any plans to abandon ship. If they could survive this, they could survive anything.

"Ready, love?" she asked.

R.J. looked directly into her eyes. His eyes transmitted all the love and caring his heart was feeling. She could see his soul and it was a mirror of hers.

"I've never been more ready for anything in my entire life," was his simple but deep reply.

CHAPTER 21

It was almost eleven o'clock when they crossed the causeway into Ocean Isle Beach. It had been a long, exciting, and stressful day for both of them. They had gone to Jillian's condo so she could pack a small suitcase for the trip. She seemed to be having trouble deciding what to take. R.J. was sure it was due to the shock she had suffered at Victor's hands. He finally told her gently not to worry about it. If she needed something else, he would take her to Shallotte and buy it. Her gratitude at not having to make any more decisions showed all over her face.

On the drive down, Jillian had alternated between constant chatter and periods of napping. Again, R.J. felt shock had her mind going in a thousand directions. He let her chatter when she wanted to and sleep when she could no longer talk. She was worried about being followed, but R.J. had carefully watched the road behind them until he was certain they were alone. They stopped once to have a quick dinner and once for a bathroom break. Each time, R.J. scanned the parking lot for cars that might belong to Victor. Each time, he saw nothing out of the ordinary. Convinced that Victor did not know they had left town, he finally relaxed slightly.

When they came over the causeway, the moon glowed bright on the calm surface of the ocean. R.J. turned to say something to Jillian, but saw she was once again asleep. His love for her surfaced and threatened to smother him with its intensity. He would give up his life for this incredible woman. Having come close to losing her today, he realized that he couldn't live without her in his life. He wanted to ask her to marry him at that moment, but knew he needed to give her time to recover. More stress was not what she needed right now.

R.J. turned left at the end of the causeway onto East 2nd Street. He followed it almost to the end, made a left onto Shallotte Boulevard, then a right on East 4th Street. Just before the street ended at a concrete barrier, there was a small dirt road with a gate. He opened the gate with a remote and drove slowly down the one lane, private road. At the end of the road was R.J.'s own personal piece of heaven.

Six years earlier, R.J. had decided he needed an escape from the crowded, crazy world of New York City. With his business booming, he had plenty of money for both a New York studio and a place of refuge at the beach. He searched for almost a year before he found this piece of land at the far eastern end of the island of Ocean Isle. There was space for a small house and it came with a private beach. He had spent another year having a house built to his specification, hoping one day to find someone to share it with. Now he thought maybe that person had finally arrived in his life.

As they pulled up to the house, Jillian woke feeling somewhat disoriented. She made a small noise of discomfort. R.J. was immediately aware that she was awake and confused. He touched her hand and leaned over to kiss her cheek.

"It's all right, baby," he whispered to her. "We're at my house now. Let's go in and get some sleep."

"I'm sorry, R.J.," she replied. "I guess I was confused by where we are. My mind is still going in circles."

"Don't worry about it," he said lovingly. "I'll get the bags and then you can follow me up the path to the house. It's dark out here but there are motion sensor lights all along the road and around the house. See, the road we just came up is all lit up. The lights came on when we drove up the road. As soon as I get out of the car, another one will activate on this side of the house."

"Do you think Victor will find me here?" Jillian's fear had surfaced again.

"Not a chance, baby. I watched the road behind us all the way down. And each time we stopped, I watched for a car to pull out behind us," R.J. revealed. "He's hiding from the police now. He won't be able to find us. He won't bother us anymore, baby. You're totally safe here."

They stepped out of the Jeep and a light on the side of the house immediately lit up the parking area. Even in the semi-darkness, Jillian could see weathered gray siding and a huge front porch that had a direct ocean view. It looked like there was even a deck off the second floor room that also faced the ocean. As tired and spent as she was, she immediately felt at home here.

They entered through a side door and once inside, R.J. turned the lights on and locked the door. He pointed out where the kitchen was and the front door to the big porch Jillian had seen from outside. She would explore the house and the beach in the morning. Tonight she was simply too tired to care.

Sensing her need to feel safe and let her mind relax, R.J. decided sleep was the best thing for both of them. He took their bags upstairs to the master bedroom. Jillian followed in his wake, not wanting to be apart from him for even a minute.

When he flipped the light switch in the bedroom, Jillian was mesmerized. The room was huge and beautifully decorated with a king sized canopy bed and local art. The floor-to-ceiling windows looking out on the beach were the main attraction. Through the windows she saw the deck that she had noticed from outside. The magnificent view of the moon glowing in the sky and its rippling reflection on the water was astounding.

While R.J. unpacked his bag and set hers up on an ottoman, Jillian stood at the windows and reveled in the beauty of the ocean at night. She felt her muscles begin to relax and her mind begin to slow down. R.J. went into the master bath and soon she heard water running. Next she heard him pad up softly behind her. His arms went around her and he held her tight against him. He whispered into her ear.

"The bath is filling for you, baby," he said. "You go slip in and let the warm water and jets relax you. I'm going downstairs to pour you some wine. I'll be back in just a few minutes."

Jillian turned and put her arms around his neck. She kissed him then, her lips gently pressing to his. She felt the electricity crackle between them and knew he did too. He broke the kiss but not the embrace. R.J. held her in his arms in the moonlight, their bodies as close as possible for several long minutes. Finally, he stepped back and gave her a small peck on the lips.

"Go get into the bath before the tub overflows," R.J. told her. "I need to do a few things downstairs and then lock up for the night. I'll be back with wine by the time you're ready to get out."

True to his word, R.J. entered the bedroom just as Jillian came out of the bathroom wrapped in a towel. He stopped for a second, her beauty and the intense love he felt took his breath away. Then he motioned towards the deck as he crossed the room. He was carrying a glass of Chateau wine for her and a Lagunitas beer for himself.

"Let's sit out there with our drinks," he suggested. "It's a beautiful, clear night and this far down the island you can see all the stars. Oh, grab that blanket off the end of the bed and wrap it around you so you don't get cold."

Jillian did as instructed and followed R.J. out onto the balcony. She sat in an Adirondack chair with soft, comfy cushions. R.J. sat in a similar chair that he moved right next to her. He handed her the glass of wine and looked at her eyes as they glowed in the moonlight.

"To us, Jillian, and our future," he said softly. "The past is the past and it will remain there. The future is unknown, but we can make it our future, a future that is exactly what you and I want."

Jillian was touched that this was R.J.'s way of telling her that her past with Victor didn't matter to him. Her love for him deepened, knowing that he understood her so well. She felt her heart swell at the thought of a future with R.J.

"To us," she replied as she touched her glass to his. "And to our future together, my love."

They sat quietly, R.J. reaching across to take her hand in his. They let the glow of the moon on the water and the twinkling of the stars soothe away the stresses of the day. When their glasses were empty, R.J. stood and took Jillian by the hand. Her eyes were beginning to droop as the last of the adrenaline drained from her body.

"Come, baby," he murmured as he gently pulled her to her feet. "Let's get you to bed."

R.J. helped Jillian into the king sized bed and climbed in after her. He pulled her close and cradled her head on his shoulder. He breathed in the seductive scent of her hair and skin. He wanted to caress her, kiss her, and make slow, passionate love to her. But he knew what she needed right now was to feel safe and to sleep.

"Go to sleep, sweetheart. Tomorrow is a new day, one that we will enjoy to the fullest," he whispered as he kissed the top of her head.

Jillian felt calm and safe. Nestled in R.J.'s arms, she was finally able to relax and let go of the horror Victor had rained down on them. She breathed in R.J.'s scent, her heart quickening its pace for a few seconds. However, the toll the day had taken was too much and her eyes closed.

In minutes, R.J. felt Jillian's body completely relax and her breathing became slow and steady. He knew she was deeply asleep and he was glad she had been able to let go. He held her close throughout the night. He didn't want her to be disoriented or scared should she wake.

Several times, he heard her make sounds of fear and she thrashed about. Each time, he spoke to her in a low voice, assuring her he was there. And each time, she quieted down and went back to sleep. It broke his heart because he knew her mind was reliving the incident in her office, but he also knew he was doing the only thing he could do……be there for her.

The next morning, R.J. woke to the sun streaming brilliantly into the bedroom. By the angle, he could tell it was late morning and he was surprised that he had slept so long. He rolled over and reached for Jillian but she wasn't there. He panicked for a moment, afraid that Victor might have found them. Then he calmed down, knowing there no way Victor could know where Jillian had gone.

R.J. rose from the bed and made his way to the bathroom. After brushing his teeth, he slipped on an old pair of jeans, a well-worn t-shirt, and the requisite flip-flops that were always by the bedroom door. As he made his way down the stairs, he realized Jillian had already been up for a while. He could hear coffee dripping into the carafe on the kitchen counter and saw the tea-kettle sitting on the stove. He poured a cup of coffee and went to the sliding glass doors.

His heart skipped a beat when he saw Jillian sitting in one of the two rocking chairs that had been hand-made for his front porch. He had paid a huge sum of money to have the teak rockers made to fit that exact spot on his porch so he could be comfortable watching both the sun and the moon rise over the ocean. Jillian looked like she belonged there. She was the picture he had always had in his mind when he imagined a life partner sitting there with him. He opened the sliding door and walked out to join her.

"Good morning, my love." She smiled warmly up at him as he came towards her. "Did you sleep well?"

"Good morning, beautiful," R.J. returned as he bent to kiss her. "I must have slept really well considering the late hour."

He gently placed his lips on hers as she reached up to cup his face. The kiss was full of passion and love. Jillian sighed as he straightened up.

"That was nice. Really, really nice," she said simply.

"Have you been up long, baby?" R.J. asked as he held up his coffee cup. "I found the coffee. Thank you."

"A couple of hours, I guess," Jillian responded. "And you're welcome for the coffee. I was restless all night and I know I kept you awake. I wanted you to sleep for a while so I've just been sitting out here. It's so beautiful, R.J. I don't know how you can stand to leave here for your trips all over the world."

"It's difficult sometimes," he conceded as he sat in the rocker next to her. "But up until yesterday, I had to work so I could keep this place. Now that I have all that money, I may never want to leave."

"I'm sorry about last night," she said softly, her eyes downcast.

"Sorry for what, baby?" R.J. asked, confused by her statement.

"I feel asleep before we could.....well, you know," Jillian murmured. "We've never spent a night together just sleeping."

R.J. sat his coffee cup on the teak table beside his rocker and rose to his feet. He stood in front of Jillian and then got down on his knees. She had her head down so he put one hand under her chin and raised her head. When she was looking directly into his eyes, he spoke quietly but forcefully.

"Jillian, I know our relationship started out in kind of a sexual frenzy but I want you to understand something. As much as I enjoy the sexual part of the relationship, as good as that is, it isn't the only thing we have between us. I feel a connection to you, a connection between our hearts, a connection that I have never, ever felt before. There will be more nights in our future with incredible sex. There will also be more nights in our future that we don't have sex. Either way, I'm still going to be here and be part of your life for as long as you want me to be."

"Oh, R.J.," Jillian cried, tears in her eyes. "You're such a special, wonderful man. Thank you for understanding what I needed last night."

"Baby, you needed sleep more than anything else in this world," R.J. stated confidently as he stood in front of her.

"No, my love, you're wrong," Jillian contradicted him.

"Yes, you needed...," he began but Jillian cut in.

"No, you're wrong," she argued, looking up at him. "I didn't need sleep. I needed to feel safe and loved more than anything else in this world. And that is exactly what you gave me last night. You took care of me, calmed me down, held me all night, and soothed me when the bad dreams came. I will never forget that, R.J. Never!"

Jillian stood then and faced him. She put her arms around his neck and kissed him with more passion than she knew was possible. His arms went around her waist and he held her tight against his body. He could feel her heart beating against his chest. At that moment, he knew…..he knew with all his heart that he and Jillian belonged together forever. And he knew that he had to tell her that he loved her. He had to let her know exactly how important she was to him.

"I was going to make breakfast," Jillian said when they finally let go of each other. "However, there isn't much in there to cook."

"I guess a trip to Shallotte is the first order of business today," R.J. laughed. "I always seem to leave my pantry bare when I go away. How about I take you out to breakfast? I know a good little place just as you go into Shallotte. Omelets to die for, pancakes that melt in your mouth, and bacon that's so fresh you can hear it oink!"

"Except for the oinking part, it sounds amazing," Jillian giggled. "Let me get dressed and then you can feed me. My stomach and I will be ever so grateful."

"How grateful?" he asked with a leer. "When we get back, you're going to have to make good on that statement and show me exactly how grateful you are."

"Don't worry, sexy man, I'll make good on it," she replied smacking him lightly on the chest. "Now get out of my way and let me put on some clothes before I get cranky from hunger."

CHAPTER 22

They made their way to Shallotte for breakfast and a trip to the grocery store. A side trip to the fish market netted some fresh scallops and shrimp that R.J. promised to cook on the grill. A few hours later, they were back at the beach house, putting the food away and planning a cookout for dinner.

"How about we take a walk on my private beach?" R.J. asked when they had everything put away. "It's so sunny and warm for the end of October that I hate to spend the day inside."

"That's perfect!" Jillian exclaimed. "I love being by the water. Just sitting on the porch this morning was so calming. If I can put my toes in the water, I'll be the happiest woman on the planet."

R.J. quickly put some water and snacks in a beach bag he pulled from the pantry. As they went out, he stopped and opened a closet built at the end of the porch. From the closet, he retrieved two canvas chairs folded into their canvas storage bags. He put the carry straps over his shoulder and turned to Jillian.

"Are you ready for a walk and then some time to put your feet in the water?" he asked as a big smile crept over his face.

"You are unbelievable," she said with a grin. "It's like you had this place built to your personal specifications. A special bag in the kitchen for beach items and now, a special place outside for beach chairs. I think I saw some rafts and umbrellas in there too."

"Yes, I did and, yes, you did," he replied. "I had the house built exactly how I wanted it. It took a year to complete, but it's what I want when I need to get away from New York. The outside closet has everything I need for going down to the beach. There's an outside shower next to that closet and another one by the side door so you don't drag sand into the house. The kitchen pantry has a place for my beach bag and shelves to hold anything I might want to take to the beach. I'm all about comfort and easy days when I'm here."

"It's an amazing house, my love," Jillian commented. "The way it's sitting on the lot, the sunrise is spectacular. You captured the perfect angle. I love the floor to ceiling windows on both floors. When I woke up this morning and saw the sun coming up, it felt like a fabulous show was being performed just for me."

"I worked with the architect very closely to capture that exact feeling," R.J. advised. "Luckily, I was able to find someone who understood my vision and what I wanted to accomplish. I love this house and have been looking for someone to share it with. I think you just might be that person."

"I just might be," Jillian smiled at him as her heart soared.

By this time, they had made their way down the path that wound through the sand dunes. A wide stretch of beach spread out in front of them. Jillian stopped dead as she took in the view. Off to the right, there was several hundred feet of beach and then water. Off to the left there was even more white, sandy beach. It looked like the beach ended at the intra-coastal waterway. There were no other houses in view, just beach, sand dunes, and water.

"Is this all yours too?" she asked incredulously. "This whole beach?"

"All mine," R.J. responded. "I own the tip of the island that extends out on the east side. The public beach is across the water on your right. Luckily the water is wide enough and deep enough that most people don't try to cross over. Those few that do, run up against a fence that you can't really see from here. The fence goes all the way around the property. It has huge signs all over it. On the other side, there's the intra-coastal. It's too shallow on that side for most boats. I've had an occasional kayaker pull up but again, I have private property and no trespassing signs posted. There are motion sensor flood lights all along the way too so anyone who might try to come in at night will get a big surprise."

"Paradise," Jillian murmured in awe.

"My own little piece of paradise," R.J. acknowledged. "And your paradise now too, baby."

They set up the beach chairs and then took a slow walk from one end of the beach to the other. Jillian was impressed with the way R.J. had made his home secure without disturbing the beauty of the area. The security features totally blended in with their surroundings. She felt her concern that Victor might disturb them slip completely away. When they came back to the chairs, she suddenly remembered something R.J. had told her that first night.

"The night I saw you at the tiki bar, didn't you tell me you lived close to there?" she questioned. "And didn't you tell me you walked to the bar?"

"I told you I walked to the bar, but I didn't say anything about where I lived," he replied. "I tend to keep that a secret most of the time. And I did walk that night. It's not far, just over a mile, so if I know I'll be having a few drinks, I walk. A DUI arrest is the last thing I want."

"You're right," Jillian was thoughtful for a moment. "You didn't even say that you lived here, just that you walked to the bar. I guess I assumed you were staying somewhere near the bar."

"Jillian, I knew you were special from the moment I laid eyes on you," R.J. said very seriously as he turned to look directly at her. "I have never and will never lie to you. I'm all about honesty in a relationship. I was in a relationship once and discovered most of what I thought I knew about her wasn't true. She had lied to me from the very beginning. After that experience, I cannot tolerate even small lies. I can deal with whatever the truth is, but a lie shatters all trust for me. And I hold myself to the same standard. I don't lie to the person I'm with."

"My love, I completely understand where you're coming from," she responded. "After my experience with Victor, I want only truth. Lies make the entire relationship ugly and sordid. There will be no lies between us. That I can promise you."

The rest of the day passed in serenity and quiet companionship. They sat on the beach, enjoying the ever-changing sights of the ocean and intra-coastal waterway. Small boats went past, seagulls swooped and cried looking for a snack, and the fall air bathed them in refreshing energy. They chatted about growing up in Raleigh, their childhoods, and their college experiences. As the daylight began to wane, they decided to return to the house for their seafood feast.

R.J. manned the grill that was on a concrete patio next to the side door. He grilled fresh asparagus and small red potatoes along with the shrimp and scallops. Jillian decided that dinner at the table on the far end of the front porch would be perfect. Even though they couldn't see the sunset, the sky over the ocean was turning pink and orange. It was too beautiful to miss out on.

Jillian busied herself in the kitchen, finding dishes, silverware, wine glasses, and candles. She hesitated over what wine to choose for dinner. He seemed to have a well-stocked wine cooler in the kitchen. She decided to see if he had a preference and opened the side door.

"I'm getting ready to set the table out here for dinner," she said. "Do you want wine or beer with dinner?"

"I forgot to tell you that we're having a special wine tonight." was his reply. "Look in the wine cooler for Chateau Kiss. I know they say white wine with fish, but I refuse to follow that rule. I know you love Chateau wines and this is one that will melt you. It's probably the best wine I've ever had."

"I was looking in there earlier and you have so many different wines!" Jillian exclaimed. "I love trying new ones from different vintners and this one sounds perfect."

"You're going to like it, baby," R.J. promised.

"If it's a Chateau and you're recommending it, I know I will," Jillian laughed as she started to go back inside. "I'll pull one of those bottles out now and open it so it can breathe for a few minutes while you finish grilling."

When R.J. came in with a platter full of grilled food, Jillian took it from him and motioned for him to follow her out to the porch. The table was set with candles, wine, and the pretty dishes she had discovered in the kitchen cabinets. She placed the platter in the center and turned to R.J.

"Thank you for a wonderful day, my love," she spoke softly as she gazed into his eyes. "This place is like a dream come true. I haven't felt so relaxed and at peace in a very long time. I love it here. It feels like home and I can see why you spent so long getting it just right."

"I loved this plot of land the minute I laid eyes on it," he too spoke softly. "It's been my haven for five years. Today, for the very first time, I felt truly and totally at home. Having you here has made me realize that. As much as I love this place, it wasn't home until you arrived."

R.J. took Jillian into his arms and held her for a long minute. He felt her heart beating against his chest and sighed in contentment. He lifted his head and looked at her, eyes brimming with love. Their lips touched and the spark between them roared into a fire. The fire not only consumed their bodies, it also consumed their hearts. Neither of them had ever experienced a passion so deep and so true. The kiss was slow and sensual with a hint that it could explode at any moment. But at that moment, the feeling of love was what each wanted. The explosion would happen later.

When they finally broke their embrace, R.J. and Jillian sat down to enjoy their dinner. As they ate and talked, the sky went from warm sunset hues to total darkness. The stars made a brilliant appearance and then the moon began its ascent, seeming to rise up out of the ocean. There was no wind and the ocean's surface shone like glass. The silver sparkle of the moon was reflected on the water in a long trail that went from the far horizon right up to the edge of the beach. Jillian and R.J. watched this display of nature's grandeur from the porch, sipping the last of the wine. They finally cleared the table and made their way upstairs. With the curtains wide open to let the moonlight shine in, their desire for each exploded into a raw passion that filled the night. When their desire was totally sated, they held each other as they slept.

The next day, Saturday, also passed in a relaxed, time-altered state. After calling her mother and Kellie, Jillian sat on the beach and then on the porch, lost in thought most of the time. R.J. puttered around the house, organizing his studio space and doing minor repairs here and there. He kept a close eye on Jillian, worried she might still be suffering from her close call, but she seemed at peace. As evening approached, he found her once again on the front porch, looking out to the sea.

"A penny for your thoughts, beautiful angel," he said, sitting down beside her in the teak rocker.

"Hi there, handsome," she replied, smiling at him. "I've been thinking most of the day about what I want to do once I leave SW&K. As much as I love to write, I honestly don't know how to begin a career in writing. Should I start with magazine articles or short stories or a book? It's kind of overwhelming."

"I have an idea that might interest you," R.J. began thoughtfully. "While I was working in my studio today, I was sorting through the photos I took the weekend we first met. I haven't really had time to do anything with them until now. I started thinking again about the book I want to do.

"I have two challenges with it. First, I have so many photos, it's going to be hard to narrow down what I want to include. It's doable, but it will take some serious focus and some time. The second challenge is that I'm a photographer, not a writer. I can barely write a check. An entire book is completely out of reach for me. I've been thinking for a while now that I'm going to need a collaborator to help me with the book. I'm going to need someone who knows how to write and writes well. Someone like you Jillian."

"What are you saying, R.J.?" Jillian's heart had almost stopped as she realized what he was asking.

"I'm saying I want you to collaborate on this book with me. I'll do the photos and you can do the writing," he answered. "We can decide together about the format. I can tell you about the circumstances surrounding the photos I decide to use, and you can write the stories to go with them. Both of our names will be on the cover, we will both take credit for it, and if it's a success, we split the royalties fifty-fifty. What do you think?"

Jillian stared at him, speechless. Her mind was processing the implications of her first book done in collaboration with a well-known photographer. People would buy his book just to see his photographs and they would see her name too. This was an incredible opportunity for a brand new author, an opportunity she could not pass up. R.J. mistook her silence as an awkward moment of deciding how to say "no thank you."

"Look, baby, if you're not interested, it's all right," he stammered, feeling embarrassed. "I totally understand if this isn't the kind of book you want to write. It was just an idea. Really, it's….."

"R.J., stop," Jillian cut in. "I'm so surprised that I had to let it sink in for a minute. I think it's a fantastic idea and I would love to do it!"

"Really? Are you sure?" R.J. asked, his face lighting up like a lighthouse beacon.

"I'm absolutely sure, but only under one condition," she replied. "You have to look me in the eye and tell me you think I'm the right person for this. I have to know this is because you think I can do a good job for you. I don't want you to let me do the book because you feel sorry for me."

"I know you can do a good job, Jillian," R.J. said looking straight into her eyes. "I first had this idea when you told me you wrote for your college newspaper. So I did some research after that and I found some of the articles you wrote in the paper's online archives. I even spoke to your former professor. Your professor was right, baby. You're immensely talented. I think together we can do an incredible book. No, that's not right. I KNOW we can do an incredible book together."

Jillian jumped up and pulled R.J. to his feet. She put her arms around him and kissed him so hard he almost fell backwards. Then she let go of him and twirled around the porch. She was happier than she could ever remember being.

"R.J. you have made me the happiest woman on this planet," she exclaimed. "Let's do a big, fat, beautiful book together!"

"Great!" he shouted as he danced around the porch with her. "Let's do a book!"

After dinner, they decided to sit on the balcony outside the master bedroom. Jillian was having a glass of wine and R.J. a beer before retiring for the night. The moon was huge and luminous once again. It was casting a radiant glow on everything as it made its way across the sky. R.J. and Jillian talked quietly about the book, throwing out ideas for the format of both the pictures and the stories they told. They found that they worked well together. They became more and more excited about the book as the time passed. Both were anxious to get started now that the ideas were flowing.

"I haven't heard back from my client yet, so tomorrow I'm going to call and confirm he will let my buddy Sherman do the shoot," R.J. decided. "That way I can clean out my dad's house while you finish up with your clients. When we're both free of those commitments, we can start on the book. I would like it if you would stay here while we work on it. The collaboration will be so much easier if we're together."

"Sounds like a good plan, but are you sure you want me to stay here?" Jillian asked. "This is your house and I don't want to intrude on your space. I could get a place somewhere close by. The tourist season is over and there are hundreds of empty places up and down the beach."

"Jillian, I want you here with me," R.J. said, his tone becoming very serious. "I want you here while we work on the book and I want you here once the book is finished. Baby, this is my clumsy way of asking you to move in with me. Please move in with me Jillian, now and forever."

Jillian was watching R.J.'s eyes as they reflected the moonlight twinkling across the balcony. She saw love and hope for their future in them. And she knew he saw the same thing in her eyes. They stared into each other's eyes for several long moments. Finally, R.J. took a deep breath and spoke.

"Jillian Stanley, I love you," he murmured softly. "I love you with all my heart and soul."

"R.J. Williams, I love you too," she murmured in return. "I love you with all my heart and soul."

R.J. rose to his feet and took her by the hand. He led her to the balcony railing and turned to look at her again. He spoke quietly and directly from his heart.

"I love this place. The sunrises, the beach, the ocean, and the moon shining over the water pull me back here again and again. It's been my own little piece of heaven for five years. Now it's our piece of heaven, yours and mine.

"The minute you walked through the door, I knew this house had been waiting for you. I knew I built this house not for me, but for us. This home will be our refuge from the world, our calm oasis in the midst of chaos. Please say you will live here with me."

"Yes, my love," Jillian responded to his plea. "When I woke up yesterday morning and walked through these rooms, I felt the love you put into building this house. I felt you in every single room, felt your calm spirit, your caring heart, your deep passion. And for the first time since I left my parents house, I felt at home. Wonderfully, truly at home. So, yes, I will be so happy to live here with you."

R.J. kissed Jillian standing on the balcony in the moonlight. It was a long, slow, sweet kiss that sealed their love for each other. It was followed by a long night of slow, sweet, passionate lovemaking. They feel asleep holding each other, words of love lingering in the air.

CHAPTER 23

Jillian took a canvas chair and her Kindle down to the beach after breakfast Sunday morning. She had downloaded *Primal Impulse Xtreme Edition*, the book Kellie had suggested. She was intrigued by the idea of a romance novel written by a man. R.J. was opening new worlds for her when it came to sex and she wanted to return that favor. She thought this book might give her some good ideas so she could surprise him that night.

Jillian was totally entranced by the story of deep emotion and explosive sex. It was exactly as Kellie had said....WOW! The more she read, the more she wanted to go back to the house and drag R.J. straight to the bedroom. She was reading a particularly arousing chapter when she heard a noise. She looked up and saw R.J. coming down the path through the dunes. He had stayed behind to wait on a call back from his client and to take care of some other business matters.

"Hey, sexy man," she said, imagining him naked on the beach as he plopped down on the sand in front of her. "What's up?"

"I have good news and I have bad news," he replied. "What do you want first?"

"Oh, well, let's get the bad news out of the way," Jillian decided, her sensuous bubble bursting.

"My client won't let me out of my contract," R.J. exclaimed. "I tried and tried but he is adamant that I do the photo shoot. If I breach the contract, he threatened to sue me for a million dollars. I have to leave tomorrow night so I can be in Texas first thing Tuesday morning."

"R.J., that's all right," she cried. "You go, do the shoot, and honor your contract. It will put our plans on hold for just a short time. You said it would take less than two weeks. Plus, I need to get back to work anyway and get my clients transitioned. I'll call Detective Oliver and see whether they have any leads about Victor."

Jillian shivered involuntarily when she said Victor's name. She could still see the maniacal rage in his eyes as he ripped off her blouse. R.J. saw her shiver and moved closer to her. He hated that this obviously insane man was still causing Jillian pain. He put a hand on her knee and spoke again.

"Now for the good news, baby," he said smiling, his finger lightly caressing the inside of leg. "I just received a call from Detective Oliver. They found Victor last night. He's in jail on multiple charges – assault, use of deadly force, stalking, violation of the restraining order – just to name a few.

"They also have him on drug charges. It seems he developed quite a cocaine habit. In order to afford his habit after the real estate market collapsed, he began selling large quantities of coke. When they finally found him, he was sleeping in his car in a city park with a big stash of coke in the trunk.

"The park is a drug free zone so that doubles the jail term for possession. Detective Oliver said his bail for all the charges is two million dollars. Victor is so broke he can't even afford a lawyer so there's no way he can afford bail. Plus he apparently owes someone a lot of money for the coke they found. He told the detective he was probably safer in jail than on the street."

"R.J. that's great!" Jillian shouted but then she turned solemn. "I guess I shouldn't be happy that Victor is in so much trouble. He is obviously very troubled."

"What you're feeling is natural, Jillian," R.J. responded, his fingers moving higher up the inside of Jillian's thigh. "He's very troubled, but he created his own problems and he made your life a living hell. You should be happy he's in jail. He needs to pay for all the havoc he caused you and his wife. Maybe he can get some help for his drug habit while he's in there too.

"The good news for us is that you can resume your life. I can go to Texas for this photo shoot and not have to worry about you. I'll miss you like crazy but at least I'll know you're safe. I was thinking that maybe when I come back, you can help me clean out my dad's house. It would be easier if someone more objective could help me make decisions."

"Of course, my love," she answered, running a finger over the hand that was still stroking her inner thigh. Without realizing it, he was fanning the flames that reading had started and a fire began to rage inside her. "I'll be there to help. It will go faster with both of us working on it and we'll be back here before you know it."

"It's a deal!" R.J. smiled at her, eyes full of love. "I have an idea. Let's go to The Isle tonight for dinner and dancing. I loved holding you that night, feeling the way your body sways, feeling the heat where we touch. What do you think?"

"I think that's perfect," Jillian said, her entire body was now engulfed in heat. "I'm ready to get out and celebrate a new beginning, a new life for both of us."

"Good, it's settled," he declared, caressing her thigh one more time before standing. "What did you have in mind for this afternoon? Some quiet time on the beach?"

"Come closer," she motioned, as the heat took over her brain. "Let me show you what I have in mind."

He looked at her in confusion and then moved toward her as understanding dawned.

"Feeling a little amorous, sexy lady?" R.J. asked as Jillian put her hands on the waistband of his shorts.

"A little amorous doesn't even begin to describe what you do to me, my love," she replied as she pushed the shorts down to his ankles. "Right now all I can think about is how you taste when I lick you."

Jillian reached out with one hand and touched his penis, stroking it softly with her fingers, examining it with her eyes. That light touch sent shock waves through R.J.'s body and he immediately began to get hard. What a turn on! Here was this beautiful, sexy woman looking at him like she wanted to devour him.

She looked up, saw him watching her, and let her tongue run the length of his penis. It was so sensual, seeing his eyes go black with desire, looking into the depths of his soul. Jillian felt wetness forming between her legs as her tongue circled the head of his hardening penis.

R.J. knees almost buckled when he looked into her eyes. She was on fire. He could see it in her eyes, feel the heat waves radiating from her tongue where it was touching him. He was a little surprised that she was so blatantly sexual outside in broad daylight but he loved it. This was a big step for her, to be this comfortable with him sexually. He wasn't sure what had aroused her so at this moment, but he would definitely enjoy the benefits.

When she took his now hard penis in her mouth, R.J. was sure he had found sensual heaven right there on his own private beach. Her mouth was hot and soft and covering him from the tip to his balls. She continued to stare into his eyes, silently speaking to him of her love and desire. Her tongue caressed him over and over, causing him to swell even more in her mouth and become harder with each gentle touch. When she reached around and grabbed his butt cheeks, he groaned in pleasure. He had never been so turned on in his life.

Just when R.J. thought he could take now more, Jillian pulled her head back until his rock hard penis slipped out of her mouth and stood fully erect directly in front of her face. Once again, she ran her tongue the length of his now throbbing shaft. Her hands moved around to squeeze his balls as she began rubbing her lips and cheeks over his hardness.

This time, Jillian groaned with excitement. She knew she had surprised R.J. but she had also surprised herself. This was so erotic, so exhilarating....and he felt so damn good as she rubbed his maleness against her cheek. She pushed him back and rose from her chair. Looking directly into his eyes, she removed her tank top and cupped her breasts for him to see. He looked down and then reached out to touch her. She shook her head no and ran her own hands over her nipples until they were hard.

"Oh god, baby," R.J. moaned, entranced by the show Jillian was putting on just for him.

She continued to fondle her breasts, watching him as he watched her. Again R.J. reached for her and again Jillian shook her head no. She stepped back slightly, slid her shorts over her hips and let them drop to the sand. She was now standing before him totally naked, her smooth skin glistening in the bright noontime sun. Her red hair was like a wreath of fire around her head. To R.J., it simply confirmed that Jillian was indeed on fire for him.

She ran her hand over her nipples once more and then let them stray over her belly. R.J. gulped air as his body reacted to the electric current that shot through him from this erotic show. He watched as Jillian's hand slid further down and her fingers disappeared between her legs. She gave a quick shiver and he knew she had touched her clit, knew she was seconds from coming.

When she withdrew her hand, he saw that her fingers were wet with her own juices. She raised her hand to his mouth and he greedily licked her fingers clean. She rubbed them across his lips when he was done and then traced a path over his chin, down his chest, and across his belly. When her fingers reached his rock hard penis, she once again stroked him lightly. It was like a feather tickling and touching him. He growled deep in his throat at the amazing sensations pulsing through him.

"Turn around," she commanded. R.J. complied instantly as he was now her willing slave.

When he had his back to her, Jillian pressed her entire body against his. Her hard nipples drilled into his back. Her hands went around his waist and found his engorged penis. She began stroking him with both hands. She pulled him closer until his firm round butt was pressing against her lower belly. She stroked him faster, licked his back with her burning hot tongue, and rubbed her nipples against his soft skin. His entire body was flushed with the heat that was bursting out of her. She was practically setting him on fire with the sparks she was generating as she rubbed against his skin.

R.J. felt her moan deep in her chest and knew she was in a state of extreme arousal. He had to make her come, had to feel her body when it spasmed in orgasm. He reached back until his hands were touching her butt. He pulled her tighter against his own butt as he pressed it back at the same time. There wasn't a millimeter of space between her overheated pussy and his firm, round butt.

Jillian spread her legs slightly and pushed up against his firm ass. She began rocking slowly, grinding her clit against it. Her hands tightened around him and each time R.J. rocked back against her, she stroked his hard shaft. Soon, she moaned again and he pressed her tighter against his butt, moving it slightly up and down. Jillian was lost. Each time he moved, his beautiful ass stroked her clit. She rocked harder against him until her entire body stiffened and she came with a scream. And then he heard another scream and another and another, a succession of orgasms that wouldn't stop.

R.J. was fighting for control. The erotic embrace they had just shared was off the charts. His penis was throbbing and begging for relief, but he wasn't allowing that yet. This was Jillian's fantasy and he would let her play it out. She would decide when it was his turn.

When her orgasms finally subsided, Jillian dropped to her knees in the sand and licked R.J.'s decidedly sexy butt. She had never experienced such a carnal desire for a man. She wanted to lick every single inch of his body and then go back and do it again. She let her tongue roam over those firm, round cheeks while one hand slipped between his legs. He instinctively spread his legs and she reached forward to squeeze his balls. Oh god, they were as hard as his penis and she knew each gentle squeeze was excruciatingly pleasurable torture for him.

Overcome with a sudden, raging need to have R.J. inside her, Jillian stood up. One more time, she pressed her entire body against his back. She transferred her heat and desire from her skin to his skin. R.J. felt her need, heard her thoughts, knew she wanted his penis inside her. He slowly turned around and pulled her against his chest. She felt him throbbing against her belly and her need for him grew exponentially.

"Tell me what you want," he whispered, peering through her eyes deep into her soul.

"I want you, R.J. I want you inside me. I want your hard penis filling me up, stroking me, making love to me. And I want it now, right now, right here," she gasped, her voice so full of need she could barely speak.

R.J. moved Jillian back until she was at the beach chair. She sat and with her eyes, she told him to kneel. He fell to his knees, his blood boiling up to the head of his penis, making it throb with a need equal to hers. She slid down in the chair, putting one leg over each armrest. Her legs were spread wide and he could see wetness running down her thighs, glistening at the entrance to her heated core. He knew she was out of control, knew she was crazed with desire for him.

Moving closer to her, R.J. let the head of his penis rub slowly over her dripping wet pussy. Jillian moaned and shivered once again. She arched her hips upward, trying desperately to push him inside her. He slowly rubbed her again and she gasped, so close to orgasm, so close to release. He leaned into her, his penis pressing into the wetness, teasing her with what was to come.

"Tell me what you want," he whispered again. "Tell me, baby."

"Make me come," she growled. "Make me come, oh god please make me come."

Pulling back slightly, R.J. leaned over and brushed his tongue over her clit. He had to have one quick taste of her. She screamed again, grabbing his hair and pushing his face into her heat. His face was instantly covered with her wetness as she orgasmed. He was amazed at how wet she was and it sent an electric current straight to his groin.

R.J. could take no more. He pulled his face away and pushed his rock hard shaft into her in one swift move. Jillian screamed with the first thrust, her muscles clenching around him as she had an immediate orgasm. He thrust in and out again and she moaned as another wave of pleasure coursed through her body. At that point, he lost all control. His hips moved without conscious thought from his brain. His penis was going deeper and deeper into her, each movement seeming to push her into a higher plane of ecstasy.

Jillian was coming nonstop, her head thrown back, her hair a fiery halo around her. Her eyes stared straight into his, feeling his thoughts of love and passion. The chair she was sitting in was in danger of collapsing but neither cared. They were on fire, their souls melting into each other, their bodies becoming one with the other. As she reached the crest of a gigantic orgasm, she cried out her final demand.

"Come baby, come for me now!"

R.J.'s body went white hot. He came with a ferocious growl, his hot juices shooting deep into her. As Jillian arched into him, screaming out his name, he felt a second wave consume him and push him over the edge. When his brain reconnected with his body, R.J. looked up at Jillian. Her head was leaning on the back of the chair, her eyes closed, her chest moving up and down as she gasped for breath. She slowly opened her eyes and looked at him. It was a look of raw sexual energy combined with pure love. It was a look he would never forget.

"Wow," she said with a soft, sensual smile.

"Yeah, wow," he agreed.

Finally, R.J. rose from his kneeling position and leaned over to kiss Jillian. She returned his kiss with one that was filled with a deep, intense passion. When their lips eventually parted, she spoke.

"Afternoon delight," she said simply as she grinned sexily at him.

CHAPTER 24

That evening, Jillian and R.J. went to The Isle for dinner as planned. With tourist season over, there were mainly locals seated at the tables and the bar. They had fresh, delicious seafood that was cooked in a light lemon sauce and served over pasta. After eating, they danced, talked, and laughed. Jillian excused herself to go to the restroom. She was feeling a little queasy after dancing on a full stomach. When she returned, R.J. was very visibly upset.

"What's wrong, my love?" Jillian asked.

"I'm so angry, I don't know if I can talk about it," he replied. "I just can't believe anyone would behave like that. And it wasn't just one of them. Both of them lied to me!"

"What are you talking about, R.J.? Who lied to you?" Jillian was confused and concerned. She had never seen R.J. like this. He was absolutely livid.

"While you were in the bathroom, I saw a girl I danced with here one night," R.J.'s voice was shaking with anger. "She gave me her phone number and the next day I texted her. To make a long story short, we texted back and forth for several weeks and even spoke on the phone once. When I met you, I broke it off with her. She told me she just wanted to be friends anyway, so it was no big deal."

R.J looked up and noticed the stricken look on Jillian's face. He thought she must be upset and was thinking he had somehow cheated on her. The last thing he wanted was to cause her any additional hurt.

"Baby, I met her before I ever saw you on the beach," he hurried to explain. "The one time we talked was before I met you too. She had just been through a bad relationship and said she could only be a phone friend.

"But once I met you here at The Isle, I knew I had to break things off. Then everything happened with my dad and I forgot. I finally texted her and told her I couldn't even be a phone friend. I didn't want anything to interfere with what I hoped would be a long term relationship with you."

"I don't understand who lied," Jillian croaked out.

But she knew who had lied. She had lied and so had Angel. R.J. Williams was Will, her phone friend. Oh god, why had she texted him back that day? And it now dawned on her why Will's name came up the night she had tried to call R.J., the night her tires had been slashed. It was already programmed into her phone.

"Angel lied," he spat out vehemently. "I guess that's her name. She gave me a fake phone number so maybe she gave me a fake name too. She made up a number and put it in my phone that night. When I saw her tonight, I tried to apologize for dropping the friendship in a text message. She laughed and told me what she had done."

Jillian sat stock still. She didn't trust her voice to sound normal so she didn't say a word. She suddenly saw her new life crumbling around her. And she deserved it. She never should have played a game with someone's life. She should have been honest with Will from the beginning.

"I don't understand why she had to lie to me," R.J. lamented. "Why not just say no thank you when I asked for her number?"

"I don't know," Jillian whispered.

"And then there's this person who pretended to be Angel," he said with loathing in his voice. "Why would she pretend to be someone else? How low is that? Why not be honest and tell me the truth? Did she think I would never find out? Was anything she told me about herself even true? And how far would she have taken things if I hadn't broken it off? I just can't understand why anyone would do such a thing. Why the need to lie? None of it makes any sense to me, baby."

At that point R.J. looked up and saw that Jillian was sitting with her elbows on the table and her head in her hands. He had been so wrapped up in his rant that he hadn't realized what was happening to her. He suddenly felt foolish for raging on and on, ruining what had been their celebration evening.

"Oh baby, I'm sorry," he cried. "I didn't mean to ruin our evening. You know how I am about honesty. I simply cannot understand or tolerate a liar."

Jillian looked up at him then, her face a mask of despair. She opened her mouth to speak but nothing came out. How could she tell him what she had done? He would never understand the depths of her sadness then or now. She knew it was too late now to be honest with R.J. And how could she continue to be with him if their entire relationship was based on a lie?

"Jillian, what's wrong?" he asked, concerned by the look on her face. "Sweetheart, I'm not upset with you."

"I'm sorry, R.J.," she muttered. "I'm sorry these women were like that."

"But it's not your fault, baby," he tried to soothe her. "I need to let it go and we need to get back to celebrating. Come on, let's dance."

"Can we go back to your house?" Jillian requested. "I'm not feeling well. I must have gotten too hot after that last dance."

"Of course we can," R.J. was very concerned now. "Do you think maybe the seafood was bad? But we ate the same thing and I'm feeling all right. Come on, Jillian, let me help you to the car."

Jillian rose on unsteady feet. Her stomach was twisted with guilt and she felt like she might throw up at any moment. She held R.J.'s arm as they went out to the parking lot. The ride back to the house was quiet. R.J. kept looking at Jillian's pale, drawn face. She looked absolutely miserable and his heart hurt for her. How could he be so self-centered that he was ranting and raving while she was obviously in some kind of distress?

By the time the short drive was over, Jillian looked even worse. She was pale, shaking, and seemed on the verge of vomiting. R.J. helped her into the house and upstairs. She dashed into the bathroom and he heard the sounds of her being sick to her stomach. He felt helpless as he waited for her to finish. When she finally came out, she looked even worse and R.J. was really concerned.

"Here, baby, lie down and let me cover you up," he said. "I'm going to get you some ginger ale from the kitchen. Do you need anything else?"

"No, thank you," she whispered as she climbed onto the bed.

When he left the room, Jillian felt the tears begin to slip out of her eyes and down her cheeks. They were going back to Raleigh in the morning and she would never see this place again. R.J. would never understand about the lies she had told him when she was pretending to be Angel. The love she had always dreamed about was gone because she had answered a text message from someone she didn't even know. Her heart was shattered and her stomach was turning inside out from the guilt. She heard footsteps on the stairs and quickly wiped away the tears. She could never explain to R.J. why she was crying.

R.J. returned with a glass of ginger ale and put it on the bedside table next to her. He slipped into the other side of the bed and pulled her close. To become sick so fast, she must have gotten a bad shrimp or scallop on her dinner plate. He couldn't think of any other reason for her to go from laughing and dancing one minute to pale, shaking, and vomiting the next. All he could do was be there if she needed him. He held her tight just as he had the night they arrived in Ocean Isle. Finally, he felt her body relax and her breathing become deep and regular. Only then did R.J. allow himself to sleep.

CHAPTER 25
THE KISS

arly Monday morning, Jillian woke to see the sun beginning to rise up out of the ocean. The sky was brilliant orange with splashes of yellow here and there. She rolled over to look at R.J. and the catastrophe of the night before came back full force. Her future with R.J. was gone before it had even begun. She had to stay calm until they got back to Raleigh. While he was in Texas, she would find a way to tell him that she was Angel. And then she would be banished from his life forever. As soon as that thought hit her, a wave of nausea swept over her and she made a run for the bathroom.

R.J. woke when he felt Jillian bolt from the bed. He heard her vomiting and felt heartsick. She had been through so much and had been so happy with him here. To have food poisoning on the last day of their long weekend was really unfair. But then he smiled. In just a few short weeks, she would be here with him all the time. And he would make her happy every single day for the rest of their lives.

Jillian finally felt her stomach settle so she rose from the bathroom floor and washed her face. She brushed her teeth and swished mouthwash in her mouth to remove any last trace of her sickness. She brushed her hair and looked in the mirror. She looked thinner and paler than she had just yesterday morning. She looked broken hearted but she couldn't let R.J. know. She took several deep breaths and made her way back to the bedroom.

As she climbed back into bed, R.J. rolled over to look at her. His eyes were full of love and concern. Jillian felt tears forming in the back of her throat but she swallowed them down. She couldn't let him know…not yet. She looked at him with such love that his breath stopped for a few seconds. He hadn't known someone could look at another person like that.

Reaching out a tentative hand, Jillian caressed his cheek. He took her hand, put it to his mouth, and kissed her palm. A flame shot through her body from that simple act. She wanted him more than she had ever wanted anyone. She needed him to make love to her one more time. She needed the memory of his lips and his hands to sustain her through the coming eternity without him. It was going to be a long cold winter and she needed to be able to remember his heat while she tried to repair her broken heart.

"Make love to me, R.J." she murmured. "Please."

"Are you sure?" he replied. "We don't have to if you're feeling ill."

"I need you, my love," was her response as she removed her nightgown.

R.J. moved closer to Jillian and kissed her softly. They were lying face to face and his hand trailed down her arm and over her hip. She put her hand back to his face and caressed his cheek again. Their lips remained together, sealed by the heat the kiss was generating in both of them. R.J. moved even closer, pressing his entire body against Jillian's. Their skin was touching from chest to toes while their lips continued a sensuous dance. R.J. gently caressed her back, from shoulders to waist, sending new waves of heat streaming throughout Jillian's body.

His hand moved lower, cupping and fondling her butt. R.J. was overwhelmed by the feelings racing through his body. He had never felt such a depth of love in his heart and soul while his body was feeling carnal shock waves from a mere kiss. But then his overheated brain realized it wasn't a mere kiss. It was a kiss filled with all the love, caring, and passion he and Jillian shared. It was a kiss filled with hope and promise as well as a deep hedonistic need for each other. He put his hand on the small of her back and pulled her body so close there wasn't a millimeter of space between them.

Jillian clung to R.J. so tightly she could barely breathe. It was as if their lips were glued together and she couldn't allow them to separate. She had to capture the heat of his lips, the taste of his breath, and the beating of his heart. She had to burn those images and feelings into her brain to sustain her when he no longer wanted her in his life.

The rest of R.J.'s body was responding to the kiss, just as Jillian's was. She felt him growing hard against her stomach and felt wetness pooling between her legs. Her body ached to have him inside her but she couldn't let his lips leave hers. This was what would keep her going when their future together turned to dust. The memory of the love between their hearts and the fire between their bodies would help her survive.

Softly and slowly, R.J. ran his tongue across the tiny sliver of space between Jillian's lips. She responded by arching her pelvis into his hard penis. The space opened slightly as she moaned and he slid his tongue into the heat of her mouth. At first she tasted of mouthwash, but in seconds the taste of her tongue and the taste of her mouth burst forth and assaulted his senses. He moaned this time as his entire body throbbed with unending desire and a passion that consumed him.

She sucked his tongue deeper into her mouth, her need to pull a part of him into her almost desperate. Jillian was on fire with a love so pure and an ardor so hot she was sure she would explode into flames. Nothing in her prior experience had prepared her for this meeting of hearts and souls. She could feel the love radiating from R.J. and knew her love was beaming back to him. As their lips and tongues continue to caress in a slow, sensual dance, she knew heaven on Earth. A kiss, so simple, yet so full of love, devotion, and desire. A kiss that neither would ever forget.

With their lips still pressed together and their tongues fanning the flames, Jillian put one leg over R.J.'s hip. He understood immediately that she wanted to feel him inside her. He knew she had heard his single thought.....his urgent longing to be inside her. His rock hard penis slid between her legs and skimmed over her clit. He felt the wetness at the entrance to her heated core and then felt her entire body stiffen as a massive orgasm rushed through her. She moaned into his mouth, but never let go of his tongue, her mouth sucking it in even further.

When her spasms began to subside, R.J. slowly moved his hips again. His penis was throbbing against her, her juices gushing out to cover it in wetness. He slid the length of his slippery shaft over her pussy lips and then her clit. With each thrust, Jillian moaned and sucked on his tongue, not letting their lips part for even a second. Their bodies were sizzling where their skin touched. His soft chest hair rubbed her nipples, making them hard knobs against his skin. His hand on her butt, holding her tight against him caused a flush to spread over her lower body. She stiffened and he felt her whole body spasm as another orgasm spread through her.

With each thrust, she groaned and came, over and over and over.

"I need you inside me," Jillian finally gasped out, barely able to breathe much less speak.

With excruciating slowness, R.J. moved his hips and began to slide into her. First the head of his hard, slick penis pushed into her. She groaned against his lips and pushed her pelvis even closer to him. Inch by inch, he entered her, the scorching flame of her wetness engorging his penis even more. Jillian felt him slipping into her, growing bigger with each inch of her pussy he captured. Her body shifted unconsciously to allow him to push deeper and deeper into it as her mouth continued to suck on his tongue.

When he was finally totally sheathed by her, he began to rock his pelvis back and forth. R.J. felt every inch of his hardness being covered by the juices gushing out of her. He felt the torrid wetness of Jillian's mouth as their lips remained sealed together, tongues reveling in unbelievable sensations. As his thrusting became more pronounced, Jillian began to move her hips to the rhythm he set.

They continued their sensual dance of love, face to face, rocking back and forth until Jillian's mouth flew open and a scream of total pleasure escaped from her. R.J. thrust harder and faster, looking into eyes that emanated an unparalleled mixture of love and desire for him. He saw her soul and knew it belonged to him. This knowledge pushed him over the edge. He groaned as he came in a giant rush of emotion, transmitting back to her the same love and desire, allowing her to see that his soul belonged to her.

They held each other for a long time afterwards. Face to face, they enjoyed the quiet return to reality. They wanted this extremely intimate moment to last forever. Such a profound expression of love was something that neither had ever known before.

After several minutes, R.J. realized Jillian was silently weeping. He pulled her closer to him and held her tight. He knew the depth of the emotion that had passed between them and thought she was overcome by it. She was, in fact, overcome by it, but for a different reason than R.J. imagined. She knew it would be the last time she would ever feel something so complex and unfathomable.

CHAPTER 26

Ten hours later, Jillian and R.J. were approaching the Raleigh city limits. They had closed up the house on Ocean Isle and stopped for a late lunch in Shallotte. Then they headed west so R.J. would make his flight to Dallas on time. They had decided that Jillian would drop him off at the airport and then go home. She had checked with Detective Oliver on the way to ensure Victor was still in jail. It looked like he would be there for a very long time and Jillian breathed a sigh of relief.

R.J. was concerned about Jillian. She was still pale and withdrawn. She hadn't talked much on the drive from the coast. He wondered if she was still feeling sick but there seemed to be something more. The sadness in her eyes and the way she studied him, like she had to memorize his features, worried him. But he didn't pursue it with her.

He was sure she was once again reliving the torment of Victor's rampage and was uneasy about being alone. He couldn't wait to return to Raleigh and take Jillian back to their home in Ocean Isle forever. He smiled as he realized he now thought of it as their home. It would never be just his home again. That thought filled him with love and happiness. When he pulled up to the departure gates, he turned and looked at Jillian.

"Do you have any idea how much I'm going to miss you, baby?" he asked with a smile. "I wish you could come with me. I don't want to be apart from you for even a few minutes. Ten days will be pure torture."

"It will be over before you know it," she responded with a forced smile. "I'm going to miss you more than you could ever imagine, my love."

"I'll call your condo when I get in, baby," he said lovingly. "I know it will be late, but I can't go to sleep without hearing your voice."

"I'm looking forward to hearing your voice too," Jillian replied, holding back tears. She knew it would be the last time she ever heard R.J.'s voice and it was tearing her heart out.

"And don't forget to call me tomorrow with your new cell phone number," R.J. reminded. "That was really nice of Kent to get that set up for you. And it was nice of Detective Oliver to offer to drop off the old one. You can get your pictures and contacts out of it, have the number disconnected, and then dispose of that part of your life for good."

"You better go, my love," Jillian said, her heart silently breaking. "I don't want you to miss your flight."

"Me either!" he exclaimed. "The sooner I get this miserable photo shoot over with, the sooner I can be with you again."

They climbed out of the Jeep and met at the back of the car. R.J. took Jillian in his arms and held her tight. She held on to him, desperate to take in his touch, his scent, his whole being. She had decided on the way from Ocean Isle that she could never see him again after he left for Texas. It would be too painful to have to tell him face to face what she had done.

R.J. kissed her gently, remembering the kiss from this morning that had propelled them to unimaginable heights of passion. He could barely wait for the time when he could reach out to Jillian any time of the day or night and know she was there beside him. He was planning to ask her to marry him as soon as they got back to Ocean Isle. He knew it was early in their relationship, but he also knew Jillian was the woman he was meant to be with. He knew she was his future.

"I love you, Jillian," he whispered as he looked into her eyes. "I'll be back before you know I'm gone."

"I love you too, R.J.," she whispered back to him. "No matter what happens, know that I will always love you."

R.J. picked up his bag and walked to the terminal door. He turned and waved, his love for Jillian ready to burst out of his chest. She waved and smiled at him, her love evident in the way her eyes shone brightly. He turned back and entered the terminal.

Jillian got in the Jeep, tears streaming down her face. When she arrived at her condo, she had no knowledge of how she had gotten there. She began unpacking but ended up on the couch in tears once again.

The next morning, Jillian returned to Stanley, Wilson, and Krenshaw. She was anxious to get her client's transitioned to new associates. During the long sleepless night before, she had decided to go see her mother once she was free of work. She would spend some time there and maybe go to the lake cabin for a few days. She could only hope she would have some divine inspiration on what to do with her life. Right now, her future looked bleak and lonely.

Talking to R.J. for a few minutes after he had arrived in Dallas the night before had been almost unbearable. However, to not have one last chance to hear his voice was even more unbearable. After their brief conversation with declarations of unending love, she had cried for hours. She knew she would love R.J. for the rest of her life. She also knew that once he realized she had pretended to be Angel, his love for her would vanish in the web of lies and deceit she had created.

The long night had also provided Jillian with a plan on how to tell R.J. that she had deceived him. She would text him from her old number while he was with his client. She would tell him that she was Angel and that she had deceived him. She would also tell him it was over between them so she wouldn't have to deal with the outrage he would feel at the deception. Then she would have the line disconnected.

Jillian couldn't bear the thought of the things R.J. would say to her once he learned she had lied to him. Even worse, she couldn't bear to hear him say it was over between them. The only way to save her sanity was to break it off with him as soon as she confessed. Text message….the coward's way out, but for this circumstance, she was a coward.

Allison knew the minute Jillian arrived that there was something horribly wrong. The smiling, happy junior partner of Thursday was no longer there. In her place was a woman who looked like death. She obviously hadn't slept well as there were huge dark circles under her eyes. And in the first hour at work, Jillian had rushed past the reception area on the way to the bathroom at least three times. Something very bad had happened, but the look on Jillian's face told Allison she had better not ask.

At ten-thirty, Jillian finally summoned the courage to text R.J. She knew the longer she put it off, the harder it would be. Detective Oliver had delivered her old phone at nine o'clock sharp. A new phone had been waiting on her temporary desk when she arrived. She transferred all the critical data, called her mother and Kellie with her new number, texted other friends to provide the number, and was now out of reasons to put off the inevitable. She picked up the old phone and typed.

I know you know I am not Angel from the tiki bar. As weird as this may sound, it's Jillian. I'm so sorry that I lied to you RJ. I didn't mean to hurt you. I realize now that the minute I pretended to be Angel, you were going to end up hurt. I hope at some point in the future, you can forgive me. I know we can't be together with this lie between us. I want you to know that you gave me the most incredible weekend of my life. I will always be grateful for that. And I will always love you RJ. Goodbye, my love.

With tears streaming down her face, Jillian hit "Send." The glorious future she had imagined with R.J. was now gone. Her own deceit had caused it and there was nothing she could do about it. She called the wireless company and had the line disconnected immediately. She went through the rest of the day in a fog of pain. She focused on the different associates who would take her clients so her mind would not spin out of control.

Late that evening, Jillian finally decided to go home. She shut down her computer and started out the door. She heard her phone ring just as she was locking the main door and decided that whoever it was could wait until tomorrow. She headed out in the darkness to her cold, empty condo.

When R.J. finished the first day of the photo shoot for this difficult client, he was happy to head back to his hotel. He could hardly wait to hear Jillian's voice on his voice mail telling him her new phone number. He was surprised that there was no missed call from a North Carolina number. He was equally surprised to see a text message from the mysterious Angel. He decided to deal with that once he got to the hotel. On the way there, he tried to reach Jillian at both her office and her condo but there was no answer at either place. He was beginning to get concerned, but told himself that she was probably having dinner with Kellie. He decided to call her at home later.

After a quick dinner alone, R.J. returned to the hotel room. He picked up his phone and opened the text message from Angel. He would call her once he read the message and demand to know who she really was and why she had lied to him. When he read the message and realized it was from Jillian, he was in complete shock.

How could Jillian lie to him? She must have realized on Sunday night that he was Will. Then it hit him. The upset stomach, her sadness, the way she seemed to be memorizing everything about him…..it was all because she knew on Sunday night. She had been caught in her lie and obviously felt very guilty. She had known all night Sunday and all day Monday and hadn't said a word.

R.J. was angry, hurt, and could not comprehend how Jillian could do this to him. His heart was shattered. She had told him goodbye without even trying to explain further. He threw the phone across the room and broke down into tears. His beautiful future was gone.

Both R.J. and Jillian spent the next days like zombies. They went through the motions of their jobs, but there was no pleasure, no happiness, no heart in their work. R.J. took the worst pictures he had ever taken, but his egotistical client didn't seem to notice. He was happy with the work so R.J. let him be. Jillian spent time with the associates on transitioning clients, but it was a rote exercise for her. She imparted necessary information and refused to engage in idle chatter.

After two weeks, Jillian had completed her promised transition and said goodbye to everyone at SW&K. They wanted to give her a going away party her last Friday there, but she simply wasn't up to it. Instead, she met Kellie for dinner. She had told Kellie what had happened the day she sent the goodbye text to R.J. Kellie was sure he would call and everything would be all right.

However, Jillian had heard nothing at all from R.J. Deep in her heart, she had hoped Kellie was right. She hoped he would call her and tell her he understood. However, in her rational mind she knew her deceit would be something he could not tolerate. All she could do now was try to move on with her life. She had money and time to do anything she wanted. She hoped a long talk with her mother and some time at the lake would help her decide what that was.

CHAPTER 27

Saturday morning, Jillian was up bright and early, preparing for her trip to Asheboro. She packed a bag, tidied up the condo, and took out the trash. After a stop at the bank, she was ready for the drive to Asheboro. It wasn't a long drive, only seventy-two miles from Raleigh, and it was beautiful this late in October. The leaves on the trees lining the highway were deep shades of red, orange, and gold. As she drove, Jillian admired the scenery, thinking that she loved the mountains of North Carolina almost as much as she loved the beaches. The thought of the beach made her heart wrench. Was R.J. back from Texas yet? Tears leaked from the corners of her eyes as she tried to stop thinking about him.

As Jillian approached Pittsboro, a small town halfway between Raleigh and Asheboro, a wave of nausea swept over her. She had been thinking about R.J. and her stomach was once again in knots. She stopped at a gas station and barely made it to the restroom before her breakfast came back up. This was becoming an almost daily occurrence, but Jillian wasn't worried. She knew that the guilt she felt over her deception with R.J. was tearing her apart. Maybe time with her mother would ease her conscience. Barbara Stanley was a wise woman as well as a loving, caring mother. If anyone could help Jillian get her life back on track, her mother was the one to do it.

Jillian arrived in Asheboro an hour and a half after leaving Raleigh. She dragged herself from the Jeep and yanked her suitcase from the back seat. She was pulling the suitcase behind her up the sidewalk when the front door of her mother's home flew open. She looked up to see her mother standing there smiling at the sight of her daughter.

Barbara Stanley was excited to see her only child. It had been months since they had spent any time together and she was looking forward to some mother/daughter time. She was also looking forward to hearing about Jillian's boyfriend, the famous photographer. When they had spoken after the problem with the deranged realtor, her daughter's voice had been full of love for this man. Jillian had seemed more subdued the last few times they had spoken, but Barbara thought this was because R.J. was out of town. She hoped Jillian finally had found her life partner....a partner like Barbara had had with her late husband, Jesse.

"Jillian, sweetheart! It's so good to see you!" Barbara cried as she ran down the sidewalk. "I've missed you so much."

Jillian dropped her suitcase and ran to her mother's embrace. She held her mother tight for a long minute, feeling loved in the way only your mother can make you feel. She stepped back and kissed her mother on the cheek.

"Mom, it's so good to see you too!" she exclaimed. "I've missed you more than you can imagine. I'm so glad we have a few days together."

"Let's get in the house, sweetie," Barbara said as she grabbed the handle of the suitcase. "I have lunch almost ready and you can tell me all about your plans to write and your boyfriend while we eat."

The ladies hurried into the house. Jillian unpacked in the small spare bedroom while Barbara finished making lunch. Jillian's mother was the consummate Southern hostess and an incredible cook. When she found her way to the kitchen in the back of the house, Jillian saw Barbara putting the finishing touches on a pot of homemade vegetable soup. Even with her recent stomach problems, the delicious smells coming from the soup pot made Jillian's mouth water.

"Set the table please, Jillie," Barbara instructed. "This will be ready in five minutes. We can eat and have a long talk. I'm so happy that you're staying for a few days. I can't wait to hear all about what's going on with you. Oh, and I can't wait for you to meet Thomas. He's such a nice man. I know you will love him."

"The soup smells wonderful, Mom," Jillian responded as she took plates and bowls from the cupboard. "I'm looking forward to your fantastic cooking, a couple days of quiet, and time to talk to the best listener I know. It's been a hectic and emotional few weeks and I definitely need some 'mom time'."

"You look thin and pale, sweetie. I'll get you fattened up a little bit before your new boyfriend gets back in town," Barbara said with a worried look at her daughter. "I've never seen you so thin, Jillie."

"I've been having some issues with my stomach for the last couple of weeks," Jillian replied. "But I'll be all right. I just need some good home cooking and some hugs from my most favorite person in the whole world. I'll be like new again."

Barbara carried bowls of soup to the table, placed sandwiches on a plate, and they sat down to eat. Jillian was suddenly ravenous and ate with gusto. She was thinking that she hadn't been this hungry since R.J. had fixed that amazing seafood grill at his house. The thought of R.J. brought tears to her eyes and she put her spoon down. Seeing her daughter's tears, Barbara became alarmed.

"Jillie, what's wrong?" she asked with concern. "Tell me what's going on. Maybe I can help."

"Oh Mom, I wish you could just kiss my booboo like you did when I was little and make everything OK," Jillian said quietly as tears streamed down her cheeks. "But the mess I've made is much more serious and it can't be fixed."

"Tell me about it, sweetie," Barbara crooned, reaching across the table and taking her daughter's hand. "We'll figure it out together."

Jillian spent the next hour sitting at the kitchen table with her mother. She told her everything – the text from Will, their brief phone friendship, how she met R.J. at the beach and then again at the office, the way their relationship progressed, their time at his house in Ocean Isle, and, finally, discovering that Will and R.J. were the same person.

"Oh Jillie, how awful for both of you!" Barbara declared. "I'm guessing he wasn't very happy when you told him you had pretended to be Angel. But it's not the end of the world, sweetie."

"Mom, I didn't tell him right then that I was Angel," Jillian confided. "He was so angry and hurt that I just couldn't do it. See, he and I had talked about honesty in a relationship. He is all about being honest and he told me he could not tolerate lies ever. He had a past girlfriend who had lied to him about a lot of things. He was so adamant that our relationship be built on honesty and trust. How could I tell him that night that I had been dishonest with him? That our relationship was built on a lie?"

"So what did he say when you told him?" Barbara asked.

"When I was back at work and he was in Dallas, I texted him from my old phone number," Jillian continued. "I took the coward's way out and told him in a text message that I was pretending to be Angel. I told him I knew we couldn't have a relationship built on lies. I told him goodbye. I had to, there was no other choice. I couldn't stand to have him call me a liar and tell me he didn't want me in his life."

With that admission, Jillian broke down and sobbed. Barbara rose and went around the table. She sat down beside Jillian and put her arms around her daughter. Jillian cried on her mother's shoulder until she was out of tears. Her heart was breaking all over again. And Barbara's heart was breaking for Jillian. When Jillian's sobs finally quieted, Barbara spoke softly.

"Have you heard from him? Did he text you or call you?" she asked.

"I haven't heard anything at all from him, Mom," Jillian murmured. "Not a single word. So I guess it's really over. Now I have to figure out what to do with my life. That's why I'm here. I desperately need some unconditional love and good motherly advice."

"I have plenty of both for you, Jillie," Barbara stated, looking at her daughter's tear-stained face. "And I always will. Let me think about it and we can talk some more later on. I think right now you could use a nap."

"I think you're right," Jillian said wearily. "I haven't slept well in two weeks and with this stomach bug I seem to have, I'm exhausted."

"You go lie down, sweetie," Barbara replied. "I'll clean up the kitchen and start on dinner. I've invited Thomas to join us tonight. Is that OK?"

"Of course, Mom!" Jillian cried. "I can't wait to meet him. If he makes you happy, he must be a good person. Wake me at least an hour before he's due to be here so I can make myself presentable."

Jillian retired to the spare bedroom and snuggled in between the covers. She was as exhausted as she had told her mother. Mentally and physically exhausted. Her thoughts drifted to R.J., wondering where he was, what he was doing, if he was back in Ocean Isle. She sighed and choked back tears, wishing that wherever R.J. was, she was with him. Soon, her eyes closed and she had the first good sleep in two weeks.

Dinner that night with Thomas was fun. Thomas was an interesting man with a lot of stories about the people in Asheboro. He was quite a good storyteller and kept the ladies entertained for several hours. During the evening, Jillian recalled meeting him once or twice when she was a child. She had come to Asheboro often with her parents to visit her grandparents. She had no idea then that this sweet man had once been her mother's boyfriend.

To be honest, she had never thought about her mother being with any man except her father. Now she realized her mother may have had her share of heartbreak before she found Jillian's father. Maybe there is still hope for me, Jillian thought at one point. And maybe she really does understand what I'm going through. Thomas left about ten o'clock after they had made plans to meet him for lunch the next day.

"Mom, Thomas is wonderful!" Jillian proclaimed while she and her mother cleaned up the kitchen. "He's so sweet and caring. I know Dad would approve, especially seeing how happy he makes you."

"I think Jesse would approve too," Barbara agreed, pleasure beaming from her eyes. "He always told me that if he went first, he didn't want me to be lonely. I could never love Thomas the way I loved your dad, but we have a mutual affection and enjoy each other's company. I don't think I will be growing old alone."

"You know, when you moved back here to Asheboro, I was devastated," Jillian said, enveloping her mother in a loving embrace. "I was so lonely. I thought you were hiding and being selfish. I was angry with Dad for dying and with you for abandoning me. I finally realized that this was what you needed to do to deal with Dad's death. Now that I see how happy you are here, I know this was absolutely the right move for you Mom. I'm glad you did it and didn't let me sway you from your decision."

"I knew you were angry, sweetie," Barbara acknowledged. "But I also knew that each of us had to find our own way back to the world of the living after your dad died. I had no thoughts of meeting anyone when I came back here. I just knew it was where I needed to be for my heart to heal.

"I also knew you would find your way too. You've done a remarkable job, Jillie. This latest set back with your young man may slow you down a little, but it won't stop you. Decide what you need for your heart to heal and then do what you need to do, my darling daughter. And know that I am always here to support you."

"I love you Mom," Jillian said. Her heart was bursting with love for her mother.

"I love you more than life itself, Jillian," her mother replied. "You are my heart. Being your mother has been my greatest accomplishment. Some day, you will have children of your own and know the unconditional love that I feel for you."

Jillian slept deeply that night. It was the first night since Ocean Isle that she didn't wake with nightmares of Victor or tears for R.J. When she woke the next morning, she felt refreshed and ready to meet the day.

The aroma of coffee drifted into the bedroom and Jillian knew her mother was up also. She sat up and was immediately seized by a wave of nausea. She dashed to the bathroom that was attached to the small bedroom and vomited. When it finally passed, she brushed her teeth, showered, and got dressed. By the time she went to the kitchen, her stomach was better but not completely settled.

"Good morning, sweetie," Barbara smiled when her daughter entered the room. "I heard the shower so I put the tea-kettle on for you. I'm making eggs and toast. I can fry some bacon if you want it."

"Morning, Mom," Jillian returned the greeting. "I think I'll make do with tea and toast. I'm still having some stomach issues this morning and I don't want to push my luck. It's odd, but this bug seems to bother me most in the morning or when I'm riding in the car. I should be fine by the time we meet Thomas for lunch."

Barbara turned and looked at her daughter. The pale skin, listless demeanor, continuing stomach issue…..it all clicked into place for her at that moment. She was unsure how to say what she thought, but knew she needed to meet this head on.

"Jillian, I don't mean to pry into your business, but can I ask you something?" she began.

"Sure Mom, what is it?" Jillian responded.

"Well, I know you've had a lot of stress lately with everything that has happened," Barbara continued. "And stress can cause physical symptoms like stomach upset. But is it possible that you're pregnant?"

"Pregnant?" Jillian was shocked at the suggestion. "Mom you know that when Gary and I were trying to have a baby, the doctors said it would be almost impossible for me to get pregnant."

"Almost impossible, but not one hundred percent impossible, right?" Barbara pushed forward. "When was the last time you had a period?"

"Ummm, it's been a couple of months I guess, but my periods are so irregular that it's not unusual for me to skip a month or two." Jillian thought for a moment. "Mom, do you think I could be pregnant?"

"Well there's one way to find out," Barbara replied. "After our lunch with Thomas, we'll go to the drugstore and get one of those home pregnancy tests. First thing tomorrow morning, you will know for sure."

Jillian sat down, shell-shocked and silent. What in the world would she do if she was pregnant? Then another thought hit her. The last time she had a period was right after Labor Day. If she was pregnant, it had to be R.J.'s baby. Oh god, what would she do?

She could never tell R.J. that he had a child. She wouldn't put that responsibility on him when she knew he didn't want her anymore. Well, she would just make it through this with her family and friends as her support system. Barbara interrupted her thoughts with a suggestion that they get ready to go meet Thomas. Jillian smiled at her mother and agreed, needing to think about something else so her head would stop spinning.

Lunch with Thomas was almost as much fun as dinner had been. He was quite the entertainer and kept them laughing. Jillian was preoccupied with thoughts of a possible pregnancy. Try as she might to focus on her mother and Thomas, her mind kept drifting to this new wrinkle. How had it happened kept coming to mind. OK, she knew how it happened, but it was something she honestly thought would never happen.

She hadn't felt the need to take precautions when she and Gary were married. That had carried over to R.J., too, and now she might be carrying his baby. Her heart hurt that she could never tell him. However, her heart also soared at the thought of having his child. She would always have a part of R.J. with her.

The next morning, Jillian removed the wrapper from the pregnancy test she had purchased after lunch with Thomas. She read the instructions, urinated on the test stick, and sat down to wait. After the allotted time, she tentatively peeked at the stick. When she saw the plus sign, she felt faint. She was pregnant! She would have a piece of R.J. to love forever!

In that moment, Jillian's whole world changed. Even though R.J. didn't love her anymore, she could love his child with total abandon. She had something more important than herself to take care of now. Her life would have a purpose.

"Mom!" Jillian called out as she ran to the kitchen, her face alight with a huge smile. "Mom, I'm pregnant!"

"Jillie, I'm so happy for you!" Barbara was almost as excited as Jillian. "Oh, I'm going to be a grandmother! How much fun will that be? I can't wait to spoil this little one. It's a grandmother's duty, you know. Oh sweetie, this is wonderful!"

Barbara stopped and looked at Jillian. She realized that she had assumed Jillian was happy about the pregnancy. Maybe she wasn't since she and R.J. had broken up. How would she handle telling him he was going to be a father? Jillian read the thoughts as her mother's face changed from happy to concerned.

"It's OK," she told her mother. "I'm so happy I may smile for the rest of my life. I know being a single mother will be difficult, but I also know I can do it. Between you, Kellie, and Mindy, I have more support and babysitters than I'll know what to do with. It's going to be wonderful, Mom. This will be one baby that will never wonder if he or she is loved."

"What about R.J., sweetie?" Barbara asked. She was suddenly worried about the path her daughter was going down. "He deserves to know he's going to be a father."

"Mom, I can't tell him," Jillian cried. "He obviously thinks he can't trust me. It clear that he doesn't want to be with me. I haven't heard a single word from him since that text message. I know I broke his trust and his heart. I don't want him to think I'm trying to trap him."

"But Jillian, he should know," Barbara exclaimed. "It's his right to know that he fathered a child. It's his right to be involved in this child's life."

"Mom, he travels all over the world," Jillian said quietly. "I can't tell him and make him feel like he has to change his life. It was my mistake that got me pregnant. I can't make him responsible for that. I can't make him be a part of my life when he obviously doesn't want to be."

"Jillian Stanley, this is not your mistake alone," Barbara proclaimed. "It takes two people to make a baby. He deserves to have the choice to be involved or not be involved. You have no right to make that choice for him. And anyway, you said he was going to stop traveling and write his book. His travels have nothing to do with the situation."

"Mom, calm down," Jillian said soothingly. "Let's not fight about it please. I promise to think about telling him. I have seven or eight months to decide so let's not argue about it today. Right now I need to call Kellie and tell her the news. Then we have to celebrate."

Jillian dialed Kellie's work number, excited with the news she had for her best friend.

"Kellie speaking."

"Hey Kell, it's me," Jillian said to her friend's terse greeting. This was how Kellie always answered her work phone.

"Hey girl, how's small town life treating you?" Kellie asked, a smile in her voice now. "You sound happier today, Jillie. Did you and your mom have a good time with the new man last night?"

"Thomas is a super nice man and makes my mom very happy," Jillian responded. "I like him a lot!"

"And how's my best friend doing, Jillie?" Kellie questioned. "I still think you need to call R.J. and see where his head is at. I can't believe he didn't even try to call you for an explanation. It just doesn't make sense to me."

"Kell, we went over all of that at least ten times in the last two weeks," Jillian replied. "He knows how to reach me if he wants to work things out. But that's not why I called. I have some really exciting news for you!"

"Ooooh, good!" Kellie cried. "I need to hear something happy and exciting coming from you. So, tell me!!"

"I'm pregnant!" Jillian shouted.

"No way! Really? Oh my God, I'm so happy for you, Jillie!" Kellie was so excited for her friend that it all came out in one long stream of babble.

"Thanks Kell!" Jillian exclaimed. "I'm so excited I could burst. A baby, a baby I never thought I would have!"

"Oh Jillie, I can't wait to be an aunt," Kellie was over the top happy for her best friend. "I'm gonna spoil that little one to death. Aunt Kellie! Has a nice ring to it, doesn't it?"

"It sure does," Jillian agreed.

"Did you call R.J. yet and tell him?" Kellie asked. "He needs to know, Jillie."

"Not yet," she said. "I'm not even sure I'm going to tell him."

"Jillian Stanley, you have to tell him," Kellie was yelling now. "He has a right to know. You can't keep this a secret from him. When you get back, we need to have a serious talk about this, girlfriend."

"You sound just like my mom," Jillian noted. "She gave me the same lecture."

"Well, you should listen to us," Kellie said. "We know what we're talking about."

"For today, just be happy for me, please Kell," Jillian requested. "When I get back we can talk about it and you can yell and lecture all you want."

"I'm over the moon happy for you, Jillie," Kellie responded.

The two women talked a little longer about the baby and all the plans Kellie was already making for taking him or her to the zoo, the park, and a dozen other places. When they hung up, Jillian was smiling at her friend's enthusiasm.

Jillian and her mother spent the rest of the day in an excited tizzy. They discussed pregnancy, childbirth, and the thrill of bringing the little one home. Jillian promised to find a good doctor as soon as she returned to Raleigh. Barbara promised to go to Raleigh to help out whenever she was needed. They even took a trip to Asheboro's quaint downtown streets to look at baby things in several shops that catered to children. Dinner with Thomas at a small local restaurant was a celebration of happiness.

The next few days passed with more shopping trips, long discussions about what Jillian would do going forward, and many loving looks passed between mother and daughter. Jillian could hardly wait to see the doctor in Raleigh to confirm what her body was telling her was true. She was still certain that she couldn't tell R.J. and her mother was just as certain that she should.

Jillian decided a few days at the Stanley cabin just on the edge of Morrow Mountain State Park was exactly what she needed. She could be totally alone with her thoughts. Not only did she have to plan for a child, but she also needed to decide what she was going to do to make money. Without the book she and R.J. had talked about doing together, she was left with no plan for how to pursue her writing career. She needed to either figure that out or make up her mind to go back to SW&K once the baby arrived.

CHAPTER 28

On Wednesday morning Jillian packed a few things in the Jeep and headed toward Morrow Mountain. She promised her mother she would be back on Friday morning and they would spend the rest of the weekend together before Jillian went back to Raleigh. Morrow Mountain State Park had always been one of Jillian's favorite places. The park had hiking trails, horseback riding, and a fabulous swimming hole where the Pee Dee and Yadkin Rivers converged. She thought she might spend the days just sitting near the water reading and thinking.

The Stanley cabin was off a rocky, dirt road about half way up the mountain. It was surrounded by trees that were showing off a breathtaking display of fall colors. When Jillian pulled up in front of it, she felt all the stress flow out of her body. She loved the peace and quiet of the cabin. Cell phone service and cable television were non-existent up here. She could be totally alone with her thoughts....no interruptions by people or electronic devices. She sat looking at the cabin for a moment. She was thinking that here she would come up with a plan to support herself and her baby with her writing talents.

The thought of the baby made Jillian smile. She put a hand on her stomach, wondering how soon she would feel the little one move. This child was at least seven months from being born but already she felt a love and protective instinct that she had never before experienced. The only sadness in all of this was that R.J. wouldn't be around to love her and the child as it grew up. She banished that thought, determined to move forward with her life in a positive way for her baby.

Jillian got out of the Jeep and grabbed the bags of food and clothing she had brought with her. She walked up the stone steps to the wide front porch made of hand-hewn oaken planks. All of the wood for the cabin had come from the forest surrounding it. The large chairs on the porch as well as most of the furniture inside had been hand made by a local craftsman. Her father had purchased the land many years before and had the cabin built once his business had started to become profitable.

The family had spent many summer days up here and down at the State Park, fishing, swimming, hiking, and picnicking. Jillian's favorite, however, had been catching lightening bugs on summer nights. She would put the glass jar of fireflies on the table by her bed and watch the flashing light show all night long. She hoped she could give her child the same wonderful memories.

Once inside, it was apparent that the cabin had been sitting empty for far too long. Jillian flipped the electric breaker, then turned on the propane tank, refrigerator, and hot water heater. She put the food she had brought with her away. She opened all the doors and windows to let the place air out. Then she busied herself with cleaning the dust from every surface until all four rooms were habitable. With the basic cleaning completed, she sat down to a tuna sandwich and glass of milk for lunch. She had to take care with her eating now that she was feeding the new life growing inside her.

After lunch, a nap seemed to be the next order of business. Jillian laid down on the twin bed that had been hers growing up. She fell into a deep sleep and dreamed she had a beautiful baby boy who looked exactly like R.J. When she woke, she knew she would tell R.J. about the baby. She understood she really had no choice. Denying him the pleasure of knowing their child was suddenly inconceivable to her.

By the time she rose from the bed, it was dark out. Jillian turned on the furnace against the chilly night air. She spent the evening writing down every idea she could come up with to get her writing career going. It was time to get serious about writing. When her eyes began to droop, she shuffled into the bedroom and slept deeply.

Thursday morning was a cool, crisp autumn day in the North Carolina mountains. Jillian woke feeling refreshed and invigorated. She had a long list of ideas from the night before and would spend the day expanding on each one that had merit. After that, she would pare the list down further until she had no more than five good ideas that had real possibilities. She drove down to Morrow Mountain Park and sat by the water.

Just like the ocean, the flowing waters of the two rivers that merged here calmed Jillian's mind. She had worked her way through half the list by lunchtime. After eating the lunch she had brought, she got back to work. By mid-afternoon, she was beginning to get sleepy, so she headed back up the mountain to the cabin. Knowing her body was demanding a nap, she complied and once again slept deeply in her childhood bed.

When Jillian woke, it was completely dark outside. She checked her travel clock to find it was nearly seven o'clock. She had slept for almost four hours! Being pregnant was certainly tiring she thought as she made her way to the kitchen. She rummaged around the fridge and put together a simple dinner of leftover vegetable soup from her mom's house and a grilled cheese sandwich. As she sat down, she realized she was famished. She also realized that she hadn't been sick all day. Maybe the morning sickness was finally ebbing.

Jillian was washing the few dishes from dinner when she heard a noise. It sounded like footsteps, but she wasn't completely sure. She went into the living room and stood still and silent, listening for the sound again. Just when she decided it must have been an animal in the woods behind the cabin, she heard the sound again. It was definitely human footsteps and they were coming up the driveway.

Panicked, Jillian didn't know what to do. Her first thought was that Victor had found her. Her second was how could he know she was here? Oh god, she hoped he hadn't found her mother and tortured the information out of her. She was frozen in place, trying to decide what she could use as a weapon, when she heard someone on the front porch. She flew to the fireplace and grabbed the poker just as a loud knock sounded at the door.

The knock startled Jillian. If it was Victor out there, he wouldn't knock on the door. He would sneak in or knock the door down. Who would be knocking on the door of a remote mountain cabin? Maybe if she ignored it, whoever was out there would leave. But that wasn't going to happen. Her car was parked outside and all the lights in the cabin were on. Whoever was out there had to know she was here. As she stood uncertainly in the middle of the living room, there was a second knock on the door but this time, it was accompanied by a voice.

"Jillian, it's me, R.J." the voice said.

Jillian was sure she hadn't heard correctly. There was no way R.J. could be there. Maybe this was just a dream, a very real dream. She was hesitating, trying to decide what to do, when a third knock sounded.

"Please, Jillian, open the door," R.J.'s voice shouted. "We need to talk."

Dropping the poker to the floor, Jillian raced over to the door and flung it open. She could not believe that R.J. was actually standing on the other side. She started to move forward to embrace him, but stopped at the last second. Maybe he didn't want physical contact with her, so instead she stepped aside and motioned him in.

"Hi," she said shakily. "Come in."

R.J. stepped inside and looked around. He took in the entire living area with an appraising glance. He seemed to like what he saw and turned to her with a smile.

"This is really nice," he noted as he walked further into the room. "I like this. It's warm, cozy, and filled with a positive, family atmosphere. No wonder you wanted to spend some time up here thinking."

"I love this place," Jillian replied, every nerve-ending on edge with curiosity. "It has lots of good memories of growing up. Um, why don't we sit down?"

They sat on the well-worn couch and faced each other. Jillian had a thousand questions but didn't even know where to start. The two most basic ones tumbled out together.

"R.J., how did you know where to find me? Why are you here?" she asked.

"Your mother told me how to find the cabin. I'm here because we need to talk," he responded.

"My mother? I don't understand," Jillian exclaimed in confusion.

"Let's start at the beginning, Jillian," R.J. said. "I got your last text message and was hurt, angry, and heart broken. It seemed like you had closed the door on us, on our future, without any consideration for what I might want."

"I'm so sorry. I knew you would be angry that I had lied to you and didn't tell you I was Angel. I just couldn't tell you on the phone. I couldn't stand the thought that you would break things off with me because I lied to you," Jillian said sadly.

"I couldn't stand the thought that my last memory of your voice would be one of anger and hurt. I had to keep the memory of you speaking words of love. It was the only way I could survive, R.J. I decided that if I broke it off with you in a text message, I wouldn't have to hear all the horrible things you were thinking about me."

"Jillian, I wasn't angry that you pretended to be Angel," he continued. "I actually understand why you pretended to be her. I realize that I kind of forced you into it with my first couple of text messages.

"Besides, I wasn't totally honest with you either. I told you my name was Will. I use that sometimes so people don't get dazzled by the fact that I'm a professional photographer. I really do understand that part. I guess I had trouble with the fact that you knew that I was Will on Saturday night and you kept it from me. That made me angry."

"Oh, R.J., I'm so very sorry," Jillian cried.

"Jillian, you don't need to apologize again," R.J. said. "I'm over that now. What really hurt me the most is that you just walked away. It felt like what we had was worth nothing more to you than a text message. I spent the two weeks in Dallas trying to understand why you would do that to me....to us.

"It took me a while but I finally figured it out. I realized that the events with Victor and all of the emotional things that happened afterwards had pushed you to your limits. You were on emotional overload. When you saw how angry I was at The Isle, I realized it pushed you over the edge.

"Then I realized something else. No one can share the connection we share and then just turn it off....just walk away unscathed. I knew you loved me then and I know you love me now. I do understand why you did what you did. I'm here because I want you to know that."

"Thank you for understanding," she replied, her heart full of love for him. "I'm so glad that you don't hate me."

"I could never hate you," he responded, looking at her with love in his eyes. "You are my heart and my soul. We belong together. I may get angry with you sometimes, but I could never hate you. I love you Jillian Stanley. For now and forever."

Jillian's heart soared. She hadn't let herself imagine this moment. She had been so certain it wouldn't happen, to imagine it would have been unbearable.

"I love you too, R.J.," she murmured as she looked into his eyes and felt the depth of their love. "I will always love you with my entire being."

Her high was quickly dashed when she remembered about the baby. How would he react? They had never discussed children. She didn't even know if he wanted any. She resolved right then to tell him very soon and see what happened. If he didn't want to be a father to her child, she would have to let him go again. It would break her heart all over again, but he had to know. Before she could say anything however, R.J. spoke again.

"You were really difficult to find once I got back." R.J. spoke directly to her heart now. "I arrived in Raleigh on Sunday afternoon and went to my dad's house. I had decided by then that we needed to talk....that we belonged together.

We could work all the rest out, but I had to know that you still loved me.

"I called your old cell number, but it was disconnected. Then I called your condo and there was no answer, so I left a message. When you didn't respond by Monday morning, I called your office number. When I heard the voice mail message that you were no longer working there, I was desolate."

"Last Friday was my last day of work," Jillian said. "I came to my mom's on Saturday. We spent some time together and then I came up here yesterday."

"I know that now." He grinned at her. "I turned into a pretty good detective trying to find you."

"How did you find me?" she asked. "My mom is the only one who knew where I went. Oh no, did she call you and tell you to come here?"

"Yes, she called me but it's not like you think," R.J. began again. "I kept calling your condo and leaving messages. I was trying to work on cleaning out Dad's house, but I was basically useless. All I could think about was how to reach you. Yesterday, I was so desperate that I went by your condo. Your Jeep wasn't there so I waited in the parking lot all afternoon and evening. The only time I left was to grab a bite to eat and go to the bathroom. I was determined to talk to you when you came home."

"By midnight last night, I realized you weren't coming home," he continued. "I didn't know what to do at that point. I barely slept all night and by this morning I had a plan. I called Allison at your office. I told her I had misplaced your new phone number and I really needed to reach you. She was sympathetic but wouldn't give me the number. So I told her I knew you were out of town and asked her if she knew where you went. She was hesitant, but finally said that she did."

"Did she tell you I was at my mother's?" Jillian was astounded at the lengths R.J. had gone to reach her. "She knew I was going there, but she doesn't know exactly where Mom lives."

"No, Allison was very professional. She didn't give out your location," R.J. went on. "She agreed to call you and let you know I was looking for you. She said it would be up to you to call me back. That was about ten o'clock this morning. At two o'clock, my phone rang. It was your mother. She apologized for taking so long to return the call. Your mother is quite an amazing woman by they way."

"Yes, she is," Jillian laughed. "I can't imagine what she told you."

"Your mother told me that Allison couldn't get you on your cell phone so she called her house. Then your mother said that you were here at the cabin. She told me I needed to get my butt up here as soon as possible." R.J. was laughing too.

"I was afraid if I made any indication that I disagreed, I would definitely be sorry. Anyway, she gave me directions to the cabin and told me that you were wandering around like a lost soul. She said she knew that you loved me deeply and that we were born to be together. She called it her mother's instinct."

"Yes, that is the indomitable Barbara Stanley," Jillian giggled. "She has a way of making you do whatever she wants and making you want to thank her for the opportunity."

"Trust me, I thanked her for the information. Then I told her that I loved her daughter with all my heart," he replied. "She told me that she was looking forward to having me in the family. Then she said if I ever hurt you, I should leave the country and prepare to hide for the rest of my life."

Jillian and R.J. were both laughing now. When they stopped, R.J. put his hands to Jillian's face and looked into her eyes. Then he leaned forward and kissed her deeply. There was such passion, love, and emotion in the kiss that when it ended, they both sighed huge, contented sighs.

"Your mother did say one other interesting thing," R.J. noted as he leaned back. "She said that there was more to it than just the two of us. I asked her what she meant, but she said to ask you."

"My mother.....sometimes I want to hug her and sometimes I just shake my head at her," Jillian replied.

Jillian was suddenly nervous. She knew exactly what her mother was referring to....the baby. She knew that R.J. had to know about it soon, but she was terrified to hear his response. However, her mother had pushed the issue, leaving Jillian no choice but to tell him immediately.

"Baby, what did she mean by that statement?" R.J. asked with a searching look.

"That's exactly what she meant," Jillian answered. "Baby."

"I don't understand what you mean," he responded, and then his eyes grew huge with understanding. "Wait, you mean baby....like you're having a baby?"

"No, I mean we're having a baby," she said, holding her breath. "You and I are having a baby."

"How? When? Oh god, this is the best news I've had in...in....in forever!" R.J. cried.

"I think you know how it happened. You were there." Jillian beamed at him and continued. "When is the baby coming? Well I'm not one hundred percent certain, but somewhere around seven and a half months from now. I took a home pregnancy test on Monday but I haven't been to the doctor yet. I'll go when we get back to Raleigh. Actually, I came up here to decide how to tell you and how to support the baby if you didn't want us."

R.J. stood and pulled Jillian to her feet. He put his hand to her stomach and lightly rubbed it. He was gazing at her stomach in complete wonder, stunned at the news that he was going to be a father. Incredible, amazing, wonderful news! He looked up at her and his eyes conveyed even more love than before. It literally took Jillian's breath away to feel so much love directed at her. Finally he found his voice again and began to speak.

"This is the best news ever, my darling," he whispered to her. "I can't believe I'm going to be a father. You have no idea how happy that makes me! Don't ever, ever think that I wouldn't want you or want our child. I want nothing more than to spend the rest of my life loving you and loving this baby. I want nothing more than for us to be a family."

R.J. looked at Jillian again, his eyes brimming with emotion. His future was again intact and wonderful. Jillian and a baby would be part of it, filling his life with love and happiness. How could he ever ask for more? He suddenly dropped to one knee, took Jillian by the hand, and looked deep into her eyes.

"Jillian Stanley, will you marry me?" he asked, staring into her soul. "Will you and our baby spend the rest of your lives with me?"

"Yes, R.J., I'll marry you," Jillian answered, feeling their souls connect. "I would be honored to have your baby and spend the rest of our lives together."

R.J. jumped to his feet and picked Jillian up. He swung her around until they were both dizzy, kissing her cheeks again and again. They fell to the couch laughing, both talking at once.

They began making plans to go to Asheboro first thing the next morning to see Jillian's mother. Then it would be on to Ocean Isle to begin their life together. They would write their book while Jillian was pregnant. They would spend lazy mornings on their private beach as their child grew in her belly. But most important, they would raise their baby together in a home filled with love, trust, and passion for each other.

Later that evening when they were all talked out, Jillian took R.J. by the hand and led him to the big bedroom. This had been her parent's room, but tonight it would be a place of love and reunion for her and R.J. She lit candles around the room while R.J. was in the shower. When he came back into the room, he pulled her close and held her for a long minute. He was so thankful that she was going to be a permanent part of his life…..her and the baby.

He kissed her hair, her face, and then her lips. His hands began to wander over her back and down to her butt. She gasped as heat raced throughout her body, his touch setting her on fire. She licked his lips and slid her tongue into his mouth. His hands became more demanding, sliding the tiny straps of her gown over her shoulders until the flimsy garment fell to the floor. He reached to caress her breasts but stopped.

"Can we do this?" he wondered. "Is it OK, now that you're pregnant?"

In response, she took him by the hand again and led him to the bed. She climbed onto the bed and pulled on his arm until he was on the bed with her. On their knees and facing each other, Jillian kissed R.J. with all the passion she possessed in her heart and soul. Their bodies melted into each other, kissing and touching until the flames became a fire that roared out of control. They were lost in each other, their world consisting of nothing but the feelings of love and desire that raged between them.

"Let's lay down, my love," Jillian murmured finally.

Lying next to Jillian, R.J. caressed her body gently with his fingers. The feathery feeling of his fingertips made her insane with need. He slowly ran his hands over her breasts, down her stomach, and across her pubic hair. When his fingers slid between her legs, she arched up against him and orgasmed with an intensity that astonished her. When she was able to think again, all she could think about was having him inside her.

As if he heard her thoughts, R.J. removed his fingers from her heat and wetness. He moved on top of her and kissed her swollen breasts. He licked her nipples, causing Jillian to moan with extreme need. He moved up until they were face to face. He looked into her eyes and sent a message of pure love to her soul. He entered her then, taking care not to break the eye contact that was connecting them as one body, one soul.

When he slid into her, they were both sure they had found heaven. R.J.'s eyes were radiating the love in his heart and his body promised to take Jillian to unimaginable heights of passion. They were locked together in an embrace of total bliss, his eyes black with the heat he felt. His hips began to move and his thrusts sent her higher and higher.

Never breaking their gaze of love and desire, R.J. felt Jillian's body begin to spasm. Her gaze deepened, her breasts swelled even more, and her muscles tightened around his hard, throbbing penis. She cried out as she came, his thrusting becoming faster and faster as he listened to her cries. Over and over, she orgasmed until her wetness was running over his balls and onto the bed. Finally, she screamed his name and this pushed him over the edge. Groaning out Jillian's name, R.J. came with a ferocious roar.

When their breathing had subsided, R.J. rolled onto his side. He pulled Jillian up until they were face to face. He put his arm around her and looked into her eyes again. The love he felt deep in his heart was mirrored in her eyes.

"I love you, Jillian," he whispered and kissed her softly. "You will always be my beautiful angel."

"I love you too, R.J." she whispered and kissed him in return.

They stared into each other's eyes until they fell asleep, their future together sealed by their love.

THE END

Did you enjoy Carolina Kiss?
If so, please go to Amazon.com or BarnesandNoble.com and write a short review.
Thank you!

Jaqueline Kiss

Find me on the web at:
JaquelineKiss.com or JaquelineKissBooks.com

Watch for **Keys Kiss***, a new Jaqueline Kiss book due out soon!*

www.ingramcontent.com/pod-product-compliance
Lightning Source LLC
Chambersburg PA
CBHW061538170626
46811CB00001B/29